Smart, Sexy, Spiritual, Strong

WRITTEN BY

BEVERLY A. BURCHETT

www.blackcurrantpress.com

BLACK CURRANT
PRESS
www.blackcurrantpress.com

Smart, Sexy, Spiritual, Strong

written by Beverly A. Burchett

ISBN # 978-0-9817111-33

PREFACE

She was completely terrified yet stiffly trying not to let it show. The wall supported her from dripping into the carpeting like a puddle of sludge. She wanted to touch herself all over to ascertain that every inch was still there, still in place, still with blood flowing through it. Yet she would not move another hair without making sure she had permission to do so. He lunged at her, his eyes glazed over, menacing and peculiarly focused like something otherworldly. He was not giving in so easily with the likes of some simple, helpless female screaming. Unfortunately, for her, he was just getting warmed up. He lifted his ax, the one they had purchased together at a yard sale, and without warning swung, this time missing her within inches but managing to mangle to bits their anniversary gift to each other. Ironically, it was a loveseat; one that she had just stood next to trembling. She managed to maneuver a duck and weave to one side just as the metal swiftly crashed down missing her head, dead center. She could feel the 'swoosh' of the swing as it cut the air making it whistle angrily. Unlike the wind, she was unable to make any vague attempt at a sound. There was a vacant space where her mouth should have been. Her legs were undecided in transforming from rubber to lead. Her heart was eager to either split in two or implode on its last breath. She had never ached so much as to be allowed yet another day, just one more, lousy day.

He spun himself and his weapon around and dragged both in her direction. There was no time to waste. She had to think quickly. She reflected, recalling the first attack narrowly scraping her right eye, then the second mighty blow barreling along the pathway towards her skull. It was a pinch of a comprehension that startled her into recognizing that he was indeed trying to kill her this time. It was so slight that in the course of his next swing, she hesitated in dodging it. Reason and logic can stall a rational person especially if they're searching for it within their horror driven circumstance. Now her equilibrium began to seep out of every pore together with burning tears, sweat and other bodily fluids. She felt reduced to the likeness of a wet paper towel, straining to remain valuable. Her mind went blank. Her mind went blank. Her mind went blank. She was actually staring at the floor when he again approached. Once more, he heaved the ax. From the corner of her eye, she saw her face distorted there in its thickness. It was wide, her eyes, glassy and swollen. As if swinging at a baseball, he hurled the tool at her side and this time it would hit something, now that she had a rigid body. It was no longer malleable in affording her absorption on impact. This swing would definitely fracture something, dislocate something, or bleed beyond a normal scrape or bruise. She could see it, the floor, come up to greet her. At first, this collision was a relief. For once the two surfaces met, her body and the ax, the entire event, so-to-speak, was at a standstill. She could, with squinted eyes, see his ankles, bear and ashy as they were commonly with more than a dab foot fungus, nails all cracked and with a greenish discoloration. Then there was the smell. She had learned to live with the rank stench, religiously believing that athletes weren't meant to possess sweet feet. He had other qualities, other, being the operative word. With him, everything was other. Other times, other cities, other moods and so on, were the trademark of the life she had created with him. She had become a consummate expert at fantasizing about the elsewhere, the anywhere else but here, and the truckload full to overflowing of regrets.

Lying in that position, she could see the blood seeping out from underneath her hair, matted and wild from the earlier pushing and shoving. She wasn't going to faint from this or anything like that. Although traumatic, it wasn't as serious as in other times when she was carrying Yolanda, their one and only child. Back then, she was always nervous about miscarrying. Now, things were different. She didn't much care for what came next. She thought, 'You cannot hurt me anymore, anymore, that is, than you already have.' He lifted her back up then hurled her back down once more all the while screaming. He was so loud that her ears were actually ringing. Thankfully, she saw the heel of his foot now as he exited into the back of the house, all the while muttering to himself. Beyond his clenched jaw was the face of a man she once knew but that was some other time, in some other place, far, far away from the present. Apparently, by leaving her slack and shattered in their untidy living room he was demonstrating that he still loved her. After all, she was, in spite of everything, still among the living.

Smart, Sexy, Spiritual, Strong

WRITTEN BY

BEVERLY A. BURCHETT

CHAPTER ONE

S he wore the poor parquet floor out behind her couch, marching, like a crazed lunatic backwards and forwards. Though her mother hadn't intended to, she had made her daughter feel trapped in a web of obligation. There she was going out with a guy she hadn't seen since the sandbox. The doorbell rang. Sarah shrugged, "Okay. Dinner? How hard could it be...one, two hours?"

While walking towards the door, she caught a glimpse of herself in the foyer mirror and wondered if she didn't look too severe. After all, with her tresses pulled back in such a well-knotted bun, she looked as if she was in the *war room* with one of her more difficult clients. Brenda, a friend, gave her some unsolicited advice once, saying that if she had any intentions of getting a man, that she was going to have to stop dressing like one. Sarah remembered nodding and marveling at how Brenda withstood living in the dark ages. She never liked the type of men who were attracted to such obvious man-traps. The whole idea of using oneself as bait was just phony fishing to her. It reminded her of those infomercials where the lure looked and smelt like a worm but was, in actuality, plastic. Enough said. She leaped to the door anxious to get the whole-contrived calamity over.

When she opened the door there stood, Jester, a skinny, soft-spoken man, her date for the evening, oddly standing a few steps down with his back turned as if he was leaving.

"Jester?" Sarah whispered, actually hoping he wouldn't answer.

Jester turned and shuffled so nervously that he nearly doubled backward down the steps. After giving each other awkward hellos, Sarah motioned for him to come inside. He stood gawky, still, but patiently waiting in the hallway as she perused her brownstone for appliances she may have left running. Having found everything in order, and with great courage she nodded, "Ready?"

Jester scurried to the front door, grabbing one of Sarah's coats from a hook on the way out. Sarah spun an enormous ring of keys around and locked all three of her doors. Jester anticipated her finishing the last lock and gently draped the acquired coat over her shoulders.

"There you go. I thought you might need this," Jester said ironically pointing to a perfectly clear summer sky.

'For what,' thought Sarah, 'suffocation?' Then she turned just enough to reveal the little cotton wrap she was already carrying. She mechanically re-opened all three doors and tossed the wrap and the coat on the wood floor. She believed in her soul that if she could just get to her car, and rush through the evening, she'd have a solid four-hour blow-by-blow to report to mom. However, as she spun her key chain around to find her car key, Jester gallantly took them right out of her hand, and proceeded to open the driver's side door. Sarah ignored her skin smarting from the friction of the metal scratching across her palm.

"You have to jiggle it a bit," she informed him as if she was now in a hurry.

"No problem," Jester proclaimed.

A grating amount of time passed as Jester tried and tried again and again to open the car door. Sarah waited and watched as he fumbled without remedy for just the right twist, just the right tension.

"MAY *I* TRY IT!" Sarah blurted.

It was supposed to sound coy, as gentle as a flower, instead of loud, curt and resounding with annoyance. She grabbed the key without apology and opened the car door. He practically pushed her over in an effort to at least hold the door open for her. She tripped under his foot, manages to recover, swiftly jumping into the car before he decided to heave her in. Jester was quicker than she realized, and manages to take the keys once more, jog around to the other side of the car and proceed to open the passenger-side door. More time passes before Sarah frustratingly reaches over and opens it for him. He pouts but finally slides sheepishly into the car.

"Tricky little locks on these things, huh?" he chagrins dropping the keys into her hand.

The engine roars to life with a blast of exhaust from the tailpipe as Sarah pushes her heel into the petal. The serge of the powerful Grand Cherokee Laredo engine beneath her sends adrenaline rushing down her spine, strangely cleansing her of all thoughts of Jester. She's a free woman now. She hardly remembers that he's still in the car.

"Those Mets are really something else, huh? I didn't see it coming with them winning any of the subway series," Jester spoke.

Sarah looked over at him with an air of caution before allowing a tiny smile to spread across her cheeks. Her old company still gave her season tickets every year to the Mets and Yankee games. She had only missed one home game since she had been attending, in any given season. She knew the stats, the names, the coaches and the recent trades. She loved, loved, loved talking about sports. She wondered if she could allow herself to hope that the evening would be that interesting. Then they rode to the restaurant having a heated debate over the year's draft picks and Sarah began to feel possibilities that the night might not be a total nightmare after all. She slowly let her foot release from the metal for a while.

"So, you don't think they have a chance against the Blue Jays? Is that what you're saying?" Sarah asked with a smile, a genuine one this time.

As she and Jester promenaded into the restaurant, it was as if they were two old friends just having a bite to eat. She observed that when Jester didn't feel the need to be a super human and when she glanced at him at a certain angle, in a dim kind of light, she saw something quite attractive about his face. With him graying at the temples, he looked very distinguished in his classically designer horn-rimmed glasses. His attire was remarkably similar to hers too, conservative tapered jacket with tailored hemmed pants. The maître d came over and escorted them to a small intimate table.

"So what is it? Come on now you have to give it up for Jeter and Wright! Come on now," Sarah teased.

"Ah…ah, I don't want to bore you any further," he announced.

"Bore me?" she asked.

"Certainly two bright people such as ourselves can find something a little more stimulating to talk about," Jester announced just as they were being seated.

"You're not boring me. You're not," she said practically begging.

"I wouldn't be any kind of gentleman if I spoke about sports with a lady all night," said Jester as if the stick up his behind just hit an eyeball.

'Back to that again,' Sarah thought, 'Why doesn't he just pretend I'm a guy?' She had had enough business talk and was not looking forward to the business of dating banter.

The maître d handed them their menus. She decided to brace herself. Ever-Ready, Jester, practically snatched hers out of her hand and stated, "I'll order for you."

"Well..." Sarah tried without words for the shock.

At the sound of the menus closing, the waiter scurried over.

"Ready?" the waiter asked, pen in hand.

Neither the waiter nor Jester acknowledged Sarah's second, "Well..."

She was invisible for the moment.

"We'll both have the Porter House steak with the potatoes ala Groton please. Also, I'd like to see your wine list," he demanded.

"Medium rare or well done?" the waiter asked.

"Medium rare, of course," Jester snickered.

Then the waiter scooped up the menus and dashed away, while Sarah got a sinking feeling in the pit of her stomach that she had no idea who she was sitting across from. Maybe he was a child of parents who sent him to military school or something like that. She wasn't sure. She wasn't a psychiatrist.

"Excuse me, ah, Jester...but...I very rarely eat red meat anymore. In fact, I can't remember the last time I have," she told him

A thought crossed her mind that he might explode at the idea of someone challenging him. It was fleeting. He lacked the nerve. 'If we were to have a fist fight, I'd send him home whining like a little girl,' she thought.

"I'm sorry," he said again so politely she felt like decking him, hard, "I thought I was being helpful. I guess I..." Jester's sentence purposely trailed off as he became painfully aware that his attempts to impress her were failing miserably. He quickly concluded that he should just talk about what he knows best -- himself.

So, without further ado he spent the rest of the evening describing his job at Dean Whirlington's, a mid-sized accounting firm.

"You know, if I do say so myself it's a great firm to work for...and not just because of the profit sharing and expense account..."

It was around about this point when Sarah's eyes began to wander around the room. There was a small circular dance floor and a live big band playing a little reggae, and a little funk. Others were laughing and swirling around. There was a group of women dancing with each another and a set of men sitting across watching them. Sarah monitored their movements to identify which woman was with which man. It was something to do.

"...That would naturally be the only reason to work for any firm. Nowadays you choose an employer just as much as they choose an employee..."

Sarah looked over and noticed the waiters serving frilly desserts and, ah ha, after dinner drinks. Oh, if only that were she and Jester. Didn't she deserve a treat for all her hard work and good behavior? Alas, she finished her large Greek salad about an hour ago even while chewing each mouthful thoroughly and completely. Meanwhile, Jester was still gnawing on his steak.

"...when I started with Whirlington, oh about eight years ago, I remember that day as clear as a bell. You may not believe this but I was very green behind the ears..."

> *green behind the ears*
> *green behind the ears*
> *green behind the ears*

'Can one be *green* behind the ears? Doesn't he mean wet behind the ears?' she thought and called the waiter over to order at least two Apple Martinis. She should at least be less coherent.

"...My mother was so proud of me for landing such a great position in such a prestigious firm fresh out of college..."

'Please don't mention the word mother,' Sarah thought. Were it not for her mother's interference, she could have been at home with her feet up watching reruns of *Prison Break*.

Finally, after five long hours, it was over. Sarah sped down the half-empty West Side Highway homeward bound.

"You sure you don't want me to drop you off?" she asked in the truest most literal way she could muster without digging through his wallet for an address and taking him home against his will.

"No, I'll be fine," Jester declared, with a tad too much self-confidence for someone who didn't have any means of getting back to Staten Island other than her generosity or public transportation.

Sarah was unsure as to why he had declined her offer and drove the rest of the way to Brooklyn weighing possible options. She wondered if Jester thought he had some chance of spending the night. Could he be that presumptuous? She grew downright angry at the thought of it.

Her car skidded to a crocked halt in front of her house eighteen minutes later. By far her best time yet for driving home from the Sugar Bar, her favorite restaurant. She actually regretted bringing him there.

Jester immediately jumped out of the car and raced over to her side. He swung her door open and literally started pulling her out.

"Jester! STOP! FOR CHRIST'S SAKE! I'm locking up my damn car. Nooooo, thank you," Sarah tried miserably to sound pleasant.

Truth was, she had had her fill of Jester. He was just one of those people who mean well but irritate the heaven out of a person in the process and meanwhile underneath it are conceited, self-involved, egotistical, and macho maniacs. Not that she wanted to talk about it, but he had never once asked her about her career. Not once.

"Just trying to be helpful," Jester bleeped as if he had a string attached that one pulled to make him speak.

Sarah got out of the car and headed straight for her front door. She turned around abruptly to say goodnight only to find Jester stumbling over her heels.

"Oh, I'm sorry, I'm sorry. Did I hurt you?" Jester babbled.

"Nooooooooooooo. I'll be fine," said Sarah sarcastically.

Undeterred by her caustic tone, he escorted her to the door. Sarah turned again but this time she made sure he wasn't under foot. 'For the love of God, what is wrong with this guy?' she thought. Then, she managed to squeeze out this lie, "I had a nice time. Thank you."

She hated lying but the truth would have been too bludgeoned. Then she whipped out her keys and opened the door.

"Thanks again," she repeated trying desperately to sum up the evening in her mind, 'once and for dang sure all.'

She hurdled inside over the threshold, just as Jester nudged forward expecting to join her. It bothered her that he was so insistent on either coming in or wanting to get a good night kiss or whatever ignorant, arrogant misguided mission he was on. Now certain that he had not understood any of her previous clues, she simply slammed the door shut behind her. It was hard for her to imagine that he felt a love connection had been forged when she had spent the whole evening listening to his life's ambition as an accountant.

"Well, good night," she barked from behind the fully latched, tightly locked and, fortified security system.

Jester stood for a long while on her landing shifting his weight from his right foot to his left foot.

"Ah...ah...you're welcome," he expressed in a stutter.

After several minutes had passed and he had finally concluded that Sarah was not going to invite him in, he slowly descended the steps. She peered through the front window to make sure, when suddenly Jester turned back around and looked up. She quickly ducked from sight. Jester dawdled for a while longer before turning around again and starting down the street. Sarah didn't know why she did it, but she snuck another peek through the curtain and as she did so Jester waved gleefully up at her. She dashed as quickly as possible, hitting her shin on one of her stereo speakers along the way. She tried not to scream out loud for fear that Jester might hear her and come running.

CHAPTER TWO

That very, next morning, Sarah needed a shot of espresso in her arm she was so tired.

"Hey, Sarah, how's it going?" Ashford asked, "Good to see you," he said sincerely.

"Fine, fine. You too," Sarah groggily replied not as sincerely, then added, "How 'bout chu?"

She was on a long unruly line at Starbucks when he just so happened by and unfortunately saw her through the storefront glass.

"Heard you got married," she offered cordially then reluctantly added, "Congratulations."

"Yeah. Yeah, thank you and happy birthday to you. Heard you just had one," he replied displaying very large, stained teeth.

"Thank you. I appreciate that," she responded with a pleasant albeit forced smile.

"You're my age. I remember," he nodded in recognition, "I…uh…" he suddenly stammered.

Sarah moved forward in line just as he was about to hesitantly divulge something of relative importance to her.

"Yes?" she inquired more interested in him leaving than anything else.

"Well, it's nothing really," he replied with a shrug.

It was the shrug that caught her attention.

"No, what is it?" she simply asked really, and truly wanting him to scurry along.

She was hung over. She was worn out. She just simply wasn't

in the mood for more *crazy* so early on in the day.

"Well, my wife, well she's younger than us..." he hedged.

"Yeah...aaannnnddd..." said Sarah watchful all the while thinking, 'What the heck is he getting at?'

"Well, I just thought that maybe, I mean, I believed that perhaps..." he paused.

"Yyeeessss..." Sarah asked while positioning her body into a kung Fu stance.

"...Well, well, you know, well, that it might have been...you..." he smiled and, of all things, winked.

She did not wink back.

"...but..." he shirked again and this time sucking in air.

"But, what?" Sarah asked meanwhile thinking, 'What the heck, I'll bite.'

"...But, it's just that...I wanted kids..." he finally answered as if slightly disappointed in the outcome of his choice.

Sarah's brow furrowed. Then her head inquisitively titled down and cocked to one side. She studied him. She was utterly confused not with what he said but with the implied message within. Suddenly speechless, she stood prepared to drop kick him if she could maneuver behind him fast enough and not be seen. If he knew what was best for him, he'd back up. Hell, everyone in the City could see that she was now a little crazy too, and definitely dangerous. Luckily for him, Ashford finally managed to see the now wickedly scathing stare Sarah was giving him and intelligently went on about his business. He waved good-bye to her from the sidewalk.

CHAPTER THREE

So there she was in a ditch.

"You're still going to be able to pick me up, right?" Karen asked, fearful of the answer.

"'Course, girl. Just like old times, I'll find a way. Besides, it's really not that bad. It sounds worst than it is," Sarah assured her.

"When you first told me I didn't know what to think. I mean, off the side of the road and all. It sounds terrible," Karen said.

"I know. I know. Girl, if anyone else was on the road, I could have been killed or worse, I could have killed somebody else," she gasped, "It's not a good place to be, you know," Sarah said shaking the whole incident off.

"But I had just talked to you. You were asleep, huh?" Karen asked.

"Evidently, knocked out," Sarah replied.

"There's only two reasons for that," Karen said.

"What's that?" Sarah asked.

"Either you're working too hard or you must have some heavy stuff on your mind," Karen probed.

"Not really. Okay, maybe," Sarah said not really wanting to get into it.

"What's up, girl? I'll show you mine if you show me yours," Karen said with a smile.

"Yeah…well…I just went on this insane date the other day and the man made me a prisoner in my own home, is all and…then the next morning I had a visit from this creep, Ashford, and…"

Sarah began but was abruptly interrupted.

"That's your problem right there," Karen interjected.

"What?" Sarah asked. Then more hesitantly, "I didn't know I had a problem."

"You need to stop dating and settle down already," Karen said bluntly.

"What?" exclaimed Sarah, defensively.

"We're not getting any younger, you know. Marriage has its problems but it's better than being out there on your own. Girl, I just don't know how you do it. I really, really just don't know," said Karen a tad condescendingly.

"Well..." Sarah uttered wanting to change the subject but to what she hadn't a clue.

"I'm sorry to leave this beautiful house. Oh, well," Karen said lazily on to her next topic.

Meanwhile, Sarah was still recovering from the euphemistic knife in her back.

"Yeah, must be nice," Sarah said thinking of Karen's ability to think on anything other than her own lingering harsh words.

"It's just perfect out here. Honestly it is. I'm going to miss all this fresh air. But I guess it's time for us to come back home," she sighed.

"Yeah. Yeah. Sure," Sarah said apathetically, still unable to let go of hurt feelings, "How's the all-American doin'?" Sarah finally tried.

Sarah realized her mistake almost immediately.

"Beautiful. Just beautiful..." Karen responded with a smile that could be seen through the phone line.

"...Now, you need to get you somebody, honey," Karen told her.

Sarah was now stunned into silence and wanted to retreat. She stood perfectly still over the receiver about to accidentally on purpose hang up the phone. She'd blame it on PMS the next time they spoke.

"Yeah, Yeah. Right away," she mused, "I'm gonna' stand in the middle of the street and snatch one from the crowd. I sure hope he fits into the tuxedo I have on lay-away at K-Mart," she joked.

"If that's what it takes, I say do it," Karen replied as if it was a viable plan.

Sarah ran right into a ditch. It was an undeniable fact. It was too late to swerve, avoid or reverse her way out of what had already occurred, literally, and figuratively speaking. She thanked God that it wasn't a terribly deep one; this trough sloped into long standing rain water. It was positioned in a shadowy corner alongside the darkened road. She thanked God for that too, no witnesses. Sure, they'd come to help after they stopped laughing at her buffoonery. By all accounts, not a great way to end a day but at least the world had stopped spinning or at any rate her car had stopped spinning, or was it most important that her head had stopped spinning? All in all, it was presumably a good thing that she and her vehicle were now in a glorious state of pause. She needed that. She wanted time to readjust herself anyway. At least that's what she told herself. She would have preferred a gentle bubble bath and a bottle of red but, alas, she was in an incline with what appeared to be tree branches peeking inside the cab through what was definitely a broken window. She was most grateful that she was in a company car, though however small, it was her own company.

She started mentally assessing the damage. She read somewhere that that was what efficient managers do; first assess damage. They don't immediately blame or admonish. There will always be time enough for those adult-sized paddles; so, she assessed. Although, with her assets in need of a tow, she couldn't help but reprimand herself for being negligent in the first place. She shouldn't have been on the road at that hour of the night. She was abnormally tired and clearly too distracted for her own good. Else, she would have kept her eyes firmly affixed to the white lines of the parkway and not thinking about other things that did not pertain to the operation of heavy machinery, i.e., a three thousand pound automobile.

Apparently, Ashford's little wicked comment that morning had more than a slight impact on her. She couldn't deny that. In fact, it was difficult for her to think of anything else. What perturbed her most about him was that what he said wasn't even factual. She was just in her thirties, hardly too old to bare a trifling Negro's kids. Besides, they had never so much as held hands and now suddenly she was on his imaginary list of wife candidates, the ego. It made her sick to her stomach that he could refer to her as a marriage reject without having given her a proper offer on bended knee, a date, a meal, some bread and water, a crumb. The most they ever did was flirt and it was the real dull kind. It wasn't the good stuff that tickles one's spine all day long, igniting singing out loud and spontaneous organisms down crowded streets. It was the kind that makes a girl have to ask, "Does he like me or what?" Apparently, she was too old for that painstaking guessing game. When did she become too old for anything?

Everything about their relationship, quote unquote, was either lukewarm or limp; a girl need only imagine the rest. Yet and still, even though Ashford was an idiot of some great and enormous proportions, that wasn't all that pained her. She just couldn't put her finger on exactly why but she was completely out of sorts in a world class phenomenon kind of way. Whatever it was it was far and away bigger than the asshole Ashford and the chestnut Jester. This, almost mid-life crisis she was experiencing was precisely why she was miles away from her house in the middle of the night down a darkened road lost in thought. An idea did occur to her while waiting for triple A but she refused to believe it. She thought, 'Am I bitter about being single?'

CHAPTER FOUR

C rystal leaned on her desk that morning feeling wonderfully nostalgic. Karen's return was making it hard for her to concentrate on anything else. The church Elders were polite enough not to say anything when her typically thirty-minute or so prayer only took five.

"God ROCKS! Amen," she prayed with eyes closed shut and her body shaking intensely.

The Elders raised their eyebrows suspiciously but agreed, "Amen."

She couldn't help herself. Her friend's impending arrival had transported her back in time. Even the dress she had on was reminiscent of the past. It had the same demure flowered print her mother bought for her when she was eight, buttoned all the way up to her neck. She had replaced the side sweep and part with a well manicured bang and the dangling earrings for cubic zirconium posts. It wasn't much of a stretch, she had only made minor changes since she and her family moved to New York. The biggest challenge was her accent. She was still working on it trying to sound more like a native born. However, over the phone it was impossible for her not to drag and drawl, like a South Carolinian. What could she say, she was a country girl at heart. Until her family moved up north, the tallest building she had ever seen was the lighthouse outside Old Sawmill Road. It was approximately a twenty-minute walk from home, overlooking the Atlantic Ocean, beckoning ships into its nearby harbor. When she closed her eyes, she could still smell the salty ocean air.

Meanwhile, across town, the only thing Brenda had on her mind was furiously searching for something in her chest of drawers. With her Razor cocked between her head and shoulder, she was flinging clothing out of it in all directions. All she had on was a flimsy gold chemise with pink, plastic peek-a-boo, high-heel fuzzy slippers.

"Yeah," she said answering the phone.

"Bree'n-da? It's may. Is that y'ou?" Crystal lazily asked.

"Jesus, Crystal," Brenda stammered and dropped the phone having finally found what she was rummaging for.

She slowly pulled out a furry, white feather boa. Handling it delicately, she flamboyantly wrapped it around her neck then picked the phone back up.

"What do you want?" Brenda barked.

"Did ya' git' up on the wrong side ov' the bed or did ya' git' up from da' wrong bed?"

"Ha, ha, ha. Really, what's up?" said Brenda bored.

"Well, Ah' jus' called 'cause Ah' jus' wanted ta' know what time Sarah was pickin' us up t-day and all..." Crystal asked staring at her pale pink polished nails.

"Why don't you call her!" Brenda snapped about to hang up the phone but she could still hear Crystal's voice.

"She leffft alreadi'!" Crystal screamed.

"Alright. Alright," Brenda fumbled, "Hold you horses. Ah...well...I believe. Let me think now..." Brenda said distractedly.

Unbeknownst to Crystal, Brenda was seductively strutting away from the dresser and towards her date, Larry, who'd been sitting patiently on the edge of her bed waiting for her. He is a golden brown vision, with overly enlarged, thick rippling muscular arms and full, juicy lips. He is bare-chested with his pants pushed all the way down to his angles. He sits obediently in his boxer shorts.

"She said something about not wanting to sit in traffic all afternoon…" Brenda told her, "…but…"

The phone begins to slide, now cumbersome, what with the boa and all.

"…Okay…Okay," said Brenda leaning into Larry showing him her feathers, "What do you think now?" Brenda moaned into his ear.

Crystal studied the phone having some slight recognition of what was going on, then started tapping her foot to the floor. Brenda couldn't help but to giggle as Larry issued several air-bites at her boa. Brenda wrapped the boa around his neck slowly teasing him with it.

"Larrrrrrrr, what are you going to do about that?" she moaned again and he sniggered.

Larry barked like a wounded puppy. Crystal's impatience mounts with every other yelp.

"Brenda!" she shouts.

"What? What?" Brenda said straightening up.

"Fo-cus, woman. Foooo-cuz!" Crystal told her.

Brenda tries to remember and playfully pushes Larry away in order to think. With that, Larry beings to stare out of the window as though he's losing interest.

"…Oh. Well, ah, she said, hum, I think, two, maybe. Maybe three o'clock. I don't know," said Brenda a little irritated with Crystal.

Larry struts over to Brenda and starts sucking her fingers from the pinky to the thumb. Apparently, he hadn't lost interest at all. Brenda stretches and contours her body undulating like a cat in heat.

"Oh! Oh! Hum," Brenda playfully growls at him completely forgetting Crystal on the other end of the phone.

"Am Ah' disturbing ya'll?" Crystal asked.

"What?   Ah…well, quite frankly…yes!" Brenda retorted deliberately dropping the phone, which Larry accidentally rolls onto, sending it sideways to the floor.

"Brenda! Bren-da! Whut in the heck 'r you doin'? Pick up dah phone…huh…. Hey? Brenda…" Crystal's voice is muffled on account of the phone being buried under tossed fluffy slippers.

Larry and Brenda are otherwise occupied. CLICK!

CHAPTER FIVE

S arah would rather watch the planes taxi to and fro than hear another iota of Brenda and Crystal bickering. As usual, there's nothing unusual about this particular quarrel. Brenda steadily denies acting like a spoiled, selfish brat, while Crystal maintains that God don't like ugly, something, something, "Saul," something, something, "King David." Sarah generally likes Crystal's Bible stories but today she's feeling pensive and uneasy, that's why her eyes are glued to the huge airport observation window.

"Ah reeelly 'iss hah."

Sarah's face contorts thinking that someone must be reading her mind. Crystal pulls a candy bar from her purse and while chewing mumbles again, "Ah reeelly 'iss hah."

Crystal sees Brenda greedily eyeballing the dark chocolate and intentionally waves it under her nose before devouring three-quarters of it in one bite.

"She said four o'clock right?" Crystal asked audibly and intentionally licking her fingers.

Twenty minutes later, their dear friend Karen appears before them, briskly walking down the long arrival ramp. When she lifts up her head, she finds Sarah, Brenda and Crystal barreling towards her gleefully screaming. She immediately drops her bags and simply allows them to engulf her in a sorely missed warm hug. She coils up a bandaged arm all the while and with the other eagerly stretches out to them as they wrap and entwine themselves around her. Karen looks leaner than they recall but still statuesque. Her tall frame could always pull off a size twelve and make it look like a size six. Now, with her face narrower, she could comfortably wear petit-sized clothing. The last time they saw her she was working on getting rid of her ten extra pounds of baby fat. She didn't look unhealthy or anything just older.

Karen too took inventory of her old friends. Everyone was a bit older, but, basically, the same. Crystal and Sarah were dressing better she noted right off. Back then, Sarah wore sneakers with everything. Karen was pleased to see that that tradition no longer remained. She still looked much too sporty for Karen's extremely conservative tastes but at least in a more tailored, feminine sort of way. Crystal still had everything buttoned up to her ears but the attire was at least a bit more modern. Brenda was the only one that didn't give her pause. Brenda had on a low cut spaghetti stringed tank top and three-inch heels. She looked exactly the same as she did the last time Karen saw her. It made her laugh almost to the point of peeing on herself when Brenda turned around and showed off a split in her shirt that went all the way up to her panty line.

Karen burst into tears at the thought of how long it had been. Then, they all hugged. Once they reluctantly let go of each other and kisses had been given all around, they strolled over to the baggage claim area to retrieve the rest of Karen's luggage. Brenda hurried to pick up the lightest bag, a make-up case, while Crystal reached for the heaviest.

"What ya' got in here?" Crystal balked.

Sarah pitched in to help her.

"It's so good to see y'all," Karen smiled with her lips tightly pressed together and cheeks moist with tears.

Sarah passed around a small package of Kleenex.

"Where's Norman?" Crystal asked, so used to seeing him and Karen together.

"Driving," Karen nonchalantly replied.

"Not from Phoenix?" Brenda asked as if to say, is that even possible, while fanning herself with her free hand, "Driving? Y'all still got that old Ford?"

"Unfortunately, he's driving it here. He hates to fly," Karen replied.

"What about my god child? How is she?" Sarah asked Karen, switching her grip on the luggage handle.

"Fine. She's with him."

Sarah squeezed Karen around the shoulders again forcing Crystal to knock into them, causing all three to stop in the middle of the terminal. They embraced once more out of sheer delight.

"Well, that gives us more time to be together then," Brenda said as she joined them forming a circle.

"That's right, girls. And we're gonna' par-tee! Do y'all still do up Friday nights?" Karen asked in between sniffles.

Back in the day, it was practically customary to go out together at least once a week.

"And Saturday and sometimes Sunday," Brenda placed the bag down and shook her hips from side to side.

Crystal didn't want anyone to think that Brenda was someone they actually knew.

"I really miss my sista's," Karen said warmly.

"They don't have no sista's in Phoenix?" Brenda asked as if she wanted a demographically studied respond.

Brenda, having never been to Arizona, assumed Karen and Norman were the only Black people there. Karen didn't have the heart to tell her she was a fool at least not to her face. Instead, Karen silently mouthed that she didn't know.

Just then, a rough looking teenage boy ran pass them and accidentally knocked Karen's purse out of her hand. They all watched it hit the floor as if in slow motion. The kid pauses but doesn't seem like he intends to pick it back up. However, upon seeing the red-eyed, mean look Karen bore into him, he reconsiders. This was the Karen that Sarah, Brenda, and Crystal remembered - tough. In fact, she was one of the toughest people in high school, a real force to be reckoned with even before she started dating Norman, head quarterback.

They all waited to see what the boy was going to do. He didn't have many options because Karen had moved close to him blocking his only route of escape. Then she snarled at him, clearly for the benefit and enjoyment of her friends. They appreciated the performance in their honor and did their best to keep straight faces.

"Pick it up!" Karen ordered the boy.

He stuck out his chest, recoiled angrily and stood his ground.

"I said, pick it up. Now!" she barked, hands raised as if she might give him a spanking if he didn't.

He hesitated for a moment before bending over, scooping up the purse and ever so gently placing it back into Karen's hand.

"Sorry," he said gruffly, glaring at Karen as if she were mad.

Then he scurried away from all of them as fast as his legs could take him. Karen bowed to her audience of three and received some applause but mostly chuckles.

As the sun was setting, Sarah's car pulled up in front of Karen's new home. All four doors flew open filling the evening air with simultaneous chattering but mostly laughter. Karen, Sarah and Crystal go to the trunk each pretending that they don't notice Brenda exiting from the back of the car to hurriedly secure the front passenger seat for the ride home. They grin as she places her pocketbook squarely on the cushion.

In retaliation, Crystal lugs one of the heaviest suitcases over to the side of the car and lowers it at Brenda's feet. Brenda dodges around the bag and Crystal and acts as if she is admiring the house. Karen looks on with a smile. Age had clearly not dampened their rousting, but perfected their comic timing. Crystal picks up the suitcase and heads towards the front door purposely pushing Brenda out of the way. Then as Brenda begins walking, Crystal stops short pretending she's catching her breath. Brenda stumbles into her, lifts one eyebrow and shoos her away.

"Thanks a lot, Sarah," Karen finally said with a hug.

"Any time."

"Nice house," Brenda said while kissing Karen on the cheek and waving good-bye.

Then she sauntered back to the car and scooted herself firmly into the front seat.

"Thanks," Karen replied all the while winking at Sarah and Crystal.

They all knew Brenda all too well. She always needed to be rewarded for her good deeds otherwise they'd never hear the end of it. Meanwhile, Sarah, Karen and Crystal successfully carry the luggage up to the front steps.

"Brenda, see you Saturday," Karen confirmed the plan.

"Right," Brenda yelled back to Karen whilst buckling herself in.

"Same old Brenda, huh?" said Karen with a grin.

"Hum, hum, lazeey," said Crystal as a matter of fact.

They placed the bags on the country-styled wooden porch that framed the entrance. Crystal immediately felt right at home.

"Thanks, Crystal. I got it from here," Karen held out her arms and gave Crystal a hug and a huge loving smile.

"Ya'll welcome. It's so nice to have ya' home again. Jus' like my Mama always used to say, 'Comin' home's like bein' reborn'," Crystal imparted true wisdom in her own gentle way as she strolled back to the car.

Karen waited until she saw Crystal get into the car before she turned and faced Sarah.

"What would I do without you?" she rhetorically asked.

She and Sarah had been friends the longest. It was more than just a reunion for them; it was a homecoming. Karen and Sarah adopted each other long ago as if they were flesh and blood sisters. Sarah was the one that Karen told all her secrets to and vice versa. They knew everything there was to know about the other. Even though they were miles apart, their conversation always picked up as if neither time nor distance mattered. Karen dug in her pockets for the keys and opened the front door. Sarah picked up the suitcases and followed behind.

"That's okay," Karen told her.

She turned and scooted Sarah from the door.

"It's okay, really. I've got it from here," she repeated then motioned for Sarah to put the bags back down.

"Are you sure?" Sarah asked.

Karen nodded, yes and pulled the door up behind her indicating that she didn't want any bugs flying inside.

"Yeah, I'm sure," Karen told her.

Karen always had a way of saying 'not to worry' that made it impossible for Sarah to challenge. Sarah leaned over and kissed her good night understanding that nothing else needed to be said.

"Oh, I meant to ask you if you needed any help, you know, unpacking?" Sarah asked while she was descending the steps.

She kind of figured that the answer would be 'not to worry' but she couldn't resist.

"The movers did everything. Can you imagine? They unpack

your boxes and put everything away. Besides, Norman will help me when he gets here. It's okay. Really."

"Well, let me at least help you bring these in."

"No, no, no, it's all-right, really. You've done more than enough already. Go home. Get some sleep."

Sarah started back down the steps.

"Alright. You get some sleep yourself, okay?" with that, Sarah headed back to her car.

"Bye, y'all. Thanks!" Karen shouted as she slowly disappeared into the house.

Sarah got in the car, started the engine, and shouted back at her just before Karen completely shut the door.

"Call me tomorrow!"

"Okay, bye. And thanks again," was the last thing Karen said before finally closing the door behind her.

Just beyond one of the many overgrown trees in the yard was a rusty blue 4-door Ford. It was noticeable because the plate hung off the back bumper and reflected glare off one of the streetlights. All three of them saw it, but it was Brenda, who was compelled to ask.

"Isn't that Norman's car?"

Sarah pulled off without saying a word. She and Crystal decided to remain silent on the subject. They refused to believe that Karen would lie to them. They just assumed that Norman was being his old self. He never liked hanging out with any of Karen's friends. It was just like him to drive clear across the country to avoid an encounter. Norman's behavior seemed exactly as they remembered from high school - selfish.

CHAPTER SIX

K aren flung the suitcases through the front door not caring where they landed. Suddenly she was weary. She really hated lying. She would eventually tell them everything she swore to herself but right now she just wanted to get settled into her new surroundings. The journey was long and she had finally made it all the way across America to her brand new home. Unfortunately, it didn't thrill her. Her eyes conveyed indifference. Her mouth lamented disappointment. In truth, it could have been a Beverly Hills mansion equipped with a sunken swimming pool, sauna and tennis court in the backyard, the works, yet it would still hold no importance to her. She had other things on her mind, she told herself. Later on, she would learn to appreciate her fully equipped three-bedroom. She told herself that too. She pushed the front door shut with her back and as it supported her from collapsing she perused her new residence and sighed.

The hallway and the living room were filled floor to ceiling with boxes. One box was torn and she could hear what sounded like cornmeal seeping quietly out of it. She listened as it made its way through a tiny hole she'd discover later at the bottom just where it was supposed to be puncture proof. She lowered her head and let the heaviness of it pull up her body. Kicking her suitcases aside she went on a hunt for the box. She's in luck. It's almost at the top of the pile. She scoops it up with her forearms and heads for the kitchen going from one end, to the other. The kitchen is also cluttered leaving no available space for the now crumbling carton. In a moment of desperation, she nudges open a closed kitchen cabinet with her elbow thinking she'll just put it in there and clean it up in the morning. Only she leans too far forward and unwittingly drops it into the sink. She takes a moment. The way lawyers do during a trial. She rests her arm against the faucet and holds her head in her hand. She wasn't displeased with the result. It had been decided for her. At least now, the cornmeal was no longer spilling all over the floor. That mission accomplished she peers out from under her fingers and pans the room. The weight of all she has to do overwhelms her.

This was not the kitchen she had always dreamt of as a young woman. She imagined it having a window positioned before a magical pond that was engulfed by trees of heights that touched Heaven. She saw Cherry Orchards, Willows, Elms and Oaks. 'Lots of Willows,' she thought. She always liked the way their branches drooped beyond their trunks as if aching to touch the soil. There would also be dozens upon dozens of birds chirping out the melodies that gently woke her without an alarm clock. She could almost hear the faint hum of children rushing outside banging screen doors with their heels and them frantically trying to escape the demands of youth, igniting the air like lightening bugs.

On that note, 'enough day-dreaming,' she thinks, especially about what could have been. She leaves the kitchen, turns out the light, and decides to take a walk upstairs rather than starting the task of unpacking. As she does so, reality sets comfortably back in place. She gently pushes open the first door on the landing. She sees Yolanda, nestled snuggly in bed. Karen merely stands there listening to her breathing as she did when Yolanda was a baby. Karen's not surprised to see her asleep. By her calculations, she and Norman probably got in five or so hours before her. She gently pulls the door close and continues down the hallway to *her* new bedroom. She can hear ferocious snoring as she approaches. She opens the door and tiptoes inside. Her eyes need a few moments to adjust to the darkness. She stumbles over to the bed. She sits down on the covers and without undressing, rolls underneath them. She slips out of her shoes and lets them fall to the foot of the bed onto the carpet. After a few seconds, Norman throws his arm around her. She's startled. She didn't want to wake him but he only stirs a bit. So, she tries to shut her eyes and to get comfortable. When her head touches the pillow her entire body sinks deep into the mattress. She's more exhausted than she thought. She didn't think she would have been because she slept the entire plane ride. She relaxes and lets the quietness of her new bedroom sounds sweep over the sounds of her husband's racket. Her eyes open and close several times before finally shutting tightly, allowing her body to meld into the springs so used to the contours of her shape. It was peaceful after-all. She didn't think it would be. Finally, she doses off imagining all the things she'll do to fix up her new home.

But as restlessness stills, Norman begins to move. He tosses and turns a few times before eventually rolling over and flopping squarely onto her bandaged arm. She shrieks with pain, while Norman, alarmed, bolts upright.

"I'm sorry, bey-bee! I was gonna' pick you up but something came up," he mumbled groggily.

Karen tries to wiggle out from underneath him. Norman senses that he may have done something else to upset her but is too tired to investigate the notion. Instead he figures that it would be easier to act out the scene they always play. If repetition is the mother of skill, Norman would receive an Academy Award for his role in this part. The short scene begins with Norman feigning sympathy and asking, "Are you mad at me?" Then he slides closer to Karen and gives her his hand caught in the cookie jar look. His finale is 'I'm a lamb and you're a wolf' look, followed by, "You're not really mad at me, are you?" Karen locks eyes with him and plainly says, without emotion as if she'd rehearsed it, "No, I'm not mad at you, Norman." How could she be? She was just carrying his heavy construction tools that he neglected to put on the moving truck, which she had thoughts of leaving along the side of a road - any road. How did he suppose she was getting home with virtually no money in her pockets?

"I made other arrangements," she told him.

Truth was, she had made her plans directly after he had made his promise. As Norman rolls back over, taking with him most of the blankets, Karen could so painfully hear him when he mumbles, "Good."

Curtain.

Karen recollects a time in their marriage when good was not simply good enough. She remembers when Norman used to take pride in everything he laid his hands to, even in the ordinary, everyday things. She was even one of his priorities. She was placed on his calendar in ink right alongside work and the *fellas*. A time, dare she think about, when it meant something to him to keep her satisfied. Now *good* is rarely a word used to describe their marriage. There was a time when she was the happiest woman alive, she thought. She had the ideal life with the ideal man. It's a classic story. They meet. They fall in love. They live happily ever after. She laughed at her own youthful stupidity. As head cheerleader, everyone respected and knew who she was but she was one of many beautiful, limber girls. Norman, on the other hand, was quarterback of a school's sports team that never lost. He was practically a god. Even Norman's teachers overlooked some of his less than scholastic conduct in an effort to keep him focused on his weekly games. To her surprise, eventually she realized that even she had succumbed to some of the star treatment. There were times when she began to strive and expect the attention that she was getting by way of her relationship with Norman. Every aspect of her life was written and/or talked about. Everyone knew who she was, respected her and treated her like she was part of some celebrity couple that resided in the hollows of Heritage High. Norman was the leading man and naturally, Karen, was the leading lady.

Karen held tightly to her bandaged arm. She had to admit that it was not just the arm that hurt but her heart, in fact, it ached.

"I'll make it up to you. I promise. You'll see," Norman yawned.

"Promise," Karen repeated under her breath.

She never liked that word. She especially hated the way Norman let it drool out of his half-opened mouth. Every time he said it, it made her feel like vomiting on his head, big chunks of beef stew if she could do it on cue and with direct accuracy.

"I promise," she whispered again.

That was an aimed and loaded gun with absolutely no likelihood of ever being fired. Norman had promised her a multitude of treasures that had as of yet to materialize. She chuckled sadly wondering how Norman failed to understand why she refused to believe anything that came out of his mouth anymore.

CHAPTER SEVEN

The bedpost rhythmically shakes to the faint whisper of two moaning voices. Two sets of feet bob in and out from underneath mangled blankets tossed atop the bed. The panting grows louder and louder and the movement of the covers shift and twist rapidly. A few candles are withering on the nightstand, as they dim against a hush of flesh against flesh, and the thumping creak of the wooden bed frame against the floor. The bedsprings nearly give way trying to support their bountiful, energetic cargo. The moaning has now escalated into words of passion and utterances of desire. The motion of the bed has become volcanic and it has begun to mount higher and higher. Now there are screams, moans and sighs of ecstasy, escalating through the entire apartment into the hallway and down into the street.

Then...complete silence.

Brenda's head pops out from beneath the sheets. She searches the nightstand for a fix. She knows it's a disgusting habit, so Crystal keeps telling her unceasingly. She finds a match, lights up, takes a drag and blows the smoke up and out of her open bedroom window. The tiny ringlets bellow out from her mouth. She closes her eyes and rests her head against the backboard. There was nothing in the world she would have rather been doing.

CHAPTER EIGHT

J ust fifty yards to go before they reach the entrance to Shea Stadium, Sarah is inching her way behind bumper-to-bumper traffic, while on the radio, "Another ninety-five degree scorcher," the announcer reports. No matter though, it is the Subway Series, the Mets verses the Yankees. Loyal fans, such as Sarah, Karen, Crystal and Brenda will brave the almost claustrophobic heat and consider it a small price to pay. Karen slumps in the passenger seat beside Sarah. She's excited because she hasn't seen a live game since she moved to Phoenix, only further confirming Brenda's notion that Karen lived in *The Land that Time Forgot.*

Crystal and Brenda squabble in the back seat the whole ride, nothing new there. Crystal is upset with Brenda over the way she rudely dismisses people whenever she doesn't want to hear what they have to say. Brenda rolls down her window to let the outside noises drown her out.

Meanwhile, Sarah's busily brooding over her date with Jester. She just can't seem to let it go. Her pursuit to find solace in her singleness seems an affliction to her mother, Millie, the one who set her up with Jester. She has other duties but none as fulfilling as marrying off her only child. This pursuit of hers would be downright impressive, inspiring even if they weren't directly affecting Sarah. It actually frightens Mille to think that Sarah is not in the least bit interested in the procurement of a husband.

Sarah isn't actually so resistance to wife-hood as one who'd be led into it kicking and screaming. She's simply in conflict over the 'til death do us part' stuff. Who could blame her? Every other news article mentions the rising divorce rate with words like alimony, palimony and custody rights. Even Millie would agree that marriage doesn't have such a grand repetition, though hers is a thirty-year old one.

Sarah believes that one day in the distant, distant future the right man will come along and she'll immediately turn to Millie and ask how many grandchildren she wants. Instead of reacting the way she normally does, as if marriage is a foreign language. Sometimes when Millie is talking to her about it, Sarah doesn't even understand what she's saying. Millie will chime, "Don't you want to settle down some day?" Sarah will pause, see her mother's mouth moving, and hear church bells and the wedding march being played on a whiney electric guitar. She'll stand there listening and swear she hears Elton John's, "Someone Saved My Life Tonight," piping right out of her mother's ears.

"Well...?" Millie will swell waiting for Sarah's reply, a reply that Sarah longed for herself.

She wished she could gather it together and present it to Millie with all haste. This answer would become more of a puzzle for Sarah to solve then a true exploration into her deepest understanding of herself. She finally just respectfully wanted Millie to stop bringing it up. In fact, the more she spoke of it the more Sarah realized that the idea of settling down was thoroughly unsettling. She wanted to settle up not down and that was the only side of the equation that she saw for herself.

"I'm not settling for some man just because you want grand kids!" Sarah blurted out.

Brenda, Karen and Crystal sat quietly absorbing the pained expression on Sarah's face. Sarah merely eased the car forward hoping that no one felt the need to respond.

"You've got to set down some rules, honey. You can't just let your motha' fix you up whenever she feels your biological clock's cracked. Gawd!"

"Don't use tha' Lord's name in vain," Crystal corrected Brenda.

"Shut up, Crystal. I'm not talking to you or the Lord. I'm talking to Sarah about her mettlesome mom," Brenda waved an apology gesture at Sarah, "No offense, Sar."

"She thinks she's helping me," Sarah retorted.

She glanced at the rearview mirror to see Brenda shrug her shoulders and dig her bottom further into the back seat.

"By the way, her club's having another party a week from this Saturday," Sarah said hoping to change the subject.

Information about a party was right up Brenda's alley.

"Helping you to do what?" Brenda interjected like a dog with a bone.

Now, in stalled traffic, Sarah turned around and pleasantly griped, "Get married. Have kids. What else?"

Then she quickly turned back around and inched up another notch.

"She thinks she's gonna' die any day now," she adds, "and how can she do that in peace without knowing that her legacy will live on."

Sarah tried her hardest to interject some humor into her explanation.

"Marriage isn't the end of the world," Karen chirped, as if awakening from a restful sleep, "You all should give it a try."

No one said a word.

Sarah simply turned and looked at Brenda and Crystal for support only to discover that they were not even listening anymore, which should have been her posture from the start.

"Not every marriage works out because people tend to get married for all the wrong reasons," apparently Karen wasn't finished, "There needs to be a course given in school, I swear to God," Karen laughed heartily, "Sorry, Crystal."

Sarah looked out of the window in the direction of the stadium. She prayed to that same God that they were nearing the entrance if for no other reason than to bury this topic and cover its dead remains once and for all with baseball enthusiasm.

"Sarah," Brenda said smiling, "I've got the perfect guy for you. No, no, he's not a mere guy at all. He's a grown man."

"I think I hear the national anthem!" Sarah tried.

"This man has got his act together too. He makes a six figure salary…" Brenda continued.

"Mon-ney ain't everythang. It can't make yah h'appi' You need da' 'word'," Crystal offered.

"A-n-y-way," Brenda continued waving Crystal off, "I'll give him a call to see when he's free. Are you free?" Brenda asked Sarah.

Sarah thought to herself, 'Am I free? Am I free? Apparently, not!'

"The game better not start without us! Less they want to hear my mouth," Karen said rather authoritatively.

Sarah yeah'd and uh ah'd, piggybacking on Karen's statement attempting to prolong the thought, but what could she say after a comment like that? Meanwhile, Brenda persisted with her probing.

"Are you free or what?" she practically demanded.

Sarah felt the work of conspirators about as she mulled over Brenda's question. 'Evidently, I am not free,' she concluded in thought. 'As long as I am single, I am always available for my kindly intentioned mother and my exceptionally helpful friends,' she thought. Without the slightest bit of effort on her part, she was about to embark on yet another Saturday night of sitting up straight and listening to yet another person's life story over cocktails.

"Alright, alright. No weirdos!" Sarah conceded, "Goodness, now I have to get my hair done."

She honked her horn, sped up, stopping short just two inches from the car in front of her.

"Get a valid license!" she screamed out of the car window.

Having given in, she's upset with herself and predisposed to take it out on anyone within striking distance.

"Speaking of men, I want to tell y'all about my date last night. I can sum it all up in three words for y'all, yum, yum, yum."

"Don't cha' mean bum, bum, bum?" Crystal smirked.

"Was I talking to you?"Brenda snapped.

Suddenly, a minivan sped up behind Sarah and ran right into the back of her car. Crystal screamed. Karen turned her head sharply to see who hit them.

"What the hell was that?" Brenda asked holding the back of her neck and breathing heavily.

Sarah grips the steering wheel with the palms of her hands, "Everybody all right?" she asked then pans the vehicle to make sure.

Karen and Crystal mutter, yes. Brenda swears while rubbing her arm, and the small of her back slowly nodding, yes. Taking a deep breath, Sarah detaches her seat belt and swings her door open. Karen follows. They immediately go around to inspect the damage, both gasping in horror seeing the back of Sarah's car smashed up like a truncated accordion, metal scratching the asphalt and something hissing out at them as they knelt down to look underneath.

"What the hell!" she yelped, "If we were going any slower we would have been parked. Look at this shit!"

The sun's glare obstructs their view as a man steps out of his minivan. All they see are a pair of snug blue jeans surrounding taut thighs. Even through the thick denims, it was hard for them not the notice that he was in shape.

"I can't believe you hit my car!" Sarah started right in on him unbidden, "Why weren't you looking where you were going? I don't believe this crap!" Sarah said pointing at her car's bumper, which had one side detached from the car, dragging on the ground.

He ignored the bumper and instead looked over his horn-rimmed shades at the emblem on the trunk.

"We were only going two feet per hour! I guess you can't handle your car at that speed, huh? Crackerjack licenses are not valid in this state," Karen added sarcastically.

The sound of horns blowing started coming from the cars behind them.

"Oh bloody hell. What have I gotten myself into? I'm terribly sorry...I..." said the driver, with an English accent.

Karen noticed that Sarah's defiant; no nonsense stance slackened a wee bit.

"Sorry' won't fix this bumper, darlin'," Karen told him.

He pulled out his wallet and with it a little burgundy woman's thong went sailing down to the ground. He quickly bent over and snatched it back up. Sarah and Karen exchanged a knowing glance -- player. Then Karen pulled out a pen and paper from her purse.

"What's the name of your insurance company?" she demanded.

"Look, huh, maybe we can work something out, you know,

without the insurance companies, you know? We all know these insurance companies and how they operate, yes?" he tried.

Karen waited for Sarah to join in, but Sarah just watched his every move.

"Are you suggesting that we do something illegal?" Karen asked.

"No, no, no. Nothing like that," the stranger replied unconvincingly.

Karen looked over at his minivan and jotted down the tag, while horns incessantly honked. Meanwhile, he tilted his head in order to get a better look at Sarah through the small opening between his face and his shades. 'She's his type,' he observes, slender long legs and a plump pouting mouth. Sarah eventually notices him showering her with this goofy, enormous grin, which in turn completely annoys her.

"I don't see anything funny about my banged up car, do you? For all I know, there could be engine damage too! Do you think that's funny!?..." she yelled.

He just stands there watching her, trying his hardest not to crack a smile as her eyes danced in the sunlight and wisps of her hair bounced when she moved.

"...But to stand in my face grinning and carrying on like it's all right. Like you got it that way. You better be counting your money 'cause this is gonna' cost. That's right! I'm not going out like this! ..." she shouts.

Even though she was now squealing at him, he liked what he saw. He was so used to American girls backing down to him as soon as they heard his accent. Sarah intrigued him.

A police officer hurriedly made his way over to them amidst obscenities being hurled his way by angry motorists.

"Look, I know this mechanic who really knows his way

around..." said the stranger, "...Grand Cherokee's."

"What on earth makes you think I would trust my car to your broke down mechanic?" now it was her turn to smile.

He had that coming. After all, he wrecked her car, dodged the point of reparation, now wants this complete stranger to believe his mechanic is the best in a land of which he, himself, is a foreigner. He knows deep in his soul that if Sarah were his sister, placed before a guy like him in a similar situation he'd already have him flung to the dirt. The police officer approaches and steps in between the two of them.

"What's the problem over here? We've got to keep the traffic moving. Come on. What's going on here?" only addressing the stranger.

Sarah glances at Karen, now angry at the flat footed cop too.

"Look, off-i-cer, this-fool-ran-into-my-car! We weren't going any faster than a crawl when he just hit me! Look at how much damage there is," Sarah complains.

"Well, when you sped up I thought the traffic was beginning to move," explains the minivan owner.

"Don't think next time, drive!" Karen says waving her forefinger in the stranger's face.

The police officer steps in between the minivan owner and Karen and blows his whistle, "Hold on now! Hold on! Okay, can both of you, get in your cars, and pull over to the side of the road. You're holding up traffic. We'll figure this out over there."

"We're gonna' miss the game!" Crystal says sticking her head out of the car window.

"Sit down, fool, and shut up. Can't you see that grown folk are trying to handle they biz-ness?" Brenda nudges her.

Finally, the minivan owner reluctantly reaches in his wallet, pulls out his insurance card and hands it to Karen.

"I didn't mean to run into your car. I was just trying to get in there so that I could see the game too. As I was trying to say to you earlier, I will pay you whatever it takes to repair the damages," he concluded.

"Mat! Mat!" called a woman popping her head out of the minivan window.

Mat, short for Matthew.

"Kelly, I've got to take care of this right now, love. I'll be there in a minute," Matthew tells her.

Sarah and Karen glance at each other again thinking, 'Kel-ly.'

"Come on now. Let's move it over there or I'm gonna' have to give you's both a ticket," the policeman yelps again.

Karen gives the police officer the *evil eye*, defiantly reaching over him and handing *Matthew* back his insurance card. Then Karen and Sarah walk around to the front of her car.

"Look girl, you should take the man up on his offer," Karen suggested once they were back inside.

Silence.

"I know, I know, *his* mechanic...but he's got a nice ride there. I don't think he trusts it to *anyolebody*. Besides, there's a lot of work that needs to be done on this one."

"Gee, thanks," Sarah smirked.

"Do you have a couple of weeks to baby-sit your car? 'Cause that's what it's going to be like. Not to mention, your insurance goes up whether you caused the accident or not. Besides, look how long it's taking your other one to get fixed," Karen reminded her.

Long pause.

Sarah had forgotten about her *company* car and immediately began to warm up to the idea.

"He did say whatever it takes for the damages, didn't he?"

"Hum, hum," Karen grinned.

Karen had always been shrewd when it came to negotiating money matters. That's why Sarah had to take a moment to reflect on that old beat up Ford parked on her lawn.

"Not a scratch on it!" Sarah said, staring at the stranger's van.

CHAPTER NINE

After all the excitement of the accident and despite the loss of their favorite team, it still turned out to be a good day. They made the best of it and ate as many hot dogs and drank as many beers as they could stomach, all save Crystal. She had Diet Cokes. Now much later, Sarah leaned out of her car saying goodnight to Karen, the last one to be dropped off. Karen was doddering on the sidewalk in front of her house wanting to linger, while Sarah was ready to call it a night. They talked about everything from the boys they dated or wanted to date in high school to careers they wanted to pursue and hadn't. It was becoming clear to Sarah that Karen didn't want to go inside.

"Oh, I don't want to go inside. It feels so cool out here," Karen said confirming Sarah's suspicion.

"Yes, it is a beautiful night," Sarah said looking up at the stars.

Then, Karen looked at driveway and stumbled backwards.

"You, okay?" Sarah asked.

Karen took a deep breath and composed herself.

"Yeah, yeah. I, silly me, I just lost my balance."

"Old age, honey," Sarah laughed.

"Wait a minute. You're older than me," Karen said most proud of that little detail.

"A few months don't count," Sarah informed her.

Karen studied her house once more. A light had just gone out in the living room.

"I...huh, girl, just remembered...You know, I'm so tired all of a sudden. I've got to go to bed," Karen said a bit too hurriedly.

"Okay. Okay, old woman," Sarah teased.

"I know, once upon a time we didn't go home to sleep but to change clothes," Karen laments.

"Please don't remind me," Sarah agreed.

Karen bent over and kissed Sarah on the cheek.

"Listen, thanks for everything. Peace, girlfriend and sorry about your car," and with that quick good-bye, Karen walked to her front door.

"Yeah, me too. Bye," Sarah said honking her horn.

Then she leaned over and yelled out of the window.

"Hey, Karen!"

"Yeah?"

"Just like old times, huh?"

It was then that Sarah noticed the living room drapes quickly dropping back into hanging position.

"Yeah, just like old times," Karen said waving good-bye to Sarah, while studying the window of her house before stepping inside.

Once Karen closes the door, she finds Norman slouched on the sofa in the dark with his eyes closed.

"Norman? Norman?" she whispers, hoping all the while that he's asleep.

He doesn't move. She slips upstairs and walks over to Yolanda's room. Peeking in, she sees Yolanda curled up like a ball underneath the covers clutching her favorite stuffed animal, a fuzzy panda. Karen sits on the edge of her bed watching her sleep. Her breathing is slow and steady with the tiniest little whistle coming from her delicate little nose. To Karen, it seems to be making music with its evenness. Each time she looks at Yolanda, she can't help but see her as an infant. No matter how big Yolanda grows, Karen still remembers the sweet face and angelic eyes that would stare up at her from the crib. She wishes she could have embraced that period of time a while longer.

When Karen turns to leave, she finds Norman standing in the doorframe.

"Where you been?" he belches.

Karen swiftly walks pass him heading towards their bedroom.

"I told you, me and the girls went to the ball game. They lost."

Norman grabs her arm and turns her around to face him.

"What friends are those?"

"Sarah, Brenda, Crystal, you know."

Satisfied with her answer, he releases her. She walks into their bedroom and hangs up her baseball cap. He follows her and stands tightly beside. She turns to go out again and he blocks her exit.

"You didn't fix me dinner tonight!"

Karen weaves him and goes into the bathroom.

"That's why I left the chicken in the sink to thaw out. Didn't Miss Davidson feed my baby?"

Karen walks downstairs to investigate but stops abruptly in the hallway. She senses that Norman is not very far behind. As she suspects he's at the top of the stairs gawking at her.

"All she had to do was put it in the oven..." Karen says defensively.

Norman comes slowly down the steps. Now Yolanda emerges at the railing half-asleep wiping her eyes.

"...That's why I left the directions on the refrigerator, so that she could..."

"There was no god damn chicken in the sink," Norman

shouted at her, his voice inflamed with rage.

His face is practically disfigured with anger as he barrels down the staircase toward Karen. Yolanda only sees their shadows against the hallway wall, as Norman slaps Karen with such force that she's hurled three steps down to the foyer.

"Next time you'll stay your ass at home and fix me some dinner like you supposed to," Norman concludes as he stretches his leg over her and snatches his car keys from the top of a pile of boxes in the vestibule.

He steps outside, slamming the front door as he goes, jarring Yolanda entirely out of her sleepiness. She comes rushing down the stairs to see about Karen.

"Mommy, I'll make us some dinner. Mommy, I'll make us some dinner," she cries.

She helps Karen up and takes her to a chair in the hallway. Karen sits and stares blankly into the darkness of the living room. Then Yolanda goes into the kitchen and pulls a loaf of bread from the cupboard. She lays it on the table. Then she goes over to the refrigerator and gets a premixed jar of peanut butter and jelly. She prepares two sandwiches, places them on a plate and brings them out to Karen. Yolanda sees some blood trickling down Karen's chin and realizes that she will have to help her mother eat hers. So she guides the sandwich into Karen's partially swollen bottom lip. Karen bursts into tears as she sloppily eats the token meal. Yolanda starts to cry also but she is unaware of the tears flowing gently down her youthful cheeks. Karen takes another bite of the sandwich and blood now comes spurting out of her mouth.

"Mommy, you're bleeding!"

Yolanda jumps up and heads over to the phone, hung on the kitchen wall. There's a list of numbers on the refrigerator. She dials.

"Yes, we need a taxi, please. 101 Carlson. Yes, please, an emergency, yes."

Yolanda hangs up and walks over to Karen. She helps her to her feet then she picks up the unfinished food and brings it into the kitchen. With some aluminum foil that was underneath the sink, she wraps the partially eaten sandwiches, takes a sponge and wipes off the counter tops after sticking the food into the refrigerator. Then she turns off the light. Karen is leaning against the wall for support, unable to stand with her legs wobbling.

"They're just around the corner, Mommy. They'll be here any minute, okay?"

Yolanda, having brought some paper towels from the kitchen, starts wiping off her mother's face. A car pulls up in front of the house.

"Ready, Mommy," Yolanda says like a command.

Then she holds Karen up as she brings her to the door. She helps her out then runs back to get Karen's purse. The cab driver sees that Karen's having some difficulty walking to the car. So, he hurries out to assist her. Yolanda locks up the house then joins the cab driver and Karen. Yolanda and the cab driver place Karen in the back seat then they walk around and take their seats.

"The nearest hospital is St. Claire's. Is that fine, Miss?" speaking to Karen.

Yolanda replies, "Fine."

"What happened to your mommy, little lady?" asked the curious cab driver.

Yolanda glances up at Karen.

"She fell."

Yolanda never lies outright. Karen instructed her over the years that if she answers the questions directly enough that she doesn't have to divulge any of their family business.

"They say that most accidents happen in the home," he replied.

"Yes," Yolanda responded politely hoping the driver wouldn't ask her any more questions.

She glanced down at her pajamas and at Karen's bloody blouse and even she knows that the questions have just begun.

CHAPTER TEN

Delroy, and his family back in Nine Miles, Jamaica, were so miserably poor, that he swore he'd one day have his own business in America no matter what it took. The previous owner died three years ago bequeathing Delroy his automotive garage. Delroy had no idea at the time that it came with a two hundred and seventy-one thousand dollar bank debt attached, not to mention ten to twelve irate vendors who were unwilling to extend Delroy a line of credit. Delroy was undeterred with such trifles.

He sat down after paying his respects to his deceased boss and wrote to everyone he knew in Jamaica telling them that he was finally a business owner in America, as he had promised. For him, being bankrupt was a step up.

"Ah gon' tel ya like dis, it need a hol lotta wark," he explained to a very silent Sarah and Matthew.

Matthew had already told her that he was the kind of mechanic who'd work around the clock if need be and that he knew more about cars than the manufacturers. He also said that Delroy was fair and genuinely cared about service, in other words, a car owner's dream. Despite his rather thick accent, Sarah hung on every word he spoke and liked him right off. She could practically taste the green, leafy, steamed sautéed callaloo and salt fish he spoke of, that is, until she looked up and saw Matthew's aplomb stare. She placed her hands on her hips, reared her head back and sneered. If looks could kill, he'd be hoisted up and thrown into a gob of spilled engine oil.

"Do whatever it takes, Delroy," she told him, then looking in Matthew's direction, "Money is no object," she said confidently. Delroy replied humbly, "Ah do me best far yur' car'e."

Sarah appreciated the intelligence Matthew displayed by remaining silent. After all, she was the one who was being totally inconvenienced. Then she waved good-bye to Delroy and left the shop. It didn't occur to her to wave at Matthew. 'Why bother.' she thought. They had been standing in the shop all morning while Delroy combed over every inch of her car. As much as she loved her car, between the paint and engine fumes she had had enough. Once outside, she searched for the nearest bus stop. Meanwhile, Matthew let Delroy continue telling him about probable damage to the chassis and what he needed to do to fix the frame. Matthew didn't want any surprises when the bill came.

Once they finished with the assessment, Matthew immediately exited the shop looking for Sarah. His mind was made up to beg her leniency on the finer points. Unbeknownst to him, she had practically sprinted in order to avoid any further contact with him. He looked up the street, and caught her walking briskly toward the next corner.

"Sarah!" he yelled.

Sarah heard her name but didn't bother to turn around. She had an inkling it might be him trailing behind, so she sped up. She had had enough shoptalk for one day. In her mind she'd done her best to operate in all fairness and forgiveness and yada, yada, yada. Now, she wanted her car back without having to learn car repair from the timing belt up. As much as she hated to admit it, she just wanted to get in and drive. She could kick herself for sounding so much like a typical female driver but under the present circumstances she could appreciate where that line of thinking came from. Somewhere a well-intentioned man in an effort to impress his woman dug underneath his car and lived to tell the tale. What he failed to realize was that his woman wasn't interested in the least in automotive theory; she listened because her man was finally uttering words. All she really wanted from her car was a key and a driveway.

Sarah pretended that her impulse to break into a full fledge run was an approaching bus. To her utter frustration, Matthew caught up with her anyway.

"For a minute there I thought you were running away from me on purpose. Wow, you American girls are fast," he said a bit winded.

Sarah blamed it on her two-inch high heel boots that Brenda bade her buy, saying she looked like a model in them. After running in them, her feet hurt. Then together she and Matthew walked to the bus stop side by side.

"That could be misinterpreted," she said sharply.

"Quite. Sorry," he said with a smirk.

They arrived at the bus stop and stood at opposite ends beneath the hooded Plexiglas awning. Sarah waited to hear his automotive genius but he just stood with his hands scrunched deep inside his pockets. She observed him with raised eyebrow and queried gaze, still nothing. Then she just looked for the bus. The thought of him trying to act like a gentleman, waiting with her for the bus, was more than she could stand.

Unbeknownst to her, Matthew was presented with a peculiar dilemma. He had the perfect opportunity to talk to Sarah alone, but faltered. 'Why?' he thought. He didn't know. He had arguably been around more women than most men would be in their lifetimes. Why this sudden hesitance, he couldn't fathom. He just knew that he couldn't approach this one the way he did all the rest. The most he got from Sarah was a snide grimace when she laughed haughtily in his face. He wasn't used to that. If he didn't know any better, he would swear that his charm was almost a repellent to her.

"Did you want something?" Sarah asked so directly that Matthew felt goaded into speech.

"Yes, yes. Well…well…I wanted to know if you think, perhaps, that you could be a little less expressive with Delroy."

Sarah gaped into Matthew's face. 'Expressive! Expressive,' she thought, 'how dare he criticize me. This impertinent British snob, who has the audacity to crash into the back of my car, convince me to use his mechanic, then to tell me how I'm supposed to act!'

"I mean, he really doesn't know what 'do what ever it takes' means. He'll probably…"

"He'll probably what, fix my car properly?" Sarah managed out of her dry rage-filled mouth.

"Well, no, no, no that's not what I mean. I want him to fix your car correctly. I do. He's the best mechanic quite possibly in the whole world…"

Sure, Matthew was exaggerating a tad but Sarah liked the sound of it nonetheless. Delroy never talked down to her or speed talked her like she was some dizzy bra'wd. He treated her with respect, a rare phenomena for a woman in a body shop. 'But this character, on the other hand…' Sarah thought, looking at Matthew in wonder, '…just who does he think he is?'

"I'm just saying," he continued, trying to save face, "that he will spend two weeks on something that could take him two days to repair."

"Look, we can settle this whole damn thing through our

respective insurance agents. No problem!" Sarah squealed
through gritted teeth.

A bus pulled up. Unfortunately, its door swung open showing
every inch of space filled with people. Although Sarah tries,
there's no way for her to get on the bus. It pulls off, leaving her
standing in the street with her mouth agape. Matthew waits for
her to walk back under the awning then continues his thought
right where he left off.

"What I'm trying to say is, that although it is admirable that he
takes his repairing seriously, it could raise the price and keep you
riding buses for a long time," Matthew said.

Sarah actually begins to listen.

"I know him very well and I know how he thinks. If you could
see your way clear to stay away from, I mean, to please refrain
from, that is to say, let's discuss together what we will say to
Delroy first. That's all."

Sarah picked over each and every word Matthew said like a
detective waiting for a criminal to incriminate himself.

"See, he will put the most expensive parts on that car even if
he has to import them from another country. No doubt about that.
They'll be more expensive than your original parts too, which
means that when your car needs further repair…well you
understand," he said with a smile.

"Who the hell do you have working on my car?" she yelled.

Matthew scratches his head.

"What do you mean? You agree, he's a good mechanic, yes?"
he asked for clarification.

"What I know is that I shouldn't have done this. That's what
I know! I should have listened to my own instincts. That's what
I know," Sarah raged at the air, as yet another crowded bus came
along and didn't stop.

"I don't believe this! He didn't even slow down," Sarah shouted, "Listen, I don't have time for your *shenanigans* right now! I HAVE A DATE!" she blurted out.

Then she turned on her heels and impatiently hobbled away determined to find a taxi.

Matthew is once again taken aback. He let the vision of her eyes darting away from his and bowing in humiliation stick with him for a moment. He thought she showed a little vulnerability with that last statement. Though it was a blow to his ego that she saw him as a rat bastard, monster, and the scum of the earth, he wanted to prove to her she was wrong. Maybe he could do something, he thought.

"Listen. Listen," he called after her, "I'm sorry. I'm sorry about all of this. I wish there was some way I could make it up to you. Honest," he said undaunted by her dismissal of him.

Nothing he has said so far particularly inspires her. Then a thought does occur to him.

"Just wait right here, okay," he told her and dashed away.

Sarah doesn't pay him any mind. She just sees his lips moving and him waving at her from her periphery. He realizes that he may as well be speaking to a brick wall and still he runs off anyway. Sarah's feeling impish and continues walking, unable to see clearly due to foot pain. She's not purposely trying to be rude to him but she does notice alleviation of pain the further away from her he goes.

Two to three minutes later, Matthew darts around the corner in his van. Sarah had to admit that she was relieved to see any mode of transportation.

A few minutes after that, Matthew puts it in gear and the van goes from zero to seventy in under a minute. Sarah is thrust back into her seat being smacked about the face by a steady stream of forced air coming from the open moon roof. Sarah shifts towards him. If she could reach him, she'd smack him, but they're going too fast for her to steady her back hand. Instead she tries to close her eyes and let her thoughts drift to her impending date. As long as she keeps her expectations low, she usually ends up having a good time, the last one not withstanding. She likes listening to people's life stories exposed neatly over dinner. She thought, 'The last one notwithstanding.' Matthew reaches into the glove compartment and hands her his business card. She shoves the card into her purse without reading it. Matthew pretends that he doesn't notice by keeping his eyes on the road.

"Whenever you need a lift, I'll provide one for you, all right? Just call me," he instructed whilst pointing to her purse.

'When pigs fly over the moon, I'll call him.'

Matthew pulls in front of the address he was unwillingly given. It looks like a disco tech to him, with its black and white motif, exceedingly large windows and music trickling out onto the sidewalk. Were it not for the small block Century Gothic wording "Salon" engraved on the large brass door handles, he wouldn't have known.

"Right here?" Matthew asked to be sure.

Sarah nods, yes trying to limit the conversation to just grunts and groans.

Unfortunately, upon exiting the van, she misjudges the width of the step bar, not to mention the height of her heels and consequently goes hurling to the pavement. She lets out a panicked holler, while stumbling out of the van, and clinging to the sliding door. The door flies sharply towards her, starling her. She leaps backward and goes headfirst to the ground as her legs give way beneath her. Matthew appears out of nowhere extending his arms, sweeping her up by the waist in one smooth swoop, just as her feet are about to hit the cement. 'He's stronger than he looks,' Sarah notes and for an instant she hates the fact that his embrace is remarkably firm with his strong biceps supporting her. 'I can't be thinking this way,' she thinks, and brushes it away declaring that she's not had a decent date in a while. Matthew lifts her up and practically carries her to the salon entrance. She realizes, to her dismay, that she has the urge to hold on a bit longer. She can't imagine why of all the thoughts in the universe, those are the ones on her mind.

"Remember what I told you," he said softly in her ear and his breath and the tenor of his voice sent a tingle down her earlobe.

The sound of his vibrato seemed to fill her entire body as when following cold liquid trickling down to one's stomach. She hated him even more now. Just two minutes ago she had been biting her lip for the swear words she'd fling at him.

"All right?" he asked, "It's really no problem at all, all right. Just call any time," Matthew repeated as the closing salon door muffled his implore.

CHAPTER ELEVEN

E arlier that morning, Yolanda, with the help of the cab driver, hoisted Karen out of the back seat and assisted her through the emergency's automatic doors of St. Claire's Hospital. There was just a smattering of people waiting to be seen, most of whom are trying to sleep in a row of hard plastic chairs lined against the wall. A television set hanging overhead flashed in their blank faces. A guard, stationed a few feet from the main door was nodding. Yolanda reached into Karen's purse and paid the driver.

"Thank you, young lady. You take good care of your mommy, now," the driver instructed while waving good-bye wondering if there was anything more to say.

Karen took a seat in one of the uncomfortable chairs. Behind the receptionist desk, a nurse took an elderly lady's blood pressure. It seems the woman took a cold bath because there wasn't any heat in her building. Now, her whole body was so stiff that she could barely get out of the tub. Yolanda could relate. While in Phoenix one winter their hot water heater burst and Karen had to boil water on the stove for several weeks so everyone could take a bath. Norman stayed at a friend's.

"Honey, are you here with your mother or not?" the nurse asked Yolanda gruffly, upset from having to repeat herself.

Yolanda hadn't heard her the first time.

"We'd like to see a doctor please," Yolanda stated maturely.

"Who's we?" the nurse questioned making no effort to rise up and look around the waiting area.

"My Mommy's bleeding," Yolanda pointed out Karen, who was sitting quietly with her head balanced against the wall.

Karen wasn't paying attention to anything in particular. Her eight-year-old was in control. The nurse finally rose up from her chair and stretched her neck around the reception window. At the same time, another woman walked into the receptionist booth from the hospital side.

"Honey, your mother needs to come over here to register with me, alright?" the nurse wearily directed Yolanda.

"She's bleeding! Can she please see the doctor? Please?" Yolanda pleaded anxiously.

"Honey, everyone has to register first. Now those are the rules!" the nurse exclaimed.

The woman inside the booth with the nurse, Miss Oliver, overheard this exchange and peered over to see Karen trying to rise up out of the hard chair without success. Miss Oliver dodged out of the booth to assist her. Then ushered both Karen and Yolanda into the receptionist booth. The nurse frowns in frustration. Karen slides into the closest chair.

Miss Oliver doesn't ask any questions she simply observes the behavior of both Yolanda and Karen. She is all too familiar with the stories about to be told. And, she is not looking forward to going through the usual routine that battered wives take her through. She would spend hours trying to convince them that their husbands had no right to beat on them. Then they would spend another hour trying to convince her that the bruises all over their bodies stem from their clumsiness and nothing more. She had worked some twelve to thirteen hours that day and wasn't in the mood to have her time wasted. She had lost quite a few women to their battering spouses and she was not looking forward to losing yet another. Now she looked over at Karen with apprehension, not of Karen, per se, but of what Karen represented. She looked over at Yolanda and pitied her sweet little face knowing that her fate might be tied to the same legacy of that of her mother's. She felt no desire to rescue a family that did not wish to be rescued. She was just about to bandage Karen up and send her home when she overheard Yolanda's whisper into Karen's ear.

"Daddy didn't mean it, Mommy," Yolanda said lovingly to Karen.

Those words struck Miss Oliver peculiarly. She knew that if this little person knew what was going on in the home then there was something worth discussing. Miss Oliver had seen so often the children pretending that nothing ever happened or repeating what the parents wanted them to say to strangers. Instead, what Miss Oliver heard in Yolanda's sentence was the presence of a child who understood and who was trying to knit that family back together again. She was surprised.

"Bring them into room two," she told the nurse.

The nurse shoved a clean stack of registration papers into Miss Oliver hands.

"Okay, okay," Miss Oliver mumbled obediently.

Then they all exited the booth and went onto the emergency ward.

Four-thirty that same morning, seven stitches and a bandage on her chin, Karen and Yolanda were finally making their way out of the hospital. Paramedics bumped into the security guard, and woke him up while they were wheeling a wounded man into an operating room. The guard struggled out of slumber long enough to shift positions. Karen and Yolanda observed this with exhausted indifference as they approached the automatic front doors. That's when Miss Oliver came rushing towards them again.

"Mrs. Montgomery? Mrs. Montgomery? May I call you Karen?" she hesitated to ask more so to catch her breath than out of politeness.

"Yes," Karen answered dryly, more so to get out of there than to be accommodating.

"May I speak with you for a moment?" Miss Oliver waved towards some empty seats along the wall.

Karen couldn't wait to leave which showed in her wrinkled brow. Sensing Karen's lack of interest, Miss Oliver simply told her, "You don't have to do any talking. This will take less than a second."

Karen propped herself on the edge of one of the waiting room chairs. The coldness of the seat complicated her mood. She was uncomfortable knowing that she couldn't avoid this last erudition. 'Here it comes,' she thought, 'someone else telling her how to live her life.'

"I'm the family counselor here and I don't know if there's a problem at home but if there is and you need help, call me," Miss Oliver said handing Karen her business card and a brochure.

"Here's my number and some other information on our services. We have a 24 hour hotline, alternative housing, whatever you need if you have to get out..."

Karen was gone before Miss Oliver completed her thought.

"Thanks, but I don't need your help. Let's go, Yolanda," said Karen escorting Yolanda by the arm.

Miss Oliver watched as they sprinted out. She was still holding her business card and a now crumbled pamphlet.

CHAPTER TWELVE

arah walked into the salon, giving Matthew a brush-off good-bye and a *wish you would go away* smile. She was still trying to regain her footing, figuratively speaking. She could only surmise that the near falling experience must have temporarily made Matthew more attractive.

Immediately, Harold, her hairdresser, approached. He took one look at her and gasped. He placed his unusually large manicured fingers on his chest and began circling her slowly, and painstakingly around in a circle. His shoulder length permed hair is newly curled at the ends like Marlo Thomas in *That Girl*. He faked a cough. Sarah squinted at him trying to make out what appeared to be a definite line of mascara highlighting his feminine almond shaped eyes. She looked at the scissors-shaped handcrafted clock above his head and saw that she was indeed on time with two minutes to spare even. She can't imagine what Harold's overly punctual problem is, but as she scans her eyes down the wall to meet his gaze with her own, she snatches a glimpse of her neck in a small slither of a mirror. A neck attached to a head of hair she does not recognize as her own. Her usually tamed mane now stuck out above her scalp nearly one foot in diameter in all directions. She turned, mouth agape to see Harold's head pulled back in horror as if he'd seen a ghost. He sucked his teeth and shook his head from side to side.

"Darl-ing..." he sings.

Sarah eyelids sheepishly close.

"Now you expect Harold to do miracles, right?"

Sarah can't escape the snickers and jeers as Harold prances away from her leaving her to stand in the middle of the salon. She looks around. There's nowhere to sit, nowhere to hide. Then Harold resumes his tirade to an imaginary entourage.

"People expect so much of me. What they don't understand is that sometimes I simply cannot handle all the pressure. I'm only one person and I have to do the work of four or five as it is. Why don't they listen to me when I tell them to wrap their heads up at night or wear silk scarves, I don't know. I can only do but so much. Work with me people. Work with me. The comb is your friend," he says in a solid weep, directing that last sentence towards Sarah.

Then he signals to her that he's ready by turning his head from her and tapping twice on the washbasin chair. Sarah takes two giant steps and lands back first into the seat. He eases her into the chair by holding her head in both hands.

"Let's make magic, shall we," he says with a jerk of his head.

Sarah prepares herself for whatever embarrassment Harold has in store for her. Judging from the way he's yanking her head about, she's inadvertently given him plenty of material to work with. Meanwhile, she's perplexed by the ideology that suggests a perfect look upon entering a salon, but with her head in a sink, she can't presently find anyone to commiserate with. Instead, once again, she tries to focus on the mystery man that Brenda arranged for her to meet. Upon further investigation, he sounded better to her than when first described. Brenda gave her a few more details. Michael Wright is his name and his family hails originally from the island of Trinidad. Sarah couldn't believe that Brenda didn't want this one for herself. Brenda always had a thing for island men but apparently this one wasn't her type. She said he was too straight lace. Imagine that. Brenda also told her that Michael was a police officer who was going to law school at night and that he was nearly finished his schooling. She touted him as being her most industrious male friend and that she often came to him when she needed legal advice. Mr. Wright sounded, in fact, just right. Had Brenda finally done something right for her? Sarah thought of the possibility of him actually being *the one* and that her meeting him came from a very unlikely source, Brenda. She had to hand it to her, though; she was the closest thing she knew to an authority on men. Now with the beauty regime underway, she felt optimistic. Maybe this one really was just a friend of a friend, who managed through his own integrity not to have anything to do with a Brenda type -- someone who went through men as vending machines go through sodas.

As the water gushed down her wooly locks, Sarah heard bursts of joyful muffled squeals coming from the dryer section. Some women who were gathered there, took turns shrieking and jumping in and out of their seats. Harold cleared his throat loud enough for them to get the hint to pipe down. Then he adjusted Sarah in the wash basin. The women giggled, lowered their excitement a smidgen but not enough to satisfy him.

"We're not on a freeway, ladies! I'm gonna' need some peace and quiet!"

Harold picked up strands of Sarah's hair on his reasoning.

"If you know what I mean?" he smirked.

The ladies nodded their apologies and tried to quietly speak among themselves.

As Harold pulls her head up and down, Sarah can make out some of what the women are saying. A heavy set women marches over to the dryers. She snatches a young woman's arm and holds it up so she can see a ring she's wearing. The heavy set woman scrutinizes it carefully as if by the naked eye she can determine its value. After several moments of viewing the ring, the heavy set woman holds the younger woman's arm to her bosom and makes a gesture with her shoulders.

"You've been holding out on us, haven't you?" she declares in a big brawly voice.

Then she turns around military style and walks abruptly away. She has a limp and the floor shakes each time she lowers her right foot. Aside from what looks like her lips curling into a frown at the corners, she smiles to the other women and winks with her approval. Barely audible, the frail, little, younger woman peeks her head coyly out from underneath the hood of the dryer.

"Who me?" she asks sweetly and playfully, showing an engagement ring.

The rest of the women swarm in ogling the ring.

"That thing could cut glass," one of them ascertains while the rest shake their heads in agreement.

Then they encircle the bride in a wall of sound so loud it might actually crush the petit woman. It's obvious that the proposed bride is nervous and apprehensive about all the attention she's receiving, for she keeps retreating back underneath the dryer like a turtle to its shell. It's also obvious that her friends won't hear of it. They stake their claim next to her at the dryers and rattle off a barrage of questions and comments about their weddings and weddings that they've attended in the past. The intended bride, whose name is Angela, has her arm extended as if it's as much a part of the conversation as she. Her friends are too busy planning her wedding to be concerned with the black and blue forming around her shoulder. They're well entertained by their wedding stories. As time passes they've discussed what Angela should wear and whom she should and should not invite, what kind of food to cater, etc., etc., etc. So far Angela and her husband to be will have a priest, a witness and not much else.

Unfortunately, Harold gets annoyed by these interruptions, continually overhearing their chatter on weddings, normally his favorite subject. Business is particularly grand during the wedding season and he lives to try out new styles on the brides. That's one of the few times some of his customers will forgo their usual look and try something new. It's what he lives for as a stylist. He's an artist really, he often says to himself.

"Let *me* see it," Harold finally says to the ladies while toweling Sarah's head.

He sachets over to a very frightened Angela shyly pulling her arm away from the circle of women as Harold nears. The rest of the women part a path for him like he's their king, or in this case, queen. He extends his hand out to take Angela's. Harold inspects the ring thoroughly. He even takes a loop out of his breast smock pocket and holds Angela's finger up to the light. Twisting and turning it along with her limp fragile hand, he hems and haws as he views the ring more closely. Angela's friends look on in anticipation. While Sarah looks on humorously. After several seconds, Harold drops Angela's arm and sighs. There is a brief moment of silence. Angela sinks into her cushioned seat. Her heart crushed, her mouth contorted with embarrassment. She's humiliated and highly disappointed. The other women look at her sympathetically.

Harold clears his throat, "Darling, if he divorces you right after the wedding, you will be a very, very wealthy woman."

Angela breaks into a smile.

"Provided, of course, it's already paid for," Harold added in his best Mae West impression.

Then he dramatically struts back over to the sink. He takes one look at Sarah's hair and gasps again.

"What? What?" Sarah asked.

Harold pressed his large palm to his chest.

"After gazing at that beautiful jewel, your head de facto scares me even more," he jokes.

Sarah rolls her eyes and pushes out her lips for him to get a good look at her disapproval.

"Touchy, touchy," Harold shrugged.

Now that Harold has blessed mousy little Angela's union, she prances around the shop, hand outstretched, showing everyone her knuckles avec bling. No longer the bashful bride, she hopping from person to person as if waltzing to some music. 'Must be the bridal march,' Sarah wearily guesses while watching her just a gushing and a twirling. Sarah wished it were July already. Most weddings would have come and gone. If only she could saddle all the wedding parties and ride them out of town. She was definitely sick and tired of hearing the word - marriage.

And as that thought crossed her mind, so did Angela, she stopped right in front of Sarah. Then, she paused there, obviously hoping to hear some kind words of awe over the masterpiece she now displayed proudly, boldly — but none came from Sarah. Sarah only lifted her eyebrows ever so slightly and grinned courteously. Angela hesitated not knowing how to react to Sarah's indifference. It startled her so, that she stepped back tripping over her own feet. She wasn't sure if Sarah liked the ring or not. And that question greatly distressed her. Sarah didn't mean to but she made Angela crawl back into her proverbial shell.

The other women shook their heads from side to side disapprovingly, instantly hating Sarah. Now they had a new topic on which to focus their attention and unleashed one nasty look after another in Sarah's direction. Angela's shoulders lifted up to her ears, her tail went between her legs and she went running back to the other women again.

"Oooh, girl, Harold knows a little kitt, catty fight when he sees one, huh, huh, huh."

"Whhhhaaaaaaaat?" Sarah asked waiting for Harold's unsolicited comments.

"Marriage, girl, marriage. You have a problem with it. No need to lie to little old Harold. I can see it on your face."

Sarah doesn't say a word. Instead she surveys the room to see if anyone is within earshot of Harold. This is not the type of conversation she is interested in having with her hairdresser.

"I do not," Sarah tries to say assertively.

Now Harold doesn't respond, but gently pushes her head so that she's physically and metaphorically facing the mirror.

"Look, Harold is not trying to get into your biz'nes. I just call it as I see it and I see you like a billboard, hum, hum."

Unfortunately, so did all the other women in the salon. Sarah wanted to kick herself for not simply saying 'nice rock.'

CHAPTER THIRTEEN

The five-hour ordeal was finally over and all Sarah had to show for it was a French twist. She obediently examined it with the looking glass Harold gave her. She thought she looked like a twelve-year old, what with the wisps of hair cascading down the sides of her cheeks. It was the exact opposite persona she was going for. It made her appear as if she spent way too much time preparing for her date, never a good sign. She hoped the guy wouldn't notice but she knew he would. He'd figure she sat in the salon all day just for him. He wouldn't believe that a great many women spend an enormous amount of days in the salon without a hint of a man in sight. Way in the corner of her reflection, she caught jeers and poisoned stares from Angela and her cast of characters.

She paid the cashier, thanked Harold and walked out with the women in the salon scoffing at her as she left. She knew she messed up and she didn't know how to fix it. So she ran out of there. It had already been a long day and it was only three o'clock in the afternoon. 'Sticks and stones,' she thought. As she exited seeing her own reflection in the storefront glass, she supposed that their stares could have just as easily have been because she looked ridiculous. It didn't matter now. It would have to do for the night. Besides she wasn't about to go back in there to have Harold re-do or re-flip a gosh darn thing.

"Psssst! Psssst!"
Sarah heard someone faintly summoning her as she exited.

Initially she thought it was a man calling for her as if she was his puppy. So she didn't bother turning to see where it was coming from.

"Psssst! Psssst!"

Again she heard it but this time it was louder and more in her direction. Following the sound, she surprisingly found Karen and Brenda hiding in a nearby doorway.

"Karen? Brenda?" Sarah asked thinking it was strange behavior even from them.

They waved her over.

"Did you guys just get here?" she asked.

"No, we've been here for thirty minutes," Karen whispered.

"Thirty minutes? Why didn't you just come in? I could have used some character witnesses," she paused to consider Brenda's and Karen's crumbled expressions, " Don't ask."

Karen and Brenda shrugged then pointed at their heads. Karen's was spiked as though she's been sleeping outdoors in a forest and Brenda's was frizzy, matted and tangled. More odd behavior, given the fact that Brenda's always had to be impeccable, even when going to a bodega.

"If Harold saw either one of these heads…" Brenda confessed.

"You should have seen mine when I walked in. He was staggering and acting like he was going to have a heart attack. Honestly, it was embarrassing," Sarah told them.

Then, she looked at Karen, remembering a time when she would have never left the house unless her hair was immaculate. In fact, Karen used to teach Sarah how to do her hair and nails back in the days when Sarah loved her Afro and torn jeans.

"Anyway," Sarah went on, "Where's Crystal? I'm starving."

"Choir practice, where else," Brenda said scathingly.

"Get this, she met someone at church. Has a date with him tonight. Can you imagine?" Brenda says with a chuckle.

She hopes Sarah and Karen will join in with the amusement, but they don't. It's nothing new for them. Brenda had a well-worn disdain for men who spend too much time at church. She believed they were hypocrites of the highest order. A little bit of religion is enough, that's her motto. Sarah and Karen look elsewhere until Brenda finishes her speech. As usual, Brenda will be heard.

"When she gonna' learn. You can't meet nobody at nobody's church. Everybody knows that. I've tried to tell her but she just don't listen. She's under the misguided conception that all the good ones are there. Can you imagine?" she asks, "If that were true, *all* of women-kind would be in there with them -- okay," Brenda concludes.

Sometimes Brenda makes a good point however convoluted it begins. Karen doesn't say a word. Sarah waits a few more seconds to give Brenda the courtesy of having listened to her, using the term loosely, theory. Then she turns to Karen and asks, "Where are we going to eat?"

Sarah waits. No answer.

"Oh, no," Sarah astutely puts two and two together.

"I think I've got to cancel now," admits Karen without apology but with an air of accusation regarding Sarah's tardiness.

Brenda lowers are head in agreement with Karen. Sarah is not at all surprised of Brenda's excuses but Karen's?

"Well, I waited as long as I could. Now I have something I gotta' do," Brenda blurted out.

"Something..?" Sarah asks indicating that it might be someone.

"I just have something I have to do. It's personal," Brenda said with her lips puckered in a kiss.

"Does *it* have a name?" Sarah mocked.

Brenda tried to pull off an indignant posture but she secretly loved the ribbing she got about her love life.

Then, of all things, Sarah catches sight of a minivan pulling up alongside them from the corner of her eye.

"Oh, brother. What in the world..." Sarah says ducking behind Brenda.

Karen and Brenda stare into the tinted windows of the SUV, trying their hardest to figure out who's inside.

"That's our little car wrecker, isn't it?" Karen inquires meanwhile, recognizing the bumper that didn't even get a single scratch on it.

A minute later, Matthew steps out of it, goes around the front and leans on the van directly facing Sarah. She tries not to notice that he's sporting a pair of white, tight fitting jeans. Sarah has always loved the way men looked in white. It reminded her of the Caribbean, being on vacation where all the men wear cotton and linen to show off their sun baked pectorals. She catches herself daydreaming and immediately tries to straighten up.

"Hi, all. Name's Matthew, Matthew Thompson. Pleased to have an opportunity to formally make your acquaintance. Sorry about the other day," he said in a very *cheerio* sort of way.

"You didn't tell me he had an English accent," Brenda swooned while sauntering over to Matthew as seductively as she could.

Karen and Sarah simply watch. They've seen this behavior before. It's almost comical. She completely surrounds a man as if she's a spider spinning a web. Brenda had no concern as to whether Matthew was attracted to her or not. In her mind, all men were attracted to her. In the dream world she lives in, men looked at her first and if she didn't like them or was unavailable, they redirected their affections to her friends. Sarah heard this speech from Brenda many, many times before. And, Sarah obeyed and never dated anyone that Brenda hankered for. That made it easier on both of them and was definitely why they remained friends. Up until now, Sarah had always regarded Brenda's idiosyncrasy about men as youthful and funny but watching her slither and cozy up to Matthew made those little rules seem somehow less amusing. For a moment or two Sarah felt a tinge of jealousy creeping into the foreground of her thoughts. As ridiculous as it was for her, she didn't want to honor Brenda's precept any more. She honestly didn't know whether it was because she liked Matthew or if he just represented any random available man that Brenda was trying to get her claws on. Either way, the whole thing made her irritable, yet she knew that the whole thing was nonsensical because both Matthew and Brenda were bona fide players.

"Matthew, Brenda, and you know Karen," Sarah managed to give some kind of introduction to what she perceived as a farce.

Matthew took Brenda's hand and kissed it gently. He did it so effortlessly as if it were the most natural thing in the world. Brenda's face went from high yellow to beet red. She fanned herself and blushed like a schoolgirl. Then he took Karen's.

"Yes, yes, I know Karen," kissing her hand also, "I'm really terribly sorry about all this nonsense. We have it all worked out though, Sarah and I," he winked at Sarah.

Sarah smirked back at him," Speaking of which, what are you doing here? I said I'd talk to Delroy more diplomatically. What else do you want from me?" she practically snapped.

She was afraid that her tone with him was too harsh and cruel but she felt she couldn't help herself. Now he was evidently trying to work his little magic on all her friends and she was not about to let him.

"I don't want anything from you," Matthew said as if springing into action like a toy soldier, "Oh, no. I came here to do you a favor," he happily replied.

"A favor?"

'The impertinence of a man who could wreck your car then make it sound as if he's doing you a favor,' thought Sarah.

"I came to offer my services to you as your driver," he held out his arm and presented his van.

"All-right," Brenda jawed while scurrying her hips towards Matthew's minivan.

Matthew watched the made for men show Brenda gave with her fanny swaying demonstratively from side to side. He was all man, after all. Then he quickly swung open the sliding door and helped her in. As his hand slid across her elbow, she ooed and awed as if she were a princess. Then, to Sarah's utter astonishment, Karen too stepped over to the van and jumped right into the passenger seat. She cleverly diverted her eyes away from Sarah fearing she might receive a hearty thump on the head.

"Brenda? Karen?" Sarah queried, her mouth twisting with anguish from their obvious lack of loyalty.

"Oh, come on, Sarah. He's just trying to be nice," Brenda explained ever so timidly.

"Yes, I'm just trying to be nice," Matthew chimed in while extending his hand to meet Sarah's but she pulled hers away.

"No. No, thank you," Sarah retorted.

She would not give in. She would not be persuaded. She walked up to Karen's window.

"Karen, I thought at least we were going have lunch today? Coffee? A donut," she said desperately.

She felt undignified begging. She could feel Matthew's eyes boring a hole in the back of her head.

"I know, girl. I'm sorry. I just have something I have to do. Listen, why don't we have dinner at Jezebel's tonight," Karen offered as a compromise.

"I can't tonight," Sarah stepped back onto the curb, purposely trying to avoid Matthew's penetrating gaze.

She hated the way his eyes seemed to look right through her and she was not about to give him any reason to continue.

"That's right. You have a date with Michael. Please treat *him* nice at least. He's a good, good friend of mine," Brenda yelped from the back seat where she had sprawled herself amorously across.

She was quite content in the enemy territory. At the mention of Michael's name, Matthew's glance turned into a full-fledged ogle. Now, Sarah could feel a faint burning sensation at the base of her neck.

"Tomorrow then," Karen suggested without getting any sort of response from Sarah one way or the other.

Sarah filed away Karen's peculiar behavior as yet another characteristic that her best friend brought back with her from the mid-west.

"Are you sure you don't need a lift anywhere?" Matthew asked Sarah.

Sarah thought it strange for him to continue this absurd, seemingly innocent quest to do a good deed act.

"I'm sure," Sarah answered him with a look that told him she knew what he was up to and that she was not going to fall into the same trap that both her so-called friends had.

Matthew disappointedly said good-bye to her and climbed into his van. She watched him as he slowly pulled away while Karen and Brenda waved their almost too gleeful good-byes in her direction. As the van drove off, she felt let down by her friends and by her present transport predicament. She wasn't used to being without a car. She got her license in high school, for goodness sakes, and had been driving ever since.

Resolutely, she reached in her pocket and pulled out some change. Lucky for her, she thought, the bus stop was only a few feet away. She strolled over to it and in the name of empowerment praised her ability to cope. She opted not to take a lift from a man she barely knew. And she was determined to live with that decision and not to let anything get her down. She recognized that maybe she had been a little spoiled by her passion for driving and she realized that there were many people who never even owned a car in their lives. She almost felt guilty by how comfortable she had been in the recent past as a car owner. Thinking this was in some way a humility lesson that she was dead set on passing with flying colors.

Unfortunately, no sooner had her foot crossed the threshold underneath the bus stop awning, it began to rain – It was lucky for her that she had made it before it started coming down, it would be a short summer rain sprinkling the earth in one spot then moving on its way to its next patch of earth. But the little inkling suddenly became a torrential down pour. It rained so hard and so vehemently that the water bounced off the pavement and soared right back up into the sky. Sarah tried to find something in her purse to protect her freshly done hairdo. It was fruitless. She couldn't find anything large enough, so she took her purse and put it above her head.

CHAPTER FOURTEEN

One long bumpy, sticky bus ride later and she was finally back in the warmth of her house. The rain felt more like a hurricane and she simply wasn't prepared. Plus the rickety bus managed to hit each and every pothole along the way. By the time she got home, she was drenched down to her bra and panties and her feet ached from having to stand while being tousled about. All of those thoughts on humility and her car vanished. Now, Matthew should pay with his blood. When the doorbell rang she didn't hear it at first because she was so busy imagining Matthew emptying out his bank accounts and change jars. She had forgotten all about her date entirely. Upon hearing the now second ring, she ran to the door with a towel around her head, a housecoat and slippers. 'He's nearly thirty minutes early,' she noted. Then she panicked and was hesitant to look through the peephole.

"Who is it?"

He responded in a booming manly voice, "Hi, it's me, Mike."

She quickly adjusted and secured her robe, then opened the door. Michael smiled when he saw her and bowed his head kind of like a male model posing.

"Hey," he said plainly.

"You're a little early," was all Sarah could think and therefore, it came barreling right out of her mouth, "Come in. Come in," she continued once she realized that Mike had no intention of giving her an explanation.

He strode right pass her and ambled over to the living room.

Sarah couldn't help thinking of Carly Simon's song, "You're So Vain," as he strutted across the parquet.

"I have a habit of being unfashionably early wherever I go," he admitted coolly like a disc jockey that only plays smooth hits.

It was uncanny. He was exactly as Brenda described. Every little thing about him seemed powerful, confident. As he made his way from her door to the sofa, she looked at the goods. She couldn't help but stare. Every inch of him appeared to have been chiseled. He had on a light, cottony fabric suit and his muscular body clung to it and outlined the most amazing figure she had ever seen on a man up close. 'Thank God,' Sarah thought. She could see herself getting into him. And that was something she never thought she would experience at the hands of a Brenda fix up. And, he brought her flowers. The petals beamed over the edge of the small shopping bag he was carrying. Sarah loved it when a man brought gifts. It showed her that he had been thinking about her as much as she'd been thinking about him and more importantly, that he was prepared. He looked at her too. He was pleased with what he saw too. She could tell and blushed when she noticed a smile forming at the edge of his mouth. Then she remembered the housecoat and slippers and that quite possibly he could be laughing out loud on the inside.

"I..I got caught in the rain. I'm just...I have to blow dry...Make yourself at home," she tried to cover her embarrassment.

Sarah pointed to the sofa for him to sit. Then she dashed into her bedroom.

"Take your time," Michael said with a wave of his hand like he owned the place.

Then he headed straight for the kitchen carrying his little shopping bag, and he proceeded to place the bag on the counter. Discovering the stove, he turned it on and waited until it reached

425 degrees. He took off his jacket, rolled up his sleeves and started riffling through the cabinets. He found what he was looking for, a roasting pan and a regular pot. Then he took a carefully wrapped package containing two steaks from the bag, which had already been cleaned and seasoned. He tossed them into the roasting pan and slipped it into the oven. He searched through the cabinets again, found a vase, filled it with water and slid a batch of roses into it.

"If you want, you can make yourself a drink. There's some mixers in the refrigerator," Sarah shouted from the bedroom.

"Thanks, but I've got it all under control," Michael replied as someone sure of oneself.

He pulled out a bottle of red wine from the bag, popped the cork and ran the top of the bottle under his nose, then fetched two crystal wine glasses out of Sarah's kitchen cabinets.

About a ship

Around that same time, Crystal was on a date with her church friend, Terry, a rather attractive man too. They were downtown by the South Street Seaport, walking arm in arm along the promenade. Crystal was in her glory. She waited for the right one and she finally got what she wanted — a man who loves the Lord. Mentioning the word of God in regular conversation with Terry was no big deal. He was raised in the church. Unlike her girlfriends, if she spoke about *Paul* or *John* as though they were old friends to Terry, he would know who she was talking about and even say Amen. Another couple passed by them and the woman glanced admiringly at Terry, making Crystal feel even prouder of her wonderful catch. In Crystal's mind, Terry was about the most spiritual, not to mention the most superb looking man she had ever seen in her life. So much so that she couldn't endure looking at him when he spoke directly to her. She'd duck and dart around trying not to stare directly at him. She didn't want to seem like a crazed star struck groupie but she knew that she was every bit the screaming teenager behind the police barricade. She was in trouble. He was out of her league. She couldn't believe that anyone as sophisticated as Terry Anthony Lieland, son of the distinguished Elder Lieland, would even give her a second glance.

Growing up, her siblings used to call her Plain Jane. Back then she didn't really mind being ordinary. At least she wasn't ugly, she thought. Some of the other nicknames in the family were Tar and Ashy. Kids can be so cruel. Crystal and Terry passed a bench along the side of the walkway and Crystal thought of how romantic it would be to sit in the moonlight holding hands. But Terry had something else in mind. He sees one of the World Yacht ships docked in the harbor and proceeds to pull Crystal over toward it. When they get within a few yards from the ship's guard, Terry stops short.

"You wait here, okay," he told her.

Then he walked up to the ship's guard.

"How you doing, man?" he asked the ship's guard.

"All-right. Ticket, please," the guard says standing rigidly and intently looking forward like he's in front of Buckingham Palace.

"Hey, listen man..." Terry began.

He leans over and begins to whisper something into the guard's ear. The guard nods his head up and down continuing to keep his eyes and his face parallel with the ship.

"I understand, man, but no ticket, no ride," the guard says without the slightest hint of annoyance or agitation at Terry's request.

Crystal looked on hoping Terry was purchasing tickets as a delightful unexpected treat for her. Being on a big ship was one of the things she had never done in life and so wanted to know what it was like. Curious, she decided to take a closer look and to see who was on board. So, she approached the boarding ramp. She made it a point to glance over her shoulder from time to time to make sure Terry knew where she was. She didn't want to lose him so early on in the evening. Meanwhile, Terry was bargaining with the guard.

"Come on, man. Help a brother out," Terry pleaded.

"My brother, I'm an only child. Ticket please" says the guard, this time while planting his foot firmly in Terry's direction.

Terry took a giant step back and noticed Crystal standing near by. Upon seeing her, he began to frantically tap all of his pockets.

"I don't believe this! I don't believe this! I forgot my wallet!" Terry exclaimed loud enough for Crystal to overhear him.

At that, the guard cut his eyes away from his imaginary post to scrutinize Terry.

"How much is it anyway, man?" Terry's charade went on.

"For you and a date, fifty dollars, sir," the guard offered back in a very official tone.

Terry then screams even louder so there's no way for Crystal not to hear him, "Fifty bucks!"

Crystal, as if on cue, reaches in her purse and pulls out her wallet. She feels proud as she counts off fifty dollars and hands it over to the guard. The guard raises an eyebrow at Terry while taking Crystal's hand and helping her through the roped partition and onto the plank.

"God is gonna' shine on you, baby," says Terry as he kisses Crystal on the cheek and quickly ushers her onto the ship.

"Not many women would do that for a man. You're very special. It's all that Holy Spirit reigning down on you, right?"

Then he kisses Crystal again once they're firmly on board.

Crystal doesn't want to make too much of the fifty bucks. She knows Terry's family. She knows that he's good for the money and although he never actually said that he would pay her back, she just knew that it was understood, he would return it to her - eventually. Besides, she loved his little pecks of appreciation on her cheeks. He smelled so good and his face was so cleanly shaven that whatever doubt was welling up in her soon melted away. Especially as they leisurely walked arm in arm down the hallway of the first level of the ship. They stopped directly in front of the restrooms.

"Hold on a minute, baby? I'll be right out," Terry says as he goes into the men's room. Crystal could get used to him calling her baby. She liked the sound of that, 'baby.' It immediately made them sound as if they were intimate with each other, and she really liked that. They were already a couple that had pet names for each other. She never had a boyfriend before, someone who would refer to her as lovey-dovey or pookie instead of the silly nicknames she was burdened with as a child. She liked it a whole lot she thought and dutifully waited outside the bathroom door for her man so she could hear him call her that again. 'Baby,' she thought, 'that suits mey jus' fine.'

Sarah's Apartment

She hadn't had anytime to set out hor d'oeuvres for Michael before he had arrived on her doorstep and now worried that she might be starving him right out of a dating mood. Luckily, she had finally finished getting dressed.

"There's some cheese and crackers if you want," she said as she came out of the bedroom and headed for the living room. That's when she could have sworn she smelt the aroma of something heavenly coming from her own kitchen.

"Hey, what's this? I smell food," she asked Michael.

"Surprise! I thought we'd do something different on our first date, like staying in," Michael said with a manly flourish.

"In?" Sarah did her best to hide her disappointment.

"You'd rather go out?" he asked having read her expression accurately.

"No...I...no...not necessarily...but..." she knew her face told another story.

For one, had she known, she would have kept on the towel and the slippers.

"Oh, I'm sorry. I call myself being spontaneous," he explained.

"You are. We, we don't have to go out," she flipped off her high heels and warmed up to the idea quicker than even she imagined.

Michael happily walked over to her with the wine and two glasses.

"Good then. Would you like a glass?" he offered.

"Yes, please," she accepted gladly.

Michael poured her a glass. Sarah took a sip and decided to go with the flow. She knew that that would be what Brenda would tell her to do. She felt somehow obligated to make this one count for her sake.

"Very nice. Smooth. What is it?" she asked.

"L'hiver. It's from France. Let's sit, shall we?" Michael said pointing to the sofa as if he were the host. He politely allowed Sarah to sit first, and then he sat comfortably beside her.

"I've always been impressed by people who knew about wines. And this is excellent. I'm looking forward to seeing what you've made for us," she said.

At that, Michael got up to check on the meal.

"Steak with my famous green vegetable medley which, by the

way, will knock your socks off," he answered as he stood up.

"Would you mind terribly if I only ate the medley? I don't eat meat," she said cautiously.

Sarah couldn't see it, but Michael slammed his glass of wine down on the kitchen counter.

"I should have known, a vegetarian," he muttered under his breath.

Sarah took another long gulp of wine. She hadn't noticed Michael's slight irritation. As far as she was concerned, he was showing signs of being very much what she had always desired in an ideal mate, imaginative and intelligent.

"You're full of surprises, aren't you? A wine-connoisseur, a chef, a man of mystery, what next?" Sarah asked enthusiastically.

"I do my share," Michael said with a shrug of confidence.

He was a little perturbed that his perfectly planned dinner wasn't as perfect as he hoped but he would get over it quickly, he decided.

"A vegetarian, uh," he resisted the urge to prejudge Sarah but he had a real distrust of people who didn't eat meat.

It was a machismo thing for him, sure fire measure in determining the good guys from the bad guys.

"Ah, anyway, tell me, how do you know Brenda?" Michael asked wanting to keep things light and upbeat.

He didn't want to get discouraged so early on. He was going to make the most of this date and just like that he was back to his smooth, suave, self-assured self.

"Oh, Brenda and I go way back. I think I've known her for almost, well, I'm about to tell my *real* age. Well, I've known her for almost fifteen years. That makes me feel ancient just saying it," Sarah said bashfully.

"You don't look ancient and, trust me, that's all that matters," Michael said while going to stir the vegetables, double checking to make sure the flame wasn't too high.

"We went to school together; grew up in the same neighborhood," she continued.

"That's cool. I don't see anyone from my old neighborhood anymore. In fact, I wouldn't know them if I did," Michael reflected deeply in thought.

"Life is strange that way, isn't it?" Sarah responded thinking about Karen's return to town.

Michael came back into the living room and sat snugly by Sarah once again.

"It sure is," he said with an inviting smile.

Aboard the Ship

On the main level of the ship, a man walked out of the men's room, fanning his hand in front of his nose. Crystal was leaning against the wall still waiting ever so patiently for Terry.

"Is anyone else in there?" Crystal inquired struggling to regain her balance from rushing up to the stranger so quickly.

She had rested too heavily on her legs and felt pins and needles when she stood.

"Some guy," the man confirmed disgustedly then walked away coughing.

Crystal's mind began to swell with possibilities of what might be wrong with her knight in shining armor. Then she laughed to herself at the stories she would tell people who asked how they fell in love. She'll tell them that she had to rescue him from the depths of a toilet in the men's room on board a luxury liner. 'Ah' took a deep breath and swam through shark infested waters,' she'll say, 'and Ah' was mighty scared but a wo-mon's got ta' do what a woman's got ta' do.' It only took a second to realize that that story should never be told to another living soul. Besides, she had to find her date first. Her pulse quickened, as she looked left then right to see if anyone was coming down the hall. Then she pushed the men's room door slightly ajar with her numbed foot. She couldn't see inside so she pushed it a little farther but now all she saw was smoke.

"Terry. Terry! Ter-ray, is everythin' all right?" she asked with spikes of panicked shrills in her voice.

She bumped the door slightly wider with her hips and again only saw smoke.

"Terry, yu'are really scaring meh' now!" she said placing half of her body into the men's bathroom.

"Terry!" she screamed and heard it echo down the hall toward the main dining room. 'Thank God,' she thought because her screams were being drowned out by the band's "If You Think I'm Sexy." Crystal then waded through the fumes, her eyes tearing and her throat closing up trying to limit the amount of smoke from getting in. She began to choke. She thanks God again for having her be one of the fire wardens at the church for so many years. She knew the procedure well, 'Lower your body under the smoky cloud.' Although the church fire captain would have chastised her for going towards the flame she would tell him, if the subject ever arose, that she was on a rescue and recovery mission. She took each step with care as she frantically called his name.

"Ter-ray! Ter-ray! -- Terr.....rrrraaaayyyy!"

CHAPTER FIFTEEN

Sarah's Apartment

"You know, I like talking to you," Michael said sinking leisurely down into the soft leather of Sarah's couch, "You're real easy to talk to."

"Really? Thanks," Sarah blushed, raising her wine glass high as a gesture of thanks for the compliment. She's surprised too at how easy it is to speak with Michael but most of all at the aspect of Brenda having introduced them. Michael was not Brenda's usual style of male friend. Sarah reclined back and allowed herself to contemplate what it would be like if Michael and she actually did get together. She knew that Brenda would no doubt manage to mention her involvement in matchmaking at every opportunity. 'You never would have met him if it wasn't for me,' and 'You never would have had this baby if I hadn't introduced you to your husband,' Sarah thought, 'and so on and so forth.' She thought that Karen would probably not have much to say on the subject one way or the other, a fact that really began to trouble her. Crystal, on the other hand, wouldn't let her rest until she agreed to let her plan the whole wedding, it was an unwritten agreement.

"Take my wife, for example..." Michael began.

Take my wife...

Take my wife...

Take my wife...

And the words hung in the air producing a frame around

Sarah's pleasant dreams of togetherness and possible wedding trimmings and trappings. Then a needle on the record player, that played the wedding march, scratched across the album and every head turned to see Sarah's face in a wrinkle.

"...There was always something wrong..." Michael continued.

Sarah swallowed her wine realizing that an ocean of it had been sitting in her mouth ever since Michael began this particular train of thought.

Take my wife...

Michael went on, "...I couldn't say anything to her without us having a fight of some sort afterwards..."

He didn't even pause to see Sarah's reaction as he gave her his examples.

"...If I said, 'Have a good day at work, honey. Don't let those people work you too hard.' How would you interpret that?" Michael asked or, rather demanded.

Sarah proceeded cautiously.

"Well..." she started slowly, still stuck at 'take my wife.' "I guess I would try not to let people bother me that particular day?" Sarah said, awkwardly managing to make it sound like a question.

"Exactly, exactly!" Michael blurted out then stood up to act out the argument he would typically have with his *wife*, complete with hand movements and neck jerks.

"Well..." he said slowly for dramatic effect, "...she would turn around and say, 'What, you think I'm a push over or something?' And I would stand there and think, 'Where the hell did that come from?' And it was always weird like that, even from the very beginning. Only I couldn't see it until it was too late," Michael sighed as if a great weight had been lifted off his chest.

Sarah hesitated only slightly before inquiring, "Then, ah, then, ah, you ah, you got a divorce, right?"

Michael made a dash for the kitchen, his third trip thus far.

Sarah had to admit that she liked being waited on by a man, but...

Take my wife...

Take my wife...

Take my wife...

"No. No, we didn't," Michael revealed, his voice trailing off behind, muffled and ever so faintly audible.

"Well, then you had a separation, right?" she asked, still somewhat hopeful.

She disliked the fact that there was a smidgen of distress in her voice.

Aboard The Ship

Crystal finally groped her way to the back wall of the bathroom and is not prepared for what she sees; Terry's body crouched down on the bathroom floor, his head resting on a pillar and the rest of him leaning in a fetal position against the tile wall. He didn't notice her at first, so busy was he examining his hands as if they weren't a part of his body. Crystal knelt down beside him, more than a little concerned.

"Ter-ray, 're ya' all ri-ght?" not knowing what to think.

'What's wrong with him, Lord?' came to mind. She looks down at the floor and sees a clear plastic bag, empty. Beside it are ten *marijuana roaches* scattered in every direction next to it. It dawned on her that this peculiar smoke had a familiar smell. Terry finally looked up, "Hey, you're not supposed to be in here!" he yelled.

Crystal accepted what he said as the gospel and jetted out of the bathroom as quickly as she could. Terry pulled himself together and ran out after her. He caught up to her as she rounded the corner of the deck into the dining area. Then he walked alongside her for several steps without saying a word. When he slid his arm around her shoulder, she pulled away.

"I'm hungry," he sniffled and then just sat down at the first table he saw.

Crystal stood frozen, part of her wanting to cry and the other part of her wanting to poke her finger in his eye. She couldn't get over just how much he was messing up her fantasy date. His family, were pillars of the church, one of the oldest families still attending. It was a known fact that his great grand daddy owned the original deed. Then she thought about what Brenda always said about men in the church - hypocrites! She didn't want Brenda to be right, but Terry was not this cool guy she had pictured so many Sunday mornings. He wasn't the perfect Christian man either who always knew what to say when called on to do the closing prayers, as she had seen him do time and time again. She resisted the urge to think that those were just words to him and that he didn't actually believe them. 'He probably practiced them in front of a mirror,' she thought. 'God forgive me,' she repented. She used to think so highly of him, that his feet never touched the ground.

Now, she just stood there, next to a couple's table in that floating dining room and stared at her date. He was just a man. She would have to accept that as a fact, as painful as it was. She had to pull herself together. Admittedly, most of what she thought of him was her own invention. She realized that it wasn't even fair for her to ask him to live up to her wishes. Mostly she knew that if she didn't move past this, that she would be miserable for the next two and a half hours. She combated the overwhelming feeling of sobbing like a baby, rolled her chin up to the ceiling and walked over to where he was already seated. As Crystal slid into the chair across from him, she couldn't help but notice a camera and a pack of cigarettes in front of Terry as well as a partially eaten plate of food that he was now picking from. A knot formed in her stomach as she pieced together yet another disturbing realization, that Terry just walked over to this table having seen the unattended food, not even caring that it was someone else's. Crystal scanned the ballroom floor. She knew that sooner or later *that* someone would be back to collect their belongings and to finish their meal. She was panicked with embarrassment. 'What if it's some big overgrown bodybuilder?' she thought, '...Or some ruffian, that managed to conceal a weapon under his tuxedo right pass the strong men and the metal detector. She thought, 'Could the entire sum of Terry's character be a grand performance for the people of the church?' She was dumbfounded. It was like he had never been anywhere before and, therefore, just didn't know how to act. She turned and just stared at him hard, trying to put together what he must be thinking. He didn't even look up at her. He continued to consume someone else's chicken and green peas, managing to pick up each pea with a knife and fork while holding a napkin just so to periodically dab the corners of his mouth. Even his flawless table manners were disturbing.

Sarah's apartment

"Yeah, yeah, a separation. Yeah, that's what we kind of had, a separation," Michael explained before he flew into the kitchen once again to check on the status of the steaks.

He was slightly agitated by what he perceived to be the third degree from Sarah.

"A legal separation?" Sarah leaned on the word legal.

"Well, sort of," he snorted and pouted under his breath.

Sarah took another long gulp of her wine, threw her head back and laughed hysterically, "That's like being sort of pregnant, isn't it? What does that mean anyway?" she laughed.

"Well, I still see her from time to time. Old habits. But there's nothing between us now, nothing."

Sarah knew that the conversation was leading less towards romance and more towards the absurd. So she sat way back and decided to have some fun. Clearly Michael was up to something and she felt obligated to find out exactly what it was.

"You men are something else," she exclaimed in a howl.

Michael appeared in the doorway between the kitchen and the living room, more than a little peeved by Sarah's enthusiasm over this topic.

"What do you mean by that?" he asked with a great deal of attitude.

"You guys just kill me that's all," Sarah responded casually.

"What? What did I say?" Michael asked defensively.

Sarah lifted her head up and inspected his demeanor. She grimaced and waited for some sign of sensitivity or awareness about what they were discussing, but there was none.

"You honestly don't know do you?" she asked ever so sweetly.

Michael walked over and sat down next to her. He was trying to be romantic again, gentle. He lifted her hand and placed it in his.

"No, I don't. You're gonna' have to enlighten me," he said with a devious grin.

Sarah shifted her weight so she could look at him face to face. Suddenly, she felt sober.

"Well, for one thing, here you are out with a woman while you obviously have another one, your wife. No doubt, sitting around somewhere waiting for you to come home," she rattled out.

"It's not like that. I don't love her anymore," Michael said, pawing Sarah's hand and moving in closer to her.

"Besides, I'm out to have a good time not to find a wife," he offered delicately.

"Men!" Sarah joked it off though she didn't like what she was hearing.

She poured herself some more wine and began to mentally count just how many glasses she had thus far. She was up to numeral four when Michael made her loose her concentration by placing his hand upon her knee.

"As pretty as you are, don't you have a few some ones hanging around?" he grinned.

Aboard the ship

Crystal was challenged by her mounting disgust of Terry. She looked around the room observing happy couples cutting a rug. She couldn't believe how well the music sounded and how beautiful the view of Manhattan was from their conquest table. She wanted to get up and join in on the fun. She wanted to shake loose her inhibitions like some of the other women on the dance floor. Even the waiters and waitresses were dancing down the aisles as they served coffee and cake. She wanted to be like the other people milling about throughout the ship, each group or couple laughing with abandonment and joy; each person having a grand old time aboard, what seemed like to her, the most magical ship ever to set sail.

Suddenly, she caught a glimpse of Terry. He was leaning out over the side of his chair. Before falling off entirely, he caught himself and straightened up. Crystal snarled at him. She was not to be trifled with when pushed beyond her breeding. Then the stranger from the men's room passed by their table. As he did so, he lowered his eyes at Terry. Then he shook his head in disapproval and continued down the aisle. As he sat down at his lively, fun filled table, he continued to stare down his nose at Terry, and of all the nerve, at Crystal too. 'Why not?' she thought.

Terry and she looked like they were stinking up the décor. Crystal wanted to say, 'Ah'm not really with dis her'e bum.' That was not the truth but the truth was something she couldn't say to anyone either. She couldn't tell anybody that she had dreamed about Terry on more than one occasion. Sometimes even romantic ones where he would take her in his arms and pull her towards him so tight that she could feel his manhood pressed against her thighs. She couldn't tell anyone that she would wake up feeling refreshed and hot with perspiration and totally in love with him. But most of all, she couldn't tell anyone, and she meant no-bo-dy, not even her own mother, that she had paid for this abysmal trip.

She turned and looked at Terry again. He had this weird look in his eyes. It was a cross between a baby with gas pains and a miserable wet puppy. He lifted up his left butt cheek and let a fart roll out beneath the Latin bass line of the guitars. Crystal was floored, horrified, mortified and nauseated all at the same time. She jumped out of her seat about the same time Terry jumped out of his. She couldn't believe that he was going to make her pay for that one too. She refused to be accused of letting one fly in the dining room. She was going to make sure that she made it to the doorway before him. She quickly saw that the fastest route out was the aisle he was in front of, so she hurdled in front of him and made her way through the scattered chairs to the exit. As she stepped across the threshold she thought that Terry was probably still making his way from around the table. He was drugged after all and bloated, but somehow Terry had managed to make it two feet ahead of her and was already making his way to the upper deck. Crystal leaped across a dancing couple and succeeded in beating Terry to the upper deck by taking three steps onto the opposite stairwell.

Once upstairs, she was safe from him, at peace again. She told herself that she needed some sea air and that she'd dodge Terry for the remainder of the trip. It was a big boat no one need know they were together. She could just avoid him. So, she closed her eyes and put her back to the ship's rail and inhaled deeply a few times. It was exhilarating for her to feel the warm breeze on her face, while listening to the laughter and music muted down below. She opened her eyes and gazed up at the stars. It was a wonderful night for peering into the sky. There were no buildings to distract her view. She was finally beginning to enjoy some of this tragic night. She even looked straight ahead at the people strolling back and forth on the ship's walkway. She would salvage what was left of this wretched date. She closed her eyes again and took another deep breath.

As she was sinking deeper into the accentuation of the music and the rhythm of the ship, she heard what sounded like someone vomiting. It sounded as if it was just below her, somewhere on the lower deck, she thought, but then the smell suddenly overtook her. It overrode her perfume and steak tartar being eaten on the deck below. It made her want to gag for air. It was an extremely pungent. She looked around to see where it might be coming from so she could then turn and go in the opposite direction. That's when she discovered, her friend, Terry. He was leaning over the side of the rail. What could she do? If she fled the scene now, surely people would think that she *was* with him. Instead, she turned her body around slowly and inconspicuously and joined the increasingly bigger crowd now surrounding this obviously seasick *stranger*. Then she politely excused herself once the illusion was complete and headed towards the lower deck where she remained until the ship docked.

CHAPTER SIXTEEN

Terry eventually passed out. And despite Crystal's efforts to avoid him all evening, when the ship finally came to port, her conscience wouldn't allow her to just leave a urine and vomit smelling, broke down, penniless date. So, she hailed a cab, and with the help of a security guard, dragged Terry's body to it. She had a very difficult time hoisting his heavy, limp body onto the seat especially when the guard had to leave to go and break up a fight. It appeared that one guy had accused another of eating all his dinner. Crystal hid her face in shame. Then she looked to the cab driver for assistance with Terry but he perpetrated that he couldn't move from behind the wheel. So, she placed her behind in the seat and swung her legs around to the other side of the cab. She had to bend over and reach her hands to her toes in order to open the door. Then she repositioned herself and scampered back in the center of the seat. She sat for a moment catching her breath and contemplating whether or not to leave him right there half way in the cab and halfway out.

"Ah shood jus' leave yor' Chris-shian ass... God forgive mie' weakness," she prayed.

Then she reached over with all her strength and grabbed Terry's slack arms. She pulled and pulled with all her might.

"Could ya' at least take his feet?" she asked the cab driver.

"Look, lady I have a bad back," he yelled back at her.

Crystal, now devoid of all her usual ladylike demeanor, hiked up her skirt up, squatted down and with all the strength she had left, dragged Terry's body onto the cab's floor.

"Jesus, motha', Mary, Joseph. Let's go," she snapped at the cab driver then she placed her feet on top of Terry's head.

Sarah's Apartment

Sarah diplomatically removed Michael's hand from her leg pretending she was thirsty and in need of more wine. In truth, his behavior had grown unsettling to her.

"Let me ask you this," Michael moved closer to her.

"Yes," she said not knowing what to expect.

"Would you ever consider going out with a married man?" he asked.

Sarah moved away from him in order to see him squarely. She felt as if she were now on shaky ground and was unable to steady herself from falling between the cracks. She didn't like the direction of this part of the evening - at all. She preferred the light-hearted, getting to know you pleasantry to the probing into each other's love life, cross-examination style of questioning.

"Well, I don't know. I guess it just depends," she said thinking, 'What kind of question is that anyway?'

It's like asking if one likes stealing or murdering. It's just not the kind of conversation one has on a first date. 'Come to think of it,' Sarah thought, '...there were several things about this evening that indicated Michael was on a tenth date and that she was going solo with this first one.'

"No, no, it's got to be a yes or no answer," Michael tugged at his chin as if Sarah's answer was the key to some type of puzzle.

"There's no such thing as being in-between!" he demanded.

"Well, I could never tell you what I absolutely would or would not do. It does depend. I may love the guy deeply then I don't know what I would do under those circumstances. I just don't know," Sarah told him.

Michael hastened away from her.

"Yes or no? Simple," he gently requested thrashing his arms in the air.

Sarah thought about it, more so for effect than for anything else. She didn't like how the question revealed more about his values than hers. She wavered back and forth wondering whether or not to answer it at all. Michael raised his arms again baiting her to say something. So she spoke.

"Then I would have to say the answer would probably be...no. I mean, I wouldn't want to be a home wrecker or anything like that. Besides, my mother would kill me, if the wife didn't do that first," she giggled just thinking about how angry Millie would be if she brought home a married man to meet her.

That answer did not sit well with Michael. He leaped over the sofa and ran into the kitchen. He flipped off the oven and reached in and pulled out the steaks.

"Ready already?" Sarah inquired from her rather relaxed position on the couch.

"No," Michael answered sarcastically.

"Oh," Sarah sat up and waited for Michael to give her more detail.

Meanwhile, Michael wrapped the steak back up in the same aluminum foil he brought it in and spilled hot dripping oil right into the shopping bag.

"Well, this turned out to be a waste of my time. I can't believe Brenda," Michael muttered to himself as he continued to toss things into the shopping bag.

"Huh?" Sarah asked while walking towards the kitchen to see what all the commotion was about.

She heard the clanging sounds of utensils being thrown into the sink followed by a series of grunts. As she reached the kitchen doorway, she saw Michael grabbing flowers out of one of her favorite vases and chucking them into a soggy bag.

"You sound just like my wife," Michael griped at Sarah. "Always taking things the wrong way. Now look what you've done," he said with a tangled forehead.

"Michael, what are you talking about?" Sarah asked now totally perplexed.

"Wait a minute, are you still living with your wife?" she asked as if discovering the answer to the question at the same time.

Michael threw his jacket over his shoulders and headed straight for the front door with the shopping bag securely placed under his arm. He didn't bother to answer Sarah's question directly.

"What if I am?" he said snidely without turning to face her, "Are you gonna' tell me not to go out with other women too?"

"Huh?" was all Sarah could manage.

She leaned against the frame of the kitchen door and placed her hand to her hip. She was suddenly in a weird state of denial about Michael's swift shift in disposition. Just a moment ago he was cooking for her and now he was rushing towards the door.

Then without warning Michael pivoted ever so slowly and fixed his eyes on her. He had a smug look on his face like a giant towering over a small village.

"Brenda said that you needed *some*," he confessed, "I guess she was wrong."

It wasn't difficult to interpret what *some* meant, what with him thrusting his hips forward and looking down in the general vicinity of his pants. Whatever good impression Sarah had of him evaporated in an instant. Now, he resembled some thug on the street who hissed at any and all females who crossed their path. It was clear that he had no respect for women as a whole. They were on earth to please him in any way he saw fit. Sarah caught a cold chill that raced down her spine as she realized that she invited this man into her house. She backed up into the kitchen and made sure she at least had access to a weapon. She sighed with relief as she saw her sharpest knife lying on the counter. 'Michael must have used it on the raw meat,' she thought. In her heart, she knew that nothing would actually happen but she wanted to make sure nonetheless.

"Huh?" was all she could think to say.

She coughed and tried not to display too much disgust for what she was hearing. Michael opened the front door, stepped outside and with righteous indignation slammed it shut behind him. Although muffled, Sarah could still hear him yelling at her.

"And I can't believe I wasted five bucks on that bottle of wine!"

She stood still in silence for what seemed like thirty days just staring at her door, which continued to shake within its frame. She was actually waiting for the color to flow back into her face. She had never been talked to like that in her life and she wasn't at all used to it. He was insulting, and belittling. Obviously, he didn't see her as a date at all but as some kind of broke down car that was pushed into his *filling* station. Unfortunately, it didn't take long for her revulsion to rapidly shift from Michael to, her girlfriend, Brenda. She couldn't decide who annoyed more. The pendulum was sloping rather weightily towards, her girl, Brenda, who Sarah suspected had completely lost her mind. 'What if he tried to overpower me?' she thought. What on earth was she going to do then? She had invited this complete stranger into her home. He was in her kitchen, cooking her dinner. Even the female police officers called to the scene would have a difficult time with that one. She was light-headed and now uncomfortably giggled at the absurdity of it all. Her eyes landed on the bottle of wine. She put it to her lips and gulped it down.

CHAPTER SEVENTEEN

The cab swerved and ran up onto the curb in front of Crystal's apartment building. She swung her door open before it came to a complete stop, vaulted out and leaned into the cab window to pay the driver. The cab driver hesitated as he gave her the change. It was two quarters and he looked as though he wanted to keep them. Crystal grabbed her change and wondered why he thought to cheat her out of it. She stared down at the money then turned abruptly and started walking towards her apartment. The cab driver stuck his head out of the window and yelped, "Hey! What about him?" referring to Terry.

"Yu' tell mey'? My back hurts," Crystal said scurrying into her apartment building and locking the glass door behind her.

Once inside, she turned to see what the cab driver thought of her response. He was standing in the middle of the street screaming at the top of his lungs, arms flapping up and down in the air like he was about to take flight. She couldn't hear him but she knew he was hurling obscenities at her. She didn't care. She turned triumphantly and continued down the hallway to her door. As she turned the key in the lock, she heard car tires skidding against the road. She turned back around and saw the cab zooming pass. Moments later she would begin to wonder what the driver did with Terry.

But now she entered her apartment and tried her best to shake off the whole nightmare. She flung her keys into a porcelain jar and disrobed right there at the entrance. She just wanted to jump straight into the shower and then straight into bed. She knew that she had to quiet her thoughts about Terry, which were overpowering her mind. He had disappointed her more than she had ever imagined possible. Her whole Christian life had been leading her to her perfect Christian man and she thought Terry was *him*. She had invested three and a half years of quality dreaming and intense visualizing into Terry. 'H'oaw could 'ah be so'a wrong?' she thought.

It was at that point that she wondered what the cab driver did with him and decided to ease her troubled mind by going to take a quick peek. She slipped back into her clothes and stepped into the hall. She was glad that no one was around. She didn't want anyone to see her. Tonight she wanted to be anonymous. She wanted to sneak out, take a quick look and pray that if Terry was out there, that he wouldn't see her either. She tiptoed quietly down the hallway. She left her door ajar so she could slip back in quickly without detection should she need to do so. She got to the main door and wedged herself behind the frame. If Terry were out there, he would have been able to see her easily behind the glass, so she made sure to stay clear of it. She sucked in her stomach and turned sideways against the doorframe. Then, she looked out through the sliver between the door and the frame. But she couldn't see anything and was tempted to just go back into her apartment and call it a dreadful night. Curiosity was getting the better of her though; she wanted to know if he was okay. She wanted to know if he was possibly sober by now and wanted to apologize for his despicable behavior. She also wanted her money and knew that she just couldn't dismiss him altogether until she got that back. So, with all of those items on her imaginary checklist, she scooted over and looked outside.

And there he was in all his buffoonery lying on the sidewalk sound asleep with spittle erupting from the corners of his mouth. He had urinated on himself and if that weren't bad enough, his head was just above a gutter filled to the street level with trash. Crystal gasped and placed her hand to her chest in repulsion. There he was, the future father of her children, she grimaced. She couldn't believe that she could be such a poor judge of character. She watched as the filthy garbage he was lying in soaked through his pleated trousers. She couldn't stop herself from thinking back to how she had admired him from a far for so many years. She had even prayed to God that he be "the one". Then, she had waited patiently for him to notice her so he could eventually warm up to that idea. She had even dressed for him on a number of occasions. She would obsess over getting into the right seat at church so he could see the many outfits she had worn in his honor. She had practiced how she would laugh at his jokes, how she would shake her head and nod as she listened to his many stories. She adored him and the lifestyle she thought he led. Terry was the church superstar from the church celebrity family. It truly hurt her soul to see him sprawled there in the sewer.

Like the Prodigal Son, Terry obviously didn't know how good he actually had it. Crystal couldn't remember a time where friends, both male and female, didn't surround him. He could have the crème de la crème of women. He came from one of the wealthiest, most attractive families on the East Coast. His mother doted on him incessantly and often mentioned how he was her favorite of her three sons. His father referred to him as the next President of the United States or at least a member of Congress. They had big dreams for him and despite his reluctance to make any of them come true, they still showered him with love, affection, encouragement and cash. Crystal too had big dreams for him that were now lying outside in front of her apartment in a pile of soggy garbage. She actually felt betrayed by God for allowing her to get her hopes up so high only to spit them back down to earth atop her head.

She marched back down the hall to her apartment, stepped inside and cried. This night she didn't *feel* like praying. She didn't want to get down on her knees to a God who would laugh at her so loudly and undeniably. She knew she was just a silly little Southern girl with a bunch of wedding design plans and a drawer full of reception hall brochures but she didn't like being reminded that nothing she ever planned worked out the way she hoped. She didn't even bother taking her clothes back off, refusing to shower as an act of protest against cleanliness being close to Godliness. She laid face down on the bed on purpose too because she didn't even want to look up!

CHAPTER EIGHTEEN

It takes a special kind of glue to keep four strong Black women together for as long as Sarah, Karen, Crystal and Brenda have been. They all were inseparable since junior year, high school and somehow the bond got stronger with each passing year, making them more like sisters than friends. It was destiny that their friendship would last a lifetime.

Sarah and Karen met earlier while in grade school and resided in the same Brooklyn neighborhood bordering Queens. Once they became friends they literally lived at each other's houses. Their mothers joked about feeding the other one's kid on a regular basis. With Sarah being an only child, Karen could and did sleep over at her house as often as her father allowed, which became every night that Sarah wasn't sleeping at hers'.

As fate would have it, Crystal and Brenda were assigned the same homeroom as Sarah and Karen one semester. Crystal liked them right off because they were the only ones who didn't tease her about her *naws*, *ain'ts* and *cainsts*. Sarah didn't know anyone from the South and thought that Crystal sounded like she was one of the characters from "Gone with the Wind." She found her accent adorable and defended her when people said otherwise. Karen, on the other hand, treated Crystal more like the younger sister she never had, who happened to always be in constant need of her wisdom and advice. And Crystal ate up every word and held fast to it as if it were the gospel, so appreciative was she of Karen and Sarah's friendship. They were her link to this new world, New York. Unbeknownst to her, she had inadvertently selected the right people to listen to at Heritage High School. Sarah was en route to becoming valedictorian. While Karen was a cheerleader synonymous with 'every boy wanted one and every girl wanted to be one.' Crystal knew that Sarah and Karen were special because once they became friends all of the joking about her Southern drawl ceased. People even began to say hello to her in the hallways. They referred to her as Sarah and Karen's Southern friend and left it at that. That suited Crystal just fine because for the first time in her life she felt like she belonged somewhere.

Brenda was there with them in homeroom too but, at that time, traveled in different circles. Most times, she and Sarah took the same school bus home together, but by no means were they considered friends. Sarah was normally seen with people who participated in study groups. Brenda and cohorts meandered about the hallways cutting classes seeking opportunities to get high. Although, Sarah and Brenda saw each other daily, neither sought a reason for conversation. There wasn't anything to talk about. It seemed easier for both of them to just pretend not to recognize the other. Though, there were times when simply avoiding each other became awkward. Like when they had to sit together on the bus because there was only one available seat. So, they began to nod politely in passing instead. They'd lower their heads just enough to show the other that there was some familiarity present but not enough to ignite a chat. Back then Brenda was also known for showing boys her feminine goods behind the stadium bleachers. She was even reprimanded for doing so and got suspended for an entire week. News of this nature traveled fast and it eventually made its way to the ears of Sarah's mother. Millie forbade Sarah from having anything to do with Brenda, even though Sarah's sole exchange with her had been a series of head nods.

Unfortunately though, the die had already been cast. Sarah became intrigued by Brenda's audacious behavior. Every time she saw her, she was dying to ask her what it felt like to put on a show for the high school boys. Sarah, in her wildest imagination, wouldn't have dreamed of doing such a thing. She was a straight "A" student working hard to stay on the honor roll. She didn't have time for boys, thinking then that they were silly and immature. Brenda, by contrast, delighted in their silliness and immaturity. The bus rides home were always entertaining as Sarah watched Brenda go from boy to boy. Brenda wasn't altogether choosy either. One day she would sit next to a jock and the next day, a brainy sort of guy. Sarah would come to find out that Brenda's motto was, 'any man showing her any attention was worthy of hers.' Back then Sarah wasn't interested in boys like that and Brenda wanted them all to herself. To each of their surprise, Sarah was the perfect girlfriend for Brenda. Pretty soon they began to talk, a little at first.

"Hey."

"Hey."

"How's it goin'?"

"How's it goin'?"

Other girls, however, had their own agendas with respect to the male population at school. It was not long before girls starting approaching Brenda and threatening to beat her up. They were tired of Brenda and her skill at taking any boy she wanted from any unsuspecting girl.

Brenda was so popular with the boys by then though that no threat was ever carried out. The boys protected her no matter the consequence. Sarah, consequently, became guilty by association, on account of her relationship with the vixen. It didn't help matters that both were beautiful, giving some of the girls yet another reason to dislike them. Sarah fared better than Brenda in this respect only because, unlike her, Sarah didn't flaunt her looks. There were dress codes at Heritage High that Brenda enthusiastically broke. Her regular attire was simple. It consisted of a clinging blouse that revealed more than it should with a mini skirt or skin-tight denims. A typical complaint of Brenda's was her mother's endless tirade about her wardrobe. Brenda couldn't understand why she was not being permitted to express herself.

So relentless were their arguments that they had to come to some sort of deal. They struck a compromise that entailed Brenda maintaining at least a "B" average. Brenda studied hard for the first time in her life, and aced all her finals, accidentally discovering the honor roll. Once Brenda proved herself by getting good grades, she then went on to show off most of her body, which actually drew a smattering of applause occasionally as she walked down the halls. Her scholastic ability and popularity won over the teachers as well. She was definitely in her element at Heritage High School.

Sarah, by comparison, had a harder way to go. For starters, she was constantly confused as a clone of Brenda and boys relentlessly pursued them both asking for dates. Sarah always said no and Brenda almost always said yes. Brenda's only excuse was that she had another date scheduled otherwise her answer was yes. Despite their obvious differences, it took the Heritage boys a long time to distinguish between the two. Sarah fought against this bizarre case of mistaken identity but innumerable arguments ensued as a result nevertheless.

One day a guy from their football team approached Sarah. His name was Walter and he towered over Sarah's five foot six frame. He asked her out in his own unique way by grunting her name then mumbling the name of a local restaurant. Sarah could only assume that he wanted her to meet him there after school. She came to that conclusion only after asking Brenda to decipher Walter's dating code. Based on the fact that Sarah had an exam the next day and no way of reaching Walter, she decided not to show.

No one could have postulated the up-roar it inspired that following day. The school's local newspaper reporters mauled her while she was getting off the school bus that morning. They rammed a video camera in her face and said that they wanted to be the first to speak to the girl who stood-up their local hero. Ashamed and slightly afraid, she hid in the girl's locker room that morning, took her Chemistry exam and then went to the nurse's office for the remainder of the day. Walter had no idea that Sarah was not Brenda until that very moment. He actually apologized to her later that week for his error. At least that's what Sarah thought he said when he uttered, "sor...heyy."

CHAPTER NINETEEN

Norman pulls Karen roughly towards him placing her face in line with his. Her body twists awkwardly around maneuvering itself to get into his prescribed position. She tries to accommodate him but fails wretchedly when her hair gets caught underneath her own shoulder. She manages to pull her arm out and adjust her hair but in doing so, she falls back over to the other side of the bed.

"Come on, honey. Let's have another lick," Norman says amorously hugging her too tightly and slobbering kisses in her ear.

"Hug me back, damnit! Y'all think we men don't need some of that too. But we do. We do," Norman coos and cuddles.

Karen rolls her hair into a bun and lies with her back pressed flat against the freshly washed sheets. She fixes her eyes to the ceiling, takes a deep breath and holds it there as if taking a dive under water. Norman rolls on top of her and immediately reaches back to unravel it.

"Yes, yes, yes. I like it out," he explains.

She knows that he intends to sweat it out and tangle it up, thereby making it impossible for her to comb in the morning. Though she had repeatedly told him that it was falling out due to his acts of passion, he'd simply laugh at her and say she was frigid. Norman's routine was to hold onto a few strands and use them to pull her towards him. When they first starting going out together, Karen used to like it when he did this. Now, she came to immensely dislike how unattractive she looked as a result of him tugging at her as if she were a cave woman. Also, Norman was a big man, who never acquired the skill of supporting his own weight. Karen had to scramble for air as he finally reached the twirl at the back of her head and proceeded to take it down. The heaviness of his body made her feel as if her ribs would break. Yet she didn't protest. She knew better. If she so much as sighed, he would prolong his attempt at love making for another five minutes or so. She decided long ago to be a spectator during this segment of the day. She gave in to the pain she was now feeling on her sternum. And then without warning or foreplay, Norman thrusts himself inside of her. His moans of excitement were that of huffing and puffing, and over exertion. She remained focused on the ceiling, paying special attention to a small thin crack running above their heads. She mentally measured the length of it in inches and then in feet. It was approximately forty-two inches long and a third of an inch wide at the top and hardly visible at the bottom. No resonance of pleasure emanated from either Norman or Karen, only sweat. Tears moistened Karen's face but she didn't allow herself to be sensitized by them. She knew this routine well. It would only be another two minutes or so before Norman was done and rolling back over to go to sleep. She could then take all the time she needed to pick up the pieces of her self-esteem while he snored vociferously at her side.

Sarah's living room

Sarah sat slumped and blank face on the couch. A now completely empty bottle of French wine is balancing facedown on her glass coffee table. She's observing the bottle as if it were a work of art, marveling at its steadiness. Unlike her it could stand on its head motionless, while she can barely sit erectly. The phone rings and she quickly picks up the bottle before it falls from the rippling reverberation of the table.

"Hello. Hello. Michael, is that you?" Sarah inquired groggily hoping it isn't him but a wrong number.

"Michael? No, it's me, Karen," Karen said softly.

"Oh, Karen, hi. How you do'win?"

Karen looks over at Norman who is curled up spooning the pillow at the opposite end of the bed. She wants to make sure he's absolutely out cold.

"That's what I'm calling to ask you," Karen whispered.

"You mean, besides Brenda fixing me up with a married man," Sarah said satirically.

"Stop! Wait! What? Tell me what happened," Karen nearly shouted.

"Just left my apartment," Sarah burped.

Karen squeals with laughter as Sarah lays out a blow-by-blow account of her date with Michael. Only she refers to it as her close encounter with the *man who lost his mind*.

"Same old Brenda, huh?" Karen said with a sigh.

Sarah and Karen were no strangers to Brenda's many exploits. Nor was it a complete surprise to either of them that Brenda was capable of concocting something as despicable as this. Those facts not withstanding, they each vowed they would never let Brenda off the hook for it. This stunt was inexcusable even for her.

"Girl, that's why I'm so glad I'm married," Karen suddenly chirped.

Sarah's eyes grew wide and she sat straight up. She tried to breathe deeply but the air had difficulty going down, as did the words that Karen spoke. Her eyes darted all the way around the room and then down at the phone. She knew she shouldn't be but she was hurt by those words.

"I don't think I could be out there dating like you all. That's why I'm so glad I have Norman," she said with a small smattering of *one-upmanship.*

Sarah was speechless. She couldn't comprehend what being married or not being married had to do with her abysmal date with *the man who lost his mind.*

Now she was sorry she had told her. Apparently nothing could penetrate her happily married friend. What she needed was Karen's support and her friendship. She didn't need to be reminded of how hard it was to find a decent man. She wanted Karen to remember back to a time when she wasn't married and dating was a normal part of life.

She liked her life and was satisfied with her choices. Even her decision to go out with Michael was beginning to sit well with her. After all was said and done, she recognized that it was the type of experience that bore material by which legendary comedy routines were made. If she ever lost her soul and decided to eventually date Michael, she knew she could use their dates as material for soap operas.

"Hey, I got an idea," Sarah said with a desire to change the subject.

"Okay, what?" Karen queried, desperately looking for an escape.

Norman had been a little too attentive since she returned home and she was feeling slightly suffocated by him.

"Let's go down to the retro movie house like we used to and see a film," Sarah said enthusiastically.

"That's right, maybe we can catch the eleven o'clock show," said Karen, shoving Norman with her finger.

Norman's snore grew louder and he swatted his arm as if

Karen's poke was a mosquito.

"Right! Okay. I'll meet you there. Bye."

Sarah hung up the phone and sat for a while in silence. She knew she had to run if she was going to get there on time but first she had to empty her mind of her entire day. 'What was the worst part?' she thought; getting caught in the rain, her date with Michael, Matthew trying to be the consummate gentleman, and last but not least, being laughed at the hairdresser's. With all of those to choose from, the one thing that kept niggling at her was her best friend Karen's comments on marriage. She just didn't expect something like that to come out of Karen's mouth. Those words penetrated her heart, so tired was she of being made to feel incomplete without a man. Karen acted as though the times prior to her getting married never existed. Yet, she and Karen were the best of friends for many, many years before Karen even met Norman. And during those prior years they never had a single disagreement. They even had identical goals back then: to get married, have two children apiece, a boy and a girl, while maintaining their fabulous full-time careers, of course.

Sarah hadn't noticed that her friend had drifted away from those dreams or was it the other way round? She enrolled in the New School for Art and Design right after high school and pursued architectural studies while Karen became pregnant with Yolanda and stayed home. Karen had always said that she would go back to school when Yolanda was old enough for pre-school but when Yolanda turned three, Karen decided to take the tuition she'd been saving and vacation instead. She and Norman took a trip to Bermuda together by boat. The pictures were incredible. It showed them scuba diving, canoeing and jet-skiing off the coast. Sarah was so jealous of them because at the time she couldn't even take a day off. It wasn't too long after that trip that their talks became less and less frequent. Sarah began to mourn the loss of them but she never told Karen had she felt.

Now waiting in front of the movie theater for Karen, Sarah felt slightly more at peace. She refused to let it bother her that Karen was now a whole twenty minutes late. Sarah was determined to at least make the last hours of the day pleasant. She'd forgive Karen's tardiness, of course, more so because she simply refused to be aggravated further. If she was going to go ballistic over anything, she'd definitely bring up Karen's snide little theory on marriage. *That* would be worthy of a fight. Yet and still, she cursed her own impatience as she looked up and down the street again and again in both directions. There was no sign of Karen, just a few stragglers rushing through the double doors of the multiplex. The temperature had dropped and Sarah found herself standing in a sealed doorway to keep warm. Several men passed by and actually told her to put a smile on her face. Little did they know, she just didn't have it in her.

Out of Sarah's eyesight, Matthew's minivan pulled up in front of the theater, u-turned then parked diagonally across the street. He hurried out of the van and ran straight for the ticket window. A pair of long stocking clad legs swung around and were placed on the sidewalk. A woman wrenches herself out of the passenger seat of Matthew's wheels and spent several minutes trying to push her hair down and back into its intended place. The woman had a poor view of her reflection in the side mirror so she got out and looked at herself on the panel of the van.

"Honestly," she screeched between her teeth.

Matthew waves two tickets up in the air attempting to signal his lady telling her to hurry and join him at the entrance. She painstakingly finishes her primping then slowly strolls across the street. She has to be careful not to trip in her three-inch high stiletto heels. When she finally makes it to the entrance, she stops and takes a moment to adjust her skirt. The back seam has flipped all the way around on her hips and the slit is resting on her thigh. That won't do. Matthew waits impatiently but politely as she ducks behind him to twist everything forward. Matthew can't understand all the fuss because he figures they're going to be in the dark for the next two and one half-hours anyway. The reason they were late to the movies in the first place was because she had to shower first on account of her feeling too stinky from being in the sun all day. He didn't want to argue with her about the fact that she carried an umbrella, wore a hat, plus doused herself with copious amounts of sunscreen. He doubted that the rays touched her at all. Yet he figured that if he reasoned with her it would take her that much longer to get dressed, so he remained silent. He pulled out one of his favorite fluffy towels for her and hoped she'd only take five-minutes as he had. After her forty-five-minute shower, she then had to blow dry the hair at the base of her neck because it had gotten soaking wet from his 'loose' shower cap. A fact that she repeatedly informed him of while the roaring air and her high-pitched voice competed for dominance. She had a beautiful head of hair that she wore in a series of waves that hung just over her shoulder blades. Matthew liked the way it looked wet and thought it was best when a little messy. Debbie, his date, wouldn't hear of it. She said that the wet look gave her too much of a casual style. 'Again, movie theater, dark,' he thought but stayed silent. Her appearance was her job it seemed and he had to move out of the way and let her get the job done.

Matthew and Debbie walked into the theater right past Sarah. Matthew didn't notice her because he had orders to walk behind Debbie and make sure the seam of her skirt stayed where it belonged. Sarah didn't see him either because her head was down studying the numbers on her watch. Karen was now officially, really late. Sarah finally realized that that meant she wasn't coming at all. She was disappointed. It was so unlike her to just leave a friend hanging without so much as a word. In the age of cellular phones, there wasn't a legitimate excuse. Sarah reached in her shirt pocket and took hers out to call Karen's house. The phone rang fifteen times before she finally decided to hang up. It didn't really worry her; she just figured everything was fine and that when she had an opportunity to speak to her, Karen would tell her that something came up - again. Sarah looked up and down the block a few more times just in case, before walking to the ticket booth.

"Has the movie started yet?" Sarah asked with this sinking feeling that it had.

"Yeap, fifteen minutes ago. Here's your change. Enjoy the show," the cashier said in a much more pleasant of a voice than Sarah expected.

"Thanks," Sarah said to the cashier for more reasons than one.

CHAPTER TWENTY

It was dark and crowded inside. The movie had already begun. So, Sarah slowly and painstakingly made her way down the center aisle in search of a seat. She didn't see any. What made matters worst were the people already comfortably spread out covering more than one. She couldn't understand why so many people were at the late, late show anyway. "Lady Sings the Blues" was more than two decades old. She walked right pass Matthew's row. Again, she didn't see him. In fact, she couldn't see anything. After walking nearly to the screen she noticed an empty seat by a far wall. So, she squeezed down the crowded row, despite the fact of it being filled with young amorous teenagers. And they were all twisted in uniquely innovative positions, paired off and huddled. They were none too pleased with her interruption of their groping and kissing frenzy. It was now clearer to her why the theater was so packed - date night. She had forgotten the rule, "when you can't go home..." She sincerely wished they could go home, an alley, a street corner, anywhere else other than right beside her. She wasn't in the mood.

Right after plopping down in her seat, she immediately wanted to get right back up. All of a sudden, everything got to be a little too much for her. She wasn't sure what it was, the affectionate youths continuing their exploration down the backs of each other's throats or the fact that she didn't have someone to explore hers. It didn't help much that she could clearly see them out of the corner of her eye and to add insult to injury, she could hear them too, cooing in each other ears. And, although they were speaking softly, it wasn't difficult to hear every single syllable. All she could do was turn around and try to concentrate on the screen.

At this point in the film Billie Holiday, played by Diana Ross is singing at this low rate jazz club where the men were trying to convince her to accept dollar bills from them between her thighs without the use of her hands. She's poor and needs the money and has to work against her own sense of morality in choosing to accept their offer. Holiday pauses by several of their tables and the camera does a close-up on her face to show the wheels churning in her head with indecision. Billie Dee's character breaks the tension by offering Holiday money also but he places the folded bills gently in her hand. The men in the movie audience bow their heads shamefully. Holiday continues to sing in her own unique style that fuses both vulnerability and strength together. In the end, Sarah mused whether Holiday's level head would have prevailed anyway.

At that, Sarah's thoughts rested once again upon Michael and how attracted she was to him before she knew he was married. She was so glad they didn't end up necking on her sofa or worst, in bed. It would have been so easy. Sarah hadn't slept with a man in over three years and was unashamedly and eagerly receptive to the idea. She told herself that the reason for her long dry spell had been because she had gotten so busy with work. She presently averaged three-to-four accounts. The firm she had been with for six long years, Jones and Jones Architecture, known for their cookie-cutter houses, drove her to realizing that she had had enough of being on their assembly line. So she ordered business cards and went out on her own. The work was tougher, but as she had hoped, it was also more fulfilling and definitely more lucrative. One thing she wasn't prepared for, though, were the constant demands being placed on most of her free time. Now that she was her own boss, if a client called her at 6:00 in the morning that was the start of her workday. It didn't matter to them that she was still in her pajamas. And if a client called at midnight it was just the continuation of her workday.

Unfortunately, another shortcoming of the whole time issue was that it was difficult to make and keep dates. Even she was tired of hearing her own excuses. After a while saying she had to work late just sounded like a flat out lie. The entire concept of dating became one giant headache. She would sometimes go out with a man as a way of saying she was sorry as opposed to genuinely wanting to spend quality time with him. This proved to be less gratifying than she thought worth it. So, she stopped dating altogether unless someone fixed her up. Without many examples to the contrary, she had consummate proof that that too wasn't working.

A few rows behind Sarah, Matthew was also sitting up and forward in his seat. He was trying to avoid Debbie's monotone snore. It was just loud enough to be irritating. Matthew had to hand it to her though; Debbie was extremely attractive even under the dim lights. She could always keep his attention with what she wore and the way she moved in it, but where she lost him was in every other way. It was almost as if she were anti-cultural. He had never met anyone with such an undeniable lack of interest in anything that was going on in the world. Try as he might, he could never get her to go to a museum or a play or anything that had to do with broadening her mind. Even when there was music involved, which she adored, or some celebrities about, which she coveted. She was sleepy at her best and apathetic at her worst. He knew that it would only be a matter of time before he stopped asking her to join him at all but he was afraid that that would curtail their lovemaking. That part of their relationship was outstanding. It didn't make any sense to him anymore. He thought, 'Could it be possible that I can't base these things strictly on sex anymore?' He had made it his life's quest to do so but lately it was becoming more like work. Even he realized that apart from the physical, Debbie and he had nothing going on.

He had been around older men who spoke about the fallacy of developing relationships in this way. But, he had never thought that he would live to experience it. Could it be that he was finally growing up? He thought that that wasn't quite possible. How could he be? He still had an address book full of women to call and he loved each and every one of them. Right? He couldn't see himself with just one woman and had no desire to find out what it would be like to settle down. The whole idea brought on an overwhelming sense of inadequacy, perish the thought. He glanced over at Debbie, wondering what it would be like to wake up beside her for the rest of his life. The image shook him to the core. Each of the other women he frequently dated were successful and equally beautiful but he couldn't imagine waking up next to them either, day in and day out. He thought once more about the older men he knew, who always told him to enjoy his unmarried status, his freedom. He cherished those times when he would accommodate their need to live vicariously through him. They would ask him specific questions about how many women he made love to in a week and the details of every encounter. He had many stories to choose from and enjoyed seeing them drool at his every word. He laughed thinking about what they'd say if they could see him now. Debbie with her head titled backward, mouth wide open, him leaning his elbows on the back of the seat in front of him, out on a date, trying to hear a film he already had in his collection.

The theater audience filtered out of the front doors. There wasn't much conversation about the film. Doubtful anyone actually watched it. The young couples were still fawning all over each other, delaying their curfews. Meanwhile, Matthew and Debbie walked out together as if strangers. Matthew tried to take her hand but Debbie's demeanor seemed tense and standoffish. So, he backed away. He didn't know whether she was still a bit tired or if she still hadn't gotten over his hopefully passing recent lack of desire for her. She was a prideful woman and was accustomed to men falling to their knees every time they saw her. She wasn't used to a man telling her no. He let her walk a few steps in front of him while he observed the marquee. It had sepia tone vintage photographs of both Billie Dee Williams and Diana Ross. He thought, 'Once upon a time every man wanted to be Billie Dee with his smooth way of talking to the ladies. And every woman wanted to be Diana or at least to sing like her, not to mention singing like Billie Holiday.' When he turned to make mention of this to Debbie, she had already made her way back to the van. He watched her as she put on the pretence of noticing something down the street in the opposite direction. Then just as he was about to join her across the street, to his surprise he spotted Sarah looking at the marquee on the other side of the entry.

Matthew stood back and observed her for a few moments. She was wearing an old pair of denims and an over sized men's shirt. He had to admit that liked that look on her. He wondered if the shirt was a boyfriend's or, hopefully, a brother's. Even though he knew that he didn't have a chance in hell of getting close to her. She was his type, slim figure, pretty face, just like all his other ladies. Where she differed greatly, though, was in attitude. Unlike the rest, she hated his guts and couldn't stand the sight of him. This flaw in her character notwithstanding, he was slightly smitten and more than a little bit intrigued. Prior to meeting Sarah he never had to do much more than be polite and look his best when it came to engaging a female's affections. If those two things failed he would say hello and watch women swoon over his accent. Not much else was required of him other than having a decent job and a nice set of wheels. He enjoyed the ease at which he could always attain a woman's curiosity even when he wasn't trying.

Sarah sensed someone staring at her and turned to find Matthew giving her a peculiar stare. After her day, it didn't shock her that it would end with running into him. Matthew grinned uncomfortably at the sight of Sarah smiling back at him. He wasn't sure if it was a smirk or some kind of a legitimate expression of sincerity. Either way he walked cautiously towards her. His eyes kept a steady fix on her as he maneuvered his way through the teenagers. For some reason he thought that she'd try to dodge him. Then he chastised himself for feeling such insecurity about a woman. He found himself trying to muster his lioness might which he summoned whenever he was confronted by perceived opposition. Yet, as he watched her he began to feel more and more anxious and, of all things -- nervous. He couldn't believe that his heart was actually racing. He tried to calm himself down because he didn't want something idiotic to slip out of his mouth. He had to get a hold of himself.

"Fancy meeting you here, love. How are you?" he hacked out choppily.

Except the word *love* clung to the air between them like a swarm of killer bees. He was immediately sorry he had said it. He didn't want her to get the wrong idea or at least he didn't want her to think lower of him than she already did. He tried to think of a clever way of saying that in England everyone calls each other love and that it doesn't mean anything really. Then he thought against eluding that his words didn't mean anything because that would sound callous and make him seem even more insensitive than she probably believed him to be. To his surprise, Sarah simply shook her head in a gesture of both friendliness and cordiality. 'Maybe she didn't even hear it after all,' he thought.

"Well, it's been a long night," she fought back a yawn while backing away from the marquee and especially away from Matthew.

She heard it, he realized, and he was definitely being dismissed. He knew that the smile of hers was just her way of saying that she was too tired to spar with him tonight. He was saddened. He liked the heady tension that was present between them. He liked the way she tried to restrain her anger towards him in order to keep the peace. It reminded him of his father during his days at boarding school. His father would sit as still as a mountain bear bating his prey quietly listening to every morsel out of the Head Master's dry mouth. He would tweak his beard and scratch his chin but his eyes would not move from their target, young Matthew. At these times, Matthew's anxiety would overtake him and he would get the urge to wet his pants. He felt safe in school, all right, but he had a suspicion that his father could legally kill him. A fact, he repeatedly told him during afternoon tea on those days in the Head Master's office. Why he took so many chances in boarding school was a mystery even to him, what with all these eerie threats to his life from dad.

Matthew found himself looking at Sarah's face and smiling. She entertained for a moment what he might be thinking then once again stepped back and began to turn and leave. Matthew imagined her running for her car, starting it up and dashing. The image troubled him greatly until he remembered, with quite the stupid expression on his face, that Delroy had not finished it yet. He knew that it wouldn't be long though before Sarah *would* drive away from him forever. Their business would soon be at an end and Matthew wouldn't have any excuse to see her again, to his realization, this thought did trouble him.

"Well, anyway, like I said, it's been a long day for me and..." Sarah didn't bother explaining why she wasn't going to start up a conversation with him.

"What is it that you really don't like about me?" Matthew asked.

He realized that he might have sounded a girl with that question. Sarah stopped dashing away and seriously contemplated the question. She replied, "You drive too damn fast. No wonder you're having problems with your insurance company."

She thought that her humorous response accomplished two things; it answered his question and closed off the entry for farther discussion. Once again she turned and began to flee. She took a cab to the theater and searched down the road to find another. Matthew didn't like her answer and knew she was dismissing him yet again. Any other time he would have just left it alone. This time, he followed and walked alongside her trying to match her gait.

"Fast...huh?" he started, "Geeeeee, no one's ever said that to me before," he said smiling.

Sarah laughed. When he saw her laughing, he laughed too. The release felt good. She mulled over the fact that she had been saying whatever came to mind to him since she met him. And he very gingerly took it squarely. Maybe Sarah and he were destined to stay in touch from time to time? Who knows? Friends even.

Sarah stretched out her hand to shake his. A hint of electricity traveled from his hand to hers and then found its way into the pit of her spine. Matthew held it tightly for a few seconds as he experienced a touch of something between them also.

"Truce," they awkwardly said to one another.

Sarah didn't want there to be any chemistry between them. 'Sure, he's cute,' she thought. His accent alone would make practically any woman show up at his door with a raincoat on and nothing else, but then what? She wasn't like Brenda, who wanted the entire population of men to be just like Matthew, good looking, good in bed and good to go when she had had enough. Sarah told herself that she wanted a little more than that as she scanned her eyes down to Matthew's jeans, which hugged his thighs in rapture. So, she was attracted to him, she thought, so what? She couldn't take Matthew any more seriously than she could have taken Michael. 'Matthew, Michael – what's the difference?' she thought.

Matthew continued to smile and hold her gaze. He wasn't entirely sure but he got the impression that she did indeed like him a little bit after all.

"Okay...well...I'll see you down at the garage," Sarah concluded and walked down the street.

Matthew recanted. He may have misread their exchange. He was once again caught off guard and didn't know what to say.

"Hey, hey, let me give you a lift," he called out to her.

Sarah shook her head from side to side and kept walking to a near-by taxi station. Matthew ran and caught up with her.

"You shouldn't be walking around alone out here in the middle of the night. Frankly it isn't safe," Matthew warned in a very parental way.

"But..." Sarah began but to no avail.

Matthew was more persistent this time.

"I'm taking you home and that's that."

He gently took hold of her arm. Then he waited for her to resist him, to tell him all the reasons why she'd rather ride home alone. But no words of that nature came from her this time. She wearily allowed him to escort her across the street.

Now Matthew felt unsure. As much as he wanted to be with Sarah and to get to know her, he realized that he hadn't really anything to say to her. He was a photographer, who spent most of his weeks taking pictures of beautiful women. Somehow he didn't think that would mean much to her. The vain circle that he traveled in considered his kind to be god-like, after all, he was in the business of making others look gorgeous. As for the women and celebrity parties that he frequented, the newness had long worn out as did the insipid conversations. He imagined that Sarah wouldn't be impressed by any of that either. Though it had its perks, he wasn't impressed by much of it himself anymore.

As they came upon the van they could hear the faint sound of someone snoring? Matthew had been so preoccupied with Sarah that he had completely forgotten about Debbie. Then, it dawned on him that the only way Debbie could have entered his van was if she left the door open. He slid back the side door and there she was out cold and sprawled across the back seat. She was drooling, and this time on his leather upholstery.

"Ah, man. Bloody hell," Matthew blurted, "Have you got a Kleenex?"

Sarah shrugged her shoulders. She wasn't even carrying a purse.

"What's wrong?" she asked.

Matthew moved aside and let Sarah take a look inside the van.

"Sarah meet Debbie, my date for the evening," he said none too proudly.

"Oh," said Sarah.

He knew he blew it. He stepped around Sarah, opened the passenger door and helped her in. He took his seat, started the engine and pulled off without saying a word.

Meanwhile, Sarah wondered what kind of man tries to seduce one woman whilst he already has another *one* for the evening. 'For the *evening*, yes that was what he said,' she thought. As if to say, every other evening he has someone else, kind of words. Sarah continued to kick the word around in her head. She thought that if it was electricity she felt earlier it could very well have been light-headedness too. She was back to her original assessment of him. He was an incurable flirt. She was thankful that his friend Debbie was there. Debbie was a reminder of the type of man she was really dealing with.

CHAPTER TWENTY-ONE

U ptown, at Brenda's apartment everything was completely still, but it was a pensive stillness as in the scene just after a tornado. Her living room had clothes strewn over every stitch of furniture. The sink was buried under a mound of dirty dishes, with an old pair of hose dangling over the edge of one of the glasses, and a pot of coffee percolated at the corner of the counter. Steam hissed from its mouth while water dripped down its sides. Sounds of heavy breathing was coming from the bathroom, door ajar. Through the apartment's narrow hallway a thin ray of light escaped casting scary shadows about the wall. And through the crack of the door, a pair of hands, Brenda's, trembled as she examined a long plastic apparatus. She studies it closely then having identified something horrifying, she let out a siren-like, blood-curdling scream. A male emerges from the side of the tub, Wayne, and stands beside her. He too is about to let out a scream as he reads the stick in Brenda's hand. The bathroom door swings wide open, hitting the wall behind it. Brenda's face is glued to the stick now fallen in the basin while Wayne, her companion, has one foot out the door and the other not far behind. Brenda eyed the plastic applicator of the home pregnancy kit. She's woozy as if drunk or high on something but her last drink was earlier that morning when Wayne rang her bell at 1:00 am. He was brandishing a bottle of Alizé, her favorite, and speaking words of make-up sex, her other favorite. The last time they had been together was two weeks prior. Wayne wanted to be more to Brenda than that of a night crawler, his description of his role in their relationship. She didn't want to cuddle after they made love and she didn't want him to sleep in her bed. So, at her request, he went home afterwards. Wayne decided since he did enjoy being with her that he would come over in the middle of the night. This way after they made love, he could fall asleep in her bed without her feeling inconvenienced or trapped, her words to describe their relationship.

"You did this on purpose, didn't you? You women are always looking for a husband," Wayne knew that what he was saying was foolish yet it came jetting out anyway.

Brenda just stared at him. He stormed out of the bathroom in a huff and went into the bedroom. He couldn't put on his pants and shirt fast enough. He was in a hurry to dismiss this whole episode of his life. As much as he had had problems with Brenda and her extremely none committal ways, he really liked their present arrangement. He couldn't believe she was about to spoil it. Brenda rushed from the bathroom after him.

Then she mentioned ever so calmly, "Oh, and I suppose *you* didn't have anything to do with this?"

Wayne jerked his head around and faced Brenda. Then he responded with scowl, "Maybe I didn't!"

He threw things around on the bed and the chest of drawers in search of his wallet. When he finally found it he scribbled out a check and shoved into Brenda's hand.

"Here," he barked.

He was thirty-two years old, and in his mind far too young to be someone's daddy. The mere idea of it gave him the shakes. He didn't know how he could support a woman on his bus driver salary let alone a woman and a child.

"What is this?" Brenda asked.

"Get rid of it," Wayne said harshly as he spun to the front door. Brenda slumped down on her end table, crushing her last menthol filtered Winston. The check went floating slowly down to the cluttered floor. She closed her eyes and wrestled with her own confusion. She was a Girl Scout when it came to being prepared. Wayne always wore a condom and she never failed to take her pill. She had missed her menstruation by a few days and only took the test as a joke to scare him and to have some fun. This was not supposed to happen to her and the joke was supposed to end in laughter.

Debbie's house

Matthew and Debbie were saying good-byes at the front gate of her parents' two-family home. It was rudely conveyed to Sarah by Debbie that she wanted to speak to Matthew alone. She was none too pleased with Sarah's presence when she finally woke up and met her. Matthew kept quiet and tried his hardest to disappear into the jagged white line down the middle of the road. Sarah figured that she'd let them talk until she couldn't take sitting in his van anymore. Then she'd jump out and call a taxi, but she knew that she was too tired for that. So she gave them another five minutes to wrap it all up. She looked around. She had no idea what part of Brooklyn she was in. All the houses on the block looked exactly alike, again reminding her of her days at Jones and Jones. Debbie's neighborhood brought back memories of the endless amount of copycat houses that she helped create. The only distinguishable differences between them were the garages. Some were on the right side of the houses and some were on the left. Debbie's was on the left. Sarah made a game out of trying to see if she could, in fact, return to Debbie's house in the morning by remembering some perceptible features. By way of a dimly lit street lamp, she couldn't see much.

With nothing else to do, she decided to ease drop on Matthew and Debbie. If she turned her head around they would know that she was out-and-out spying. So she peeked into the side mirror instead. She saw Matthew bending forward and kissing Debbie. Debbie retreated a few steps back and rolled her eyes up, feigning her dissatisfaction. Sarah couldn't make out what she was saying, only that her body language was cursing him out. Matthew took her arms and pulled her towards him in a full body hug. Debbie wilted like a June rose petal in July and rested her head upon his chest. Sarah blushed at the intimacy of their stance and looked away from the mirror but unfortunately not before Matthew spotted her.

Their eyes locked for a second. Sarah didn't know what to do. It was awkward. She was caught. Matthew simply smiled warmly at her and kissed Debbie on the forehead as if she were a sister or a niece. A few moments later he slid back into the van and started the engine.

He was calmer now than he was during the ride over to Debbie's. One would guess he settled into the notion that there was no stopping the imaginary wrecking ball from ruining his reputation. What could he say about Debbie? She wined and complained the whole way home and was so obviously upset over Sarah that she made them all feel uneasy. He even tried putting on the radio to drown her out but she spoke at a squeaky decibel, rising above the volume. She actually said the word *hussy* but only she and Matthew could hear it when she spit it into his ear. He felt a little traumatized by the whole incident.

"How is she?" Sarah asked, more rhetorically than anything else.

Upon spending time with Debbie, she was certain of the answer and hoped Matthew wouldn't bother trying to explain. Matthew didn't answer but knotted his lips and sighed. He knew

Sarah was just being polite. He peered through Sarah's window and saw Debbie standing at the front door leaning on the buzzer. Her mother, wearing a bathrobe and slippers, came to the door. Sarah couldn't understand why Debbie's mother wasn't furious with Debbie for waking her up in the middle of the night. Instead her mother seemed loving and gentle as she scooted her little Debbie inside of the house. Sarah could just imagine Millie welcoming her in the house in that way and smiled.

"What is it?" Matthew asked.

Sarah didn't realize that her internal laugh was audible.

"Nothing," Sarah replied smartly.

She wasn't willing to conceive of a discussion about Debbie or any other girlfriend of Matthew's, for that matter, but Matthew continued to press her and appeared head set on knowing what her little laugh was all about.

"No, come on, tell me," he said as he took the car out of drive and put it into neutral.

Then he sat up and waited for her reply. He decided that the giggle had to have something to do with Debbie and was probing to see what Sarah thought of her. Mentally, he gave Sarah a compliment for showing the greatest level of maturity he had seen in a long, long while. The women he dated wouldn't have shown any restraint if placed under the same circumstances. His most recent example, having just left the vehicle.

Sarah waved her hand at the road as if to say, *we can go now*. She wasn't about to share her opinion of Debbie with him. If she were with Karen, or Brenda or Crystal, it would have been difficult for her to stop talking about Debbie. Alas, there are unwritten rules against defaming someone's character with their significant other.

After a couple of minutes of silence, Matthew saw that he wasn't getting anywhere with his delay tactics and raised his hand in a surrender pose. He could see that she was growing tired and losing steam. He didn't want to push it. Besides, he could surmise from her body language what her laugh was about. He applauded her again for having the decency and restraint not to express what they both already knew.

"Sorry. Sorry. I was just... Never mind. Really," he said.

Sarah nodded in acceptance of Matthew's apology.

"Ah, where to?" he asked.

He shifted into drive and the van throttled forward.

"Lawrence, between Church and..."

"Redmond."

"How do you know where I live?" Sarah asked in a deliberately pale way.

She guessed that he might have gotten her address from Delroy. And that idea didn't sit well with her at all.

"I *don't* know where you live. I just know that there is only one block that Lawrence and Church can have as a cross street. 'Cause if you go in the other direction, you'll run into a school, right?"

Matthew spoke very matter-of-factly. His sentences had just the right amount of forbearance. He didn't want to offend her but he didn't want her to think that he had done anything wrong either.

"Right. Right," Sarah quickly agreed and tried to move on.

She couldn't believe that she was letting her anxiety show in such a way. It wasn't dignified behavior to accuse a man of confiscating your address from his auto-mechanic. Then yet another sentence slipped out of her mouth before she could get a hold of herself.

"How do you know about that school?" she asked.

"I have a younger cousin attending classes there," he answered.

Matthew hoped to segue into a real conversation, to put an end to this indictment. He didn't want to fight with her. If he could, he wanted to shield her from any more discomfort at his hands. So, he reached over and put another compact disc in the player. As the night air began to sweep across both of their faces, *Sophia's Toy* began to play. It was hard core Rock-n-Roll and an odd choice for the ride. It was hardly the cool down music Sarah felt sure that they both needed.

"If you don't mind me saying so, I think I bring out the worst in you," Matthew said humbly.

He explored Sarah's face for a reaction to his statement. Sarah's head was pressed into the neck rest. Despite her original assessment of the music, she was being strangely lulled by it. She winked an eye and mumbled ever so softly, "I don't hate you."

Matthew drove on down the road, finding difficulty in hiding the grin that started in his belly and rose to his lips, framing the lower half of his face.

CHAPTER TWENTY-TWO

By the last song on the compact disc, Sarah and Matthew were singing at the top of their lungs and banging out drumbeats on the dashboard. The van amplifiers shook from the shear volume of the lead singer's earsplitting timbre. They both sang harmony as if they were back-up singers, Matthew's tenor to Sarah's soprano. The dial quivered beneath the word maximum on the tuner. They chuckled about their antics as the song began to fade out.

"That is fantastic!" Sarah exclaimed.

"It really is, isn't it? She really has a fierce voice. I grew up with a bloke who knew her before she started doing rock and roll. You should see her on stage. She's really something. Quite an entertainer."

"I would love to see her in concert."

"That would be lovely. I'd love to take you!"

The last audible chorus of the song was heard faintly beneath the hum of the van motor. Neither spoke for an endless haze of seconds. The silence was thick. 'Did Matthew just ask me out on a date?' was all that Sarah could think about. She started to say yes, but the words got trapped in her throat. She didn't want it to sound like she was agreeing to a real date, God forbid. Before she uttered a sound, she had to find for sure what he meant in order to make it clear that it would just be two casual friends meeting at a mutually agreed upon public place at an aforementioned time.

Matthew's shoulders tensed as he thought about how liking someone could sometimes be complex. If they were kids in a sand box he would have simply handed her his shovel. His problem in life was that he always got caught up in the moment and at that moment he was enjoying Sarah's company. He wasn't thinking about what other people would say if they went out together for drinks. He wasn't taking a survey of the consequences their friendship would bring. He didn't have assumptions of them going to a concert as the beginning of a budding relationship, but he was smart enough to know that Sarah was thinking about all of those things and much, much more. As much as women say they want a man to sweep them off their feet, Matthew knew better. The broom, in question, should come equipped with magical powers. In his experience with women, he found them to be shrewder and more level headed than men. When it came to affairs of the heart, he discovered that women at least tried to choose the best man they could find. He, and some of his friends, shamefully chose *easy* above all other qualities. He turned the corner onto Redmond and didn't bother waiting for an answer from her. He was going to play it cool and allow her to make the next move.

Sarah suddenly jerked forward in her seat.

"What's the matter? I'm driving carefully, aren't I?" he asked.

Matthew was, in fact, obeying every traffic law, and making every effort to stay within the speed limit. In truth, Sarah hadn't noticed. She was lost in the ambiance of having a somewhat pleasant time with Matt-hew and didn't quite know how to deal with that. Meanwhile, he found himself wanting to extend their evening and was equally unprepared with that budding surge of excitement.

"Oh no, no...It's just that I forgot about my girlfriend, Karen. We were supposed to go together to see "Lady Sings the Blues" tonight but she didn't show up."

Matthew was confused.

"Oh, no. She's gonna' kill me," she explained.

"She didn't show up and you're the one in trouble?" Matthew asked.

 This was yet another thing he was learning about women.

"I know. It's something we do. We have this unwritten rule that if someone is late, we wait. I tried calling but there was no answer. So, I just went inside the theater."

"American women."

"I know. It probably doesn't make any sense to you at all," Sarah said.

"Do you want to swing by her house? We could see if she's all right," he liked where this was heading, anything to spend some more time with her.

"Could we?" Sarah smiled brightly.

She was more than a little worried about Karen now. It did not make sense for her to just bail without even calling or leaving a message. She thought about some of the recent conversations she had with her. Had she missed something in their conversations, some hidden meaning? She wanted to wait for Karen to divulge information but she was becoming more and more elusive.

"Sure, where to?" Matthew said and with that, they took off once again down the darkened road.

Karen lived approximately twenty minutes away from Sarah. Matthew got there in ten. His minivan pulled up to the driveway and just as it was stopping, Sarah jumped out. As she ran down the path to the door, she thought about what she would say. She thanked God that the living room lights were still on. At least she wouldn't wake anyone unnecessarily. At three in the morning it was probably as good a time as any for her to show concern.

She would ask her to explain some of her recent erratic cancellations. 'Maybe it was nothing,' Sarah thought. Maybe she was just letting her imagination run away with her. It could simply be that Karen's a mother now with a whole host of responsibilities that arise without warning.

Sarah gave Matthew the thumbs up. He switched off the engine and made himself small behind the dash. She was kind of glad that he was with her. This way she could say that she was just in the neighborhood and decided to stop by. Also, he could be a quick getaway excuse. If she caught Norman and Karen in the throes of passion, she would need one. Having her story straight, she rang the doorbell. After a few rings no one came to the door. Sarah wondered why she even bothered, but then she heard voices from inside. As she was about to ring the bell again, her attention was diverted by something in her periphery. There was movement in the living room. She could see something through a small opening in the window shade. It was shiny and sharp. It looked like a knife but it was too big to be that. At a glance, 'it might be an ax?' Sarah thought. Then she saw something or someone falling. It was Karen. She swung headfirst into the wooden arm of the couch before hitting the floor. Sarah squinted to adjust her focus. It was definitely Karen, now trying to prop herself into a seated position. The only thing blocking Sarah's view was a slender table lamp, which was directly underneath the windowpane. Karen tried to get up but someone or something knocked her back down. Sarah couldn't see who or what. She reached over in a sheer panic and this time rested her finger on the bell. Now, Sarah could hear Norman's voice yelling about something. The words were unclear but the tone was angry and cold. Then Sarah saw Norman extend his arm and backhand Karen across the cheek. Sarah stood frozen. Then Yolanda appeared at the living room doorway. Norman yelled something at her too and she took off back upstairs.

Karen and Norman didn't hear the ringing despite the fact that Sarah had both hands on it now. Her body shook and tears moistened her eyes. She felt powerless. The door wouldn't open no matter how many times she kicked at it and screamed and hollered. It seemed the whole world wasn't listening. She swallowed in pain, mixed emotions and hurt. Her throat was hoarse and dry from calling for help until no sound escaped her lips at all.

A hand came from behind her and gently removed her sweaty palms from the doorknob. She flipped around to find Matthew. He stood very close to her and placed his fingers on her wet shoulders, now dripping with dread and perspiration. His subtlety gave her permission to relax. She longed to and, at the same time, felt sure she had forgotten how. She had just seen her best friend being brutally beaten by her husband. It didn't seem real.

"Call the police," came out in a crackled tiny voice that she didn't recognize as her own.

Matthew simply lowered his head in the direction of the living room window. Sarah was reluctant to look again. She had already been programmed to associate that window with suffering. Matthew shifted his weight and gave her some room. He peered up the street allowing Sarah to take all the time she needed. She took in a deep breath and as she was exhaling carried her attention to their window once more. She paused. She held her head in her hand and shook it from side to side. She was stunned and flabbergasted. She was floored by what she saw.

There was Norman seated snuggly beside Karen on their couch. Their arms were interlocked around each other and they were rocking backwards and forwards. Sarah thought she was going to be ill. She immediately ducked away from the window, turned and marched back to the van. Matthew was not far behind.

They got in. They buckled up. They took off.

The streets were empty that time of night as was Sarah, empty and depleted. Her stomach was a ball of twine stirred up and sickened to the core. She tried to keep her emotions from showing but they started to leak through her thin veneer. She had known Norman almost as long as she had known Karen.

Norman used to be a star in her eyes as well as in the hearts of many people who attended their school. There was no one more loved than him. Back in high school, teachers would have laid down their careers for Norman. Many figuratively had with the bogus grading they gave him. Norman lacked enthusiasm for his classes but he was by no means a dumb guy. He knew that his athletic ability was his ticket and anything he wanted to do or didn't want to do could be negotiated. His fame was so pervasive in Heritage High that if he liked someone, that special someone was liked by all, and if he hated someone, that someone was hated by all. Girls were excluded from this problem. Everyone knew that Norman loved all of the ladies.

When he started dating Karen there were girls in school who actually wanted to beat her up. They were so heartbroken and forlorn of Norman's choice. Back then, Norman and Karen were very much in love. He would do anything for her, which surprised everyone, including some of *his* best friends. Sarah couldn't fathom how their relationship degenerated to the display she witnessed tonight. Except that hidden amongst his many qualities blurred his perfect love for himself. He was pummeling her as if she was a guy and not the prom queen he danced with all night at Tavern on the Green or the mother of his lovely little daughter. How could something like this happen? The more Sarah thought about it, the sadder she became. She didn't even notice when they pulled up in front of her house.

She maintained focus on the scenery of the quiet Brooklyn streets. Matthew didn't really know what to say so he remained silent for the entire ride. During the trip he thought about extending his arm to comfort her. He was genuinely concerned about her and wanted her to know that. He watched the incident from the street and from that distance it looked like something out of a movie. He couldn't imagine what it must have looked like up close.

Slowly, Matthew began to realize that his passenger wasn't moving. He looked for the address sign on the building and was certain that he went to the right house. Sarah wasn't paying attention. She was still looking out of the window. He could tell that her mind was a million miles away. So, he detached his seat belt, then hers. He slipped out of the van, then went around and helped her out. She was spent. She was sure that she hadn't the energy to make it to her door. Matthew stood beside her and waited for her to move forward down the little pathway to her stairs. Instead, she vacantly looked up at the stars. Matthew followed her lead and scanned the sky also. It was a clear brilliant night, on the eve of a full moon. Matthew drew an imaginary line connecting the stars of the big dipper as he had done so many times as a boy. He stretched and rolled his neck around. He felt tired too.

"Would you like to come in?" she asked and didn't wait for an answer.

She proceeded up the stairs, opened the door and stepped inside. Matthew timidly walked in after her. By the time he entered, Sarah had already disappeared into another room. He closed the door behind him and politely waited to be led all the way into her home. He couldn't presuppose anything with her. He had been incorrect so often that this time he played it safe and let her take control.

"Want Blackforest or Apple Manor?" she called out to him.

He peeked around a column and saw her in the kitchen putting a kettle on the stove. Two boxes of tea were displayed in the kitchen doorway for his approval. He hadn't a clue what flavor they were.

"Blackforest," he shrugged.

Sarah stayed in the kitchen messing about. Matthew could hear the refrigerator door open and close several times but not much else. Now, that he had confirmation that his presence was indeed requested he began to take a look around the place. It was a photographer's dream. Her ceilings were at least fifteen feet high. She had windows on three of the four living room walls, which for Matthew, meant she had sunlight all day long. He took a quick but thorough inventory of her record collection and then her books.

"<u>All It Takes Is Guts</u>, excellent," he mumbled.

Sarah came from around the opaque glass wall that separated the kitchen from the living room carrying a tray of crackers and cheese.

"What?" she asked.

"Oh," Matthew said.

He was startled from his snooping.

"I loved this book," he replied pointing at the shelf.

"One of the best I've read."

"Me too," he said.

They stared at each other uncomfortably for a few seconds. Sarah couldn't help but compare him to Michael who walked in and plopped his behind on her sofa.

"You have an amazing home. It's huge. I'd love to photograph it one day if that would be okay?"

Sarah nodded in all directions. Neither she nor Matthew knew if she was saying yes or no. She asked herself repeatedly why she was being so standoffish towards his advances. Then she asked herself if they were, in fact, come-ons or if he really found her place spectacular.

"I was lucky. It was pouring rain and I was the only one who answered the owner's ad."

"Really?"

"Yeap. Anyway, I'll go and get the tea."

"Fine."

Sarah walked back into the kitchen and Matthew continued looking around. Shortly after, she came back in and placed two cups on the coffee table. She sat on the sofa. He sat on a sectional.

"Thank you," he said as he sank into the velvety leather.

"Thank you for dropping me off," was all Sarah could manage before she felt like crying.

She laid both hands on the coffee table and let them settle from shaking before attempting to pick up her teakettle. Once again her thoughts were back on Karen and Norman as if they had never left. The image of Karen falling to the floor was now outlined with much more detail. Sarah's mind took that event and slowed it down in instant replay. As Norman's hand swept across Karen's face, an imprint remained from the blood just beneath the surface of the skin. Sarah could see in her minds-eye that Karen was not caught off guard. She had braced herself and prepared for the blow. Sarah held her stomach and rocked back and forth on the couch. Each revelation about Norman and Karen sent her insides into spasms. Matthew sat and watched her. It was clear to her that he might have thought she was having a nervous breakdown. She jumped up and put the radio on. A news broadcast was underway reporting a violent armed robbery that took place up town. She turned the dial three times before leaving it on a Hispanic station. She didn't speak Spanish. She didn't want to understand what anyone was saying anymore. She just wanted to hear some noise, any noise.

"Have you two been friends a long time?" Matthew gently asked.

Sarah paused and mulled over the question for a while before responding.

"A life time."

CHAPTER TWENTY-THREE

There's a thump at Karen and Norman's front door. Norman's eyes jet open. He pulls his arm out from underneath Karen's limp body and ambles over to the window. He hisses when he sees the paperboy making his rounds down the street. He can't help but count the number of times that he and his neighbors cautioned him against breaking a window. The stringy, twelve-year-old boy, who pitches for a little league team, swore his throwing was accurate within a margin of error of five percent. Norman opened the front door and there it lay. The newspaper wrapped in a thin sheet of plastic, in the same spot it had always landed since their young friend had his route. Norman swooped down and scooped it underneath his arm. He remembered a time when he too could be depended on for his precision. His teammates said he had the hands of a surgeon. They marveled at his ability to have them run to the exact yard line he instructed and as they got there the ball would float into their arms as if a gift from heaven. His timing they said was as perfect as Timex. He had the rare talent of knowing where everyone was on the field at all times. When it came to football, he had a photographic memory.

Norman glanced at the staircase in the hallway and imagined he could see the bleachers of his high school football field filled with screaming fans and cart wheeling cheerleaders. His daydream is so vivid that he can make out the individual faces. He sees himself with the football on his shoulder. He is just about to throw it to a running back. Norman puts the newspaper in that position and pretends he's out there again. He draws his arm way back and releases the paper. It spins perfectly from his grip and slices the air in a brilliant rounded arch and into the nervous palms of a teammate who stands by the goal-line, touchdown. In reality, it actually lands on the couch, inches away from Karen's head. Karen pries open one of her eyes. Both are swollen. She sees Norman with his hand just above her head and flinches. He grabs the paper and puts both arms in the air.

"It's okay," he yelps.

Karen relaxes her tense arms, which were raised up protecting her face.

"It's okay. I'm not gonna'…" Norman lets the sentence trail off.

He wants to forget about last night. He wants to tell Karen that he had too much to drink and that he wasn't completely himself. Remorse wells up in his throat with extreme sincerity. Would he cry? He could never give anyone that benefit. He would never let Karen see him in any vulnerable state. Instead, Karen fights back tears for both of them. She fears that there may be something really wrong with her eyes. She can't seem to open one of them and she begins to worry about blindness.

"Are you hungry?" Norman asked as if everything was as per usual.

Norman can't even find the stove so Karen surmises that he wants her to fix breakfast. She tries to stand but her stomach muscles still ache from Norman's blows. She cups her palm over her eye and gently rubs until she senses some feeling there. She's relived to find that it's caked with pus and not blood. She licks her fingers and soaks the eyelid with her own saliva. The room comes into focus. She would give anything to be able to just stay on the couch for the rest of the day.

"Why don't I fix you breakfast for a change?" Norman

suggests.

Then he jumps up and walks into the kitchen. Karen can judge the damage he has done to her by his sudden acts of kindness. Usually their arguments continue well into the next day. Either Norman feels guilty or his hangover isn't so severe. Karen has learned to take advantage of any peaceful moments she has to herself. She knows that it will not be long before Norman requests her presence in the kitchen. As much as he wants to make amends, cooking is not the way to do it. Karen reflected upon the recent hours. She held her chin in her hands and sighed. Her life was unbelievable to her. Nothing in it made sense anymore. Yolanda came into the living room and stood at the entrance. Her black Barbie doll was clutched in her hand and dragging behind her as she slowly walked up to Karen. She jumped up on the couch and sat extremely close. Karen roped her arm around her and held her tightly.

At a downtown clinic

"June Adams," the nurse hollered in a way that indicated just how much her feet hurt.

A young girl about three-months pregnant stood up and walked through a door marked private. Brenda and Crystal overhear her say to the nurse that this had been her third time. The nurse listened without judgment and followed her through the door. Brenda will be next. The waiting area didn't take long to empty out. When Brenda and Crystal first got there at least thirty young girls were wandering about the corridor. Each of them looked nervous and withdrawn. Crystal spoke in tongues quietly every time one of the girl's names was called. She believed that they needed to be prayed for because no one even bothered to accompany them to the clinic. It didn't surprise her that Brenda allowed her to be spiritual. That's because Brenda was just as scared as the young girls. It did come as a shock to her. However, that Brenda asked her to escort her there and not Sarah or Karen. Usually she was the last to know the secret goings-on of her girlfriend, Brenda. She knew better than to feel too honored though. Brenda had an ulterior motive. Naturally Crystal became her intermediary. Now that she was in a jam that she couldn't talk her way out of, she believed in God. Crystal didn't mind. She worked in a church and was used to people who only wanted God when there was a mess to bless. The nurse poked her head into the waiting area once more.

"Brenda-sue James," she shouted.

Crystal eyed Brenda curiously.

"I prefer Brenda, just Brenda," Brenda corrected.

The nurse ignored her request while pushing the door open for her with her hips. Crystal motioned to the nurse that she wanted to go with her. Brenda waved at her telling her not to bother. Crystal obeyed. Then Brenda followed the nurse into the examination room.

The 5'x5' room is jammed with reproductive related paraphernalia.

"Please sit down. Did you fill out a pink form?" the nurse asked as routine.

Brenda gave her the form and allowed her to evaluate it. The nurse never looked up from the paperwork to address her. She took a moment reviewing Brenda's application and stopped when she saw Brenda's age.

"Occupation?"

"Student, full-time."

"Married?"

"No."

"Are you having problems with the father?" the nurse asked somewhat indignantly.

Brenda could see that the nurse was getting heated.

"Well, no, not really. Why?" Brenda asked.

The nurse paused before speaking.

"Then why are you doing this? Usually women *your* age make the choice to have the child," the nurse said letting the words echo off the walls.

Brenda thought it was very unprofessional of her. After all, wasn't she forbidden from giving her own opinion or something?

"I'm just asking," the nurse remarked smugly when she saw that she couldn't get anything out of Brenda except a blasé gaze.

Brenda was cool and collected. She didn't even raise an eyebrow. She was prepared for this moment. All through high school enemies of hers anticipated her eventually getting pregnant and what a scandal it would be. She knew this to be true because word got back to her one day that someone told someone else that she had missed her period. That nosey someone overheard her say to Sarah that her cycle was a day late. She missed the part when she told Sarah that it came the day after that. Before she knew it the rumor mill churned out a charming little story of her having twins for someone on the basketball team. She couldn't refute the basketball team part. She had dated several of its members. Then for weeks Brenda experienced a dating dry spell. Apparently, the boys who liked her were afraid of being beaten up by the mysterious daddy. Brenda watched as girls snickered behind her back or walked around giving her pitied glances. She was disgusted by the whole thing and learned how easy it was to sully someone's reputation. She remembers finding it particularly interesting that she couldn't get any support from females for a female dilemma. Instead, these girls were basking and gloating in her troubles. On occasion she could hear them say things like,

'Well, she brought it on herself,' or 'She got what she deserved.' She refused to confront the busybodies because that would be a sign of defeat. She wouldn't give them the satisfaction of knowing that they were winning. One day in gym class Brenda made sure she got a seat directly in front of the girls responsible for the lie. Then she waited for just the right moment to raise her hand to ask permission to go to the bathroom. She spoke loudly and clearly as if she were making a public service announcement. The entire class, which comprised really three classes altogether, turned and stared, with hand raised high, Brenda held up a huge box of over night Kotex maxi pads. She used the great big ones that looked like diapers for dramatic effect. She looked like she was doing a commercial where the advertisers insist on seeing their product in every shot. The rumors stopped immediately.

"Just tell me what I have to do, okay?" Brenda huffed.

"Okay," the nurse replied.

Jezebel's

Jezebel's, New York City's perfect chic hush-hush ambiance, a heavy metal door painted gray and exterior nondescript with a raised bronze sign sporting its name. Thick opaque curtains cover its gigantic storefront windows protecting its patrons from prying eyes. As it is with many well-to-do eateries, only those who know where the restaurant is will be able to find it. Once inside one could do quite a bit of celebrity hobnobbing but for Sarah and Karen it was all about the food. There isn't many places in the City that served catfish and grits for dinner.

As Karen approached the restaurant's entrance, eating was all she had on her mind. Norman tried his best to fix breakfast that morning but Karen didn't have the heart to tell him that the meal wasn't fit for human consumption. So, she hadn't eaten all day.

Now she just stood in front of the restaurant salivating. It was dusk, yet she wore huge sunglasses that wrapped half way around her face, and the ace bandage supported her wrist. Despite the enormous size of the lenses, they aren't doing a very good job of covering a patch of make-up on the lower portion of her chin. She took off the shades, reached into her purse and pulled out a compact mirror. It was hard for her to comprehend who was in the reflection. She imagines an abstract painting where the eyes are off to the left of the head. The lips are rounded beyond that which is possible. Karen wipes the mirror off with her sleeve and apprehensively holds it up once more. She blinks rapidly to clear off any residue from underneath her eyelids. This time when she looks into the glass she recognizes herself but doesn't know where to begin applying yet another layer of foundation.

"Damn!" she says taking a powder compact from her bag and hurriedly concealing every rough area.

Now she glows like an apparition. She will need something to lean on tonight, she resolves, a crutch. She makes her mind up to drink heavily and to remind herself later to break anything that she can see herself in. She refits the glasses around her ears and walks inside. The maître d informed her that Sarah was already seated at one of the tables having soup. Karen assuredly waves the host aside and strolls up to Sarah's table feigning cheerfulness.

"Hey, how are you? Sorry 'bout last night. Got tied up. Norman wanted to do it all night. If, you know what I mean? I'll make it up to you, though, okay," said Karen with a wink.

'What a pile of horse manure,' Sarah thought, looking up and only seeing her own face glaring back at her from Karen's eyeware. She was glad they were in Jezebel's. Maybe everyone would mistake Karen for a celebrity.

"That's...never mind. Sit. Sit," Sarah instructed her in a way that was too much like telling a prisoner to sit for his/her last meal, "It's...okay," she said.

Karen slid her jacket off and lowered herself into the seat. Sarah pretended not to notice when Karen winced as she bent over. Once again Sarah mentally replayed in slow motion Karen crashing to the floor. She shook off the sharp sympathetic jabs penetrating her insides by holding her breath and exhaling with a spurt.

"Please. Come on. Let me make it up to you. I really will you know," Karen reiterated.

Sarah inched her lips into some semblance of a smile.

"Okay," she said, resigned to play along with Karen's annoying pretense at normalcy, at least for a while. After dinner Sarah thought she would have her opportunity to say what was on her mind.

"Where is everyone?" Karen asked.

Sarah examined Karen's face. It had all the signs of a battered wife. Why hadn't she noticed it before?

"I don't know," she replied lost in thought, "Brenda called and said she had something else to do, as usual, and that Crystal was with her. They said they would try to make it later."

"Well, I'm gonna' order something now. I'm starving," Karen said.

While Karen perused the menu, Sarah watched her behavior for anything inconsistent but Karen didn't seem out of the ordinary at all. Karen was completely pulled together. Not one hair was out of place on her head. Sarah was baffled. She wondered how long it might have been going on. Did it start in high school? They'd have to be pretty good actors to pull that one off. The thought that someone could get used to severe punishment crossed her mind, but she believed that that someone could never be Karen.

"Karen, how are you?" it was a good direct question, Sarah

thought.

"Good. Can't complain. Well, actually I could complain but I won't. What kind of soup is that? It looks and smells really good."

It was Karen's incessant happy tone that finally started to get to Sarah. It was annoying and absurd and disturbing. How could she be happy? Sarah pushed her bowl aside. She figured this was a good a time as any.

"What would you complain about?" Sarah asked, again trying to create an opening to delve deep whilst treading lightly.

Karen adjusted her back and sat in a more upright position.

"What, something wrong?" Karen asked in a concerned manner.

Sarah placed her hand onto Karen's and held it there firmly. Her heart was filled with empathy and she struggled to keep an ocean of tears from gushing forth.

"Karen, hum..." Sarah said with her throat constricted.

Suddenly it didn't seem like such a good idea now that she had the floor. She had to be cautious. Karen and she were the same age. What can a peer reveal to another peer? Then Sarah wondered whether she was the right person to give advice on marriage. She had never even been proposed to. Sarah's hesitancy became awkward for both of them. Karen slowly eased her hand from underneath Sarah's.

"Sarah, whatever you are, baby, we can still be friends but I don't go that way," Karen joked with a fluttering of her eyes.

Then Karen studied her menu again and laughed. Sarah tried to join in on the laughter but instead went stone-faced.

"Gees, can't take a joke. What is it? Is everything all-right?" Karen asked more concerned for her friend.

Sarah didn't answer. She bowed her head instead cowering underneath her own self made pressure. Her expression betrayed her all the while. She was never any good at hiding what she was feeling. She was transparent and thought for sure that Karen could read her thoughts.

"Is everything all-right with you?" Sarah said almost whimpering.

There was a long silent pause between them. Karen looked around the restaurant agitated.

"Look, I don't know how to say this," the words trailed off as Sarah lifted her head and fixed and locked eyes on Karen, "except to just say it."

"Say what?" Karen munched on the breadsticks in a basket on the table.

Sarah took a long deep breath before she went on.

"I came by your house last night."

The sentence shot out faster than a derailed locomotive. She figured that she'd let Karen tell her what happened that she would have to confess.

"Why, why didn't you ring the bell?" Karen's voice cracked but other than that, not a hint of distress showed.

Sarah remained focused on Karen's eyes. They were darting about the restaurant. Karen shifted position. It was a strain for her to look directly at Sarah.

"I did," Sarah declared now visibly upset

"You couldn't have. Me and Norman would have heard you." Karen dismissed the notion.

Sarah rested her forehead in her hand. She tried to think of exactly when she and Karen stopped having truthful discussions with one another. They had stayed best friends for so long because they were completely honest with one another. Sarah didn't know who she was talking to any more. Karen was emotionally backing away from Sarah and Sarah couldn't understand why. It hurt.

"Karen, you two couldn't possibly have heard me. Norman was…"

Sarah's pitch was so high that she had to swallow before finishing her sentence.

"…Norman hit you."

Karen fell back into her chair and bellowed with laughter. The laugh was loud, somewhat shaky, and dishonest.

"Sarah, come on? Norman..?" she asked.

Then she leaned her head back and roared until tears came to her eyes. It echoed off the ceiling and ricocheted in Sarah's gapping mouth.

"…hitting me?"

Karen shook her head from side to side and wagged her index finger.

"You've got to be kidding. What makes you say that? Did somebody tell you something? I don't know what they could have told you, but no. No one's hitting on me," said Karen so sternly that even Sarah was having second thoughts about what she saw.

She looked around the room to see if anyone else noticed how pale Karen appeared. She hadn't been aware of it when Karen first sat down. It was only after Sarah saw her neck that she realized that her face was completely discolored. Sarah was torn between blowing the lid off their casual chat or just letting the whole thing play out the way Karen described. After all, she wasn't married to Norman and didn't have to suffer through his fits of rage. In all honesty, she knew that it would be easier on both of them. And why not have things be easy? Karen could blissfully continue in her sham of a marriage and Sarah could make believe that she had faith in it. But it pained her deeply to know that she was right and that Karen was busily trying to refute the truth.

"Then take off your sunglasses," Sarah told her.

"What is this, you feel like beating up on someone and I just happen to be here? What ever happened between you and Brenda is between you and her. And you should take it up with her! I feel like I'm on trial here or something," Karen barked.

Then, she rolled her head from side to side as if she was gearing up for a fistfight. Sarah didn't move. Karen slouched in her chair and went on speaking composedly.

"Look, I don't know what somebody's been telling you but I've just been a little clumsy lately, you know? Moving back home after all these years is a little unsettling."

Karen had told so many people this story so many times that even she was beginning to believe it. And, although she sounded persuasive, Sarah never doubted that it was Norman beating up her last night. She saw it with her own eyes, eyes that wept in agony for her friend all night long. Now, she knew that it was her mission to get Karen to acknowledge the truth. Karen needed to get it off her chest too, she decided, and it didn't matter that Karen didn't know that herself. She was going to be the one to tell her. Sarah believed that Karen had fallen so deep into a sea of denial that it had impaired her vision.

"Take off your sunglasses, Karen," Sarah simply told her.

Karen turned away from Sarah.

"When you got off the plane your arm was all bandaged up. I didn't think about it at the time. Then it was your hand. And now, and now your whole face is covered up."

"What are you a private detective or something? I fell! That's all there is to it. Give it a rest," Karen pleaded.

"I saw you last night. It was you," Sarah continued.

Karen stood up.

"Just drop it, all-right? Look, I don't want to talk about this anymore," Karen said fuming.

Sarah slammed her hand down on the table angrily. Some people directly next to them shuffled in their seats at the outbursts.

"I'm worried about you, damn-it! What am I supposed to do?"

Then she rose and placed her hands on Karen's shoulders.

"Should I let him hit on you? I don't know if I can do that."

Karen yanked her body from Sarah's arms and walked away.

"Don't walk away from me," Sarah said just loud enough for Karen to hear.

Karen stomped her feet while whipping back around to pick up her jacket. Now some other people in the restaurant took notice of them.

"Karen, how you just gonna' walk away from me?" Sarah asked.

Karen turned sharply and faced her.

"He's a good man. He takes care of Yolanda and me. I don't ask him to, he just does it. He's my husband. He loves me and I, I love him. I don't expect you to understand. He-'s-always-been there-for-me, always, without question, without a word. How many men out there would work two sometimes three jobs, just to make sure that you didn't have to want for anything? How many would, tell me that? He never complains, not even once. And I put him through it too. I ask for the world! And I want him to put it right in my lap," Karen's speech is choppy and uneven.

Her legs are wobbly so she holds onto the back of the chair for support. She looks as if she's about to faint. Sarah listens and tries to hold herself steady.

"And sometimes, I don't even want him to touch me," Karen goes on, "Sometimes I think I deserve what I get," she says without apology.

Sarah plops back down in her seat, just as the host scurries over to their table to ask if they can take their conversation outside. Neither, Sarah nor Karen pay any attention to him. He repeats it several times. Again, nothing. Sarah waits until he's out of earshot before continuing.

"You do not deserve this, Karen. My God, you do not deserve some man beating up on you in your own home. I don't care if he built the house, everything in it and a whole neighborhood to put it in," Sarah spoke softly and gently.

Karen was unglued.

"This is none of your business!" Karen shouted.

"I'm your friend! I'm your friend! Please don't tell me it's not my business!" Sarah shouted right back.

Karen threw her arms up. She's had enough of this cross-examination. She turned and went towards the door just as the host approached their table again. The host sees her exiting, and is satisfied enough to return to his post. He's pleased that the disruption is over. Though Karen stops in the middle of the restaurant before reaching the door as if she's forgotten something, makes a ninety degree turn and struts back over to Sarah.

"You're my friend, huh?" she said smugly, "Look at you, little miss prim and proper. You know so much, don't you?"

Sarah began to seethe uncomfortably now that she's being attacked for telling the truth.

"You don't have a husband, do you?" Karen asked deliberately laying out her argument for effect.

"You don't even have a boy friend, do you?" she let her words penetrate and wound.

"How could you possibly understand what this is all about?"

"We're not talking about me. We're talking about you," Sarah said defensively.

"Well, let's talk about you for a goddamn minute, shall we?"

Karen turns a chair around and straddles it.

"Can't find the right man to love you? Oh, poor baby. That's really a God damned shame," again Karen wanted to make the point stick, "There must be something wrong with all of them, right? Oh, such a shame. Poor you!"

The gloves were off. All Sarah could do was recoil into her seat.

"Maybe, it's because you're a stuck-up-bitch, always have been, always will be. Even in high school no man could stand how cold you were. They would come to me first and say, 'I like Sarah. Can you ask her out for me?' Can you imagine? No one could get next to you, let alone date you. You haven't a clue what marriage is all about. You don't even know what having a relationship with a man is like. You don't have the slightest idea because you've never had one. So you can't tell me a Goddamn thing 'bout what's going on. 'Cause you don't know, now do you?"

Karen acted as if she was waiting for an answer but she knew Sarah wouldn't give her one.

Then Karen again grabbed her belongings and stormed out of the restaurant. Sarah sat with her chin to her chest. She saw people staring at her from out of the corner of her eye. So, she waited until they rejoined their own conversations before lifting her head back up. The harsh words and tone spoken by Karen would not be soon forgotten. She flagged the waitress to her table. This episode had been exhausting and when the waitress walked over she couldn't remember why she had called her.

"Bring me a shot of Tequila - and keep them coming," said told her.

Later that evening Sarah exited the restaurant just before closing and leaned against the building wall for an hour. Her diet was all liquid - runny soup and Tequilas. She swaggered to the curb and held out her hand for a cab. No vacant taxis on the road tonight. After several minutes, Sarah began to lean against a street light pole. She straightened up, though, when her head smacked into it. In doing so she tries to shake off the numbness and spots a pay phone a few feet away in the process. She drags her body towards it, picks up the receiver and holds it up to her ear. It was heavy in her grasp and sticky at the bottom. She listened for several seconds before realizing that she hadn't call anyone yet. She laughed dryly at herself, searched through her purse and pulled out Matthew's card. She read it and tossed it to the ground. Then she pulled out her phone book and thumbed through it. She couldn't find what she was looking for so she dropped the phone book back in. It missed the purse and fell to the ground too. She slowly bends over to pick it up and in the process, picks up Matthew's card again, then calls him.

CHAPTER TWENTY-FOUR

Unenthusiastically, Crystal entered the dank smelly bar. If it weren't for Brenda's incessant pleading and whining, Crystal would not have been in such a place. She didn't think it was improper for her to visit a bar, she just knew that it wasn't quite what God had in mind when he said, 'Go ye into the world.' If she saw anyone she knew and they asked her, she would say that she was trying to console a sick friend. Then she would point to Brenda. Brenda was not by any means her usual self. As much as Crystal liked the new Brenda, who wasn't wearing anything sexy tonight, she knew that this change in her was an indication that something was drastically wrong. She couldn't refuse her invitation. Besides, Brenda always knew the right buttons to push. Brenda told Crystal that they would only go for one drink. Then she told her that she really needed someone to talk to who would listen without judgment. Crystal loved this kind of talk, which fueled her wish to be nurturing. Brenda also told her that she didn't have to worry about transportation and that she would pick her up and take her home safely. Even with all of those promises, Crystal was still not persuaded to go. Then Brenda told her not to be so heavenly bound that she is no earthly good. That cinched the deal. One thing Crystal would not stand for was being called self-righteous by a back sliding Christian. She was determined more than ever to be the best friend she could be to Brenda. She even prayed and repented for feeling otherwise during Brenda's little crisis. Deep in her soul, she always knew that with Brenda always playing with fire she'd eventually get burned. However, this was not the time for her to give Brenda a sermon, nor to chastise her for previous deeds. She couldn't say no. She had a commitment to her faith to show love and compassion to those in need. Besides, she hadn't talked to God in a while since her date with Terry. She had to do something to re-establish their relationship. She was so very sorry that she had blamed Him in the first place. God had nothing to do with her poor choice. She finally admitted that to herself. In recent days, she had taken a closer examination of Terry and discovered whole truckloads of lies and inconsistencies that she hadn't seen in her three years of adoring him from afar. She thought that with all her good church teachings, it would have prevented her from making such a huge blunder. She was happy that Terry had forgotten most of the evening but remembered just enough to pay her back her money and leave her alone.

As soon as they walked into the club, Crystal immediately ushered Brenda to two empty stools at the long wooden bar. She wanted Brenda to slurp down a non-alcoholic beverage, then they'd talk for a while, then they'd call it a night. No sooner had they sat down, though, Brenda began flirting with a stranger seated directly across from them. Crystal tried to be big about it. He seemed nice enough but Crystal wondered why Brenda wanted to complicate her life further with yet another man. She kept thinking that if she were in Brenda's shoes she wouldn't want to entertain even the possibility of other men let alone have one in the flesh. Brenda was unique in this way. She always wanted a man around to validate her existence. Crystal saw that her mission was clear. She figured that her job was to keep Brenda focused on the moral dilemma at hand – to abort or not to abort. Crystal glanced across the bar at the man in question.

"Du' ya' know 'em, Brenda?"

"No, I don't but I sure would like to."

"Jus' rememba' that ya'll in no condition ta' get ta' know anybody new right now," declared Crystal.

Then she spun around on the barstool several times allowing Brenda time to soak in her pearls of wisdom. As Crystal turned, she noticed a little sign displayed on the wall that read, 'No dancing.' Meanwhile, the entire club was boogying down in every available inch of space. The bartender had a compact disc player wedged between the cash register and the liquor where he pre-selected a number of hit songs that played one after another. The crowd was really getting into his medley too. Each time one came on that, they liked; a roar of ahs filled the room. Crystal turned to tell Brenda about the little sign but Brenda wasn't paying attention to the music, the dancing, the people, nor Crystal. She was busily ogling the man at the opposite side of the bar.

"Brenda, what did ya' want ta' talk to mey about?" Crystal asked bluntly.

It was time for tough love. She deliberately stuck her head out blocking Brenda's view of the stranger. Brenda counteracted by sitting further forward on her stool to see the stranger mime offering her another drink. Brenda said yes with a shake of her head and mouthed Coke Cola very suggestively with her lips. She made sure to wet them as she did so. Crystal fumed with nausea and couldn't believe she took her hair out of rollers to come and keep Brenda company. Crystal had been looking forward to sitting in front of the television that night with a pint of Hagen Daaz strawberry. Instead, she sees that she's nothing more than decoration. A prop, so Brenda won't have to look like a desperate woman alone for the evening.

"Brenda, did ya' or did ya' not sey ya' needed someone ta'

tawk to tonight?" Crystal's southern charm was fraying at the seams.

Brenda didn't even hear her. She was saying thank you to the stranger as the bartender handed her a glass of soda. It took a while but it was becoming clear to Crystal that Brenda's concentration laid elsewhere. She knew that no matter what she said, Brenda was going to talk to this man first. Therefore, she decided to wait it out. She knew it wouldn't take long before Brenda was bored with this one and moved onto the next. Crystal would see her at intermission.

"Look, Ah'm goin' over there," Crystal said while pointing to the other side of the makeshift disco.

"It looks like they'all havin' fun over there," Crystal emphasized *they'all* to make the point that she was not.

"Besides, if Ah'm gonna' ta' be here by myself, Ah' may as well be by myself," she goaded Brenda to lead her in the direction of being conciliatory.

Crystal had lost. Brenda was not falling victim to any of Crystal's guilt laden traps. Crystal slid down from the barstool and shuffled to the downbeat through the dense crowd.

"We'll use this here spot as home base, okay? Jus' tell me when we're leavin'. Yu' have the ride," Crystal said as she went to the other side of the room.

"Okay. Okay. We're not leaving anytime soon so cool your heels," Brenda answered never once taking her eyes off the handsome stranger the whole time.

When it came to Brenda, Crystal had developed a particular way of viewing things over the years. If she really wanted to push the point, Brenda would eventually give in. Crystal knew that. She was out now and didn't want to get into anything with her. She would let it go and bring it up another time. She didn't expect much from her other than an occasional night out on the town with the girls. They always had a good time and because they had such a long history, they never ran out of things to talk about. Crystal could never tell other women some of the things Brenda did though because they'd inevitably ask why she kept Brenda as a friend. How does one say that when you've known someone for so many years, you can't just toss them out of your life. At some point they, in effect, become like family - for better and for worse. There may be limits placed on the amount of time spent with them, just as a way of keeping the peace, but disowning them wouldn't be an option. Besides, Crystal had fond memories of Brenda. After all, Brenda, Sarah and Karen were really like sisters to her. Crystal loved the fact that she could say anything to Brenda and that Brenda wouldn't get offended. She didn't have that kind of freedom and ease of speech with anyone else. However, of late, Brenda had been extraordinarily irksome and difficult to read, leaving Crystal with many matters of conflict to express to her. Crystal rested on the notion that their friendship was built on open lines of communication and that's what made it last so long. Then she continued strolling over to another section of the club, swaying to the music as she went.

As soon as Crystal was out of sight, Brenda's stranger came around the bar and sat down next to her.

"I thought she'd never leave," he said with a sparkling smile, "What is she, your chaperon?"

"Sometimes more like a ball and chain but she's good people," only Brenda was allowed to speak badly of Crystal.

"Too bad you're not here alone. I'd like to protect you," he offered.

"Funny, I didn't think I needed any protection," she bantered.

"You do from men like me," the stranger said with a mischievous growl.

Brenda twisted up her mouth and gazed at him through one eye.

"Promises, promises," she smirked.

The stranger coughed out a laugh and draped his arm around her chair. Brenda rested her shoulder on it to see how strong he was. He saw what she was attempting to do and flexed his muscles just for her. She turned and tapped his pecks.

"My, my, my. You're a healthy one aren't you?" Brenda became flush.

"I know the ladies like a man who's physically fit," the stranger responded confidently.

"How many ladies are we talking about?" Brenda spoke firmly letting him know that she did not like the aspect of being one of many.

"There's only one lady I'm interested in tonight and she's sitting right beside me," the stranger leaned in a little closer to Brenda and gave her a reassuring grin.

She knew it was a lie but she had a few of her own.

Meanwhile, on the other side of the club, a man danced up to Crystal. Crystal didn't quite know what to do with herself as he approached. He hadn't asked her to dance or anything and she wasn't sure if what he was doing was an invitation. She figured it must be. So, she started moving awkwardly to the music in his general direction. He was more aggressive than what she was used to. At one point, he stepped on her heels and tried to rub up against her behind. She put her handbag up to block him and about faced. He perceived what she was doing as some kind of a challenge. He tried to get up close to her again. Crystal then held out her hands prohibiting him from moving within three feet of her.

"Damn, girl! You're playing a serious game of hard ta' get," the man said.

"Ah don't wount to danz that close to yuwa'. Ah' don't know ya'," Crystal's southern accent whistled and spurred.

"We's just dancin'," he said while backing up to give her some room.

Now that she could take a decent look at him she decided that he wasn't a total thug, but not much better than one either.

"But when a pretty lady says no, she mean no. I'm cool with that," he said while backing away some more.

Crystal smiled admiring him for immediately recognizing that she was uncomfortable and for him continuing to dance with her anyway. He stopped pushing up on her and toned down his dance moves entirely. Crystal still couldn't move as quickly as some, who could maul a complete stranger on the dance floor. It was harder still, she thought, because of the way he was dressed. His pants were practically down around his thighs and his sneaker shoestrings were untied and purposely loosely laced. Crystal didn't know what to make of him. He looked like the type of guy who would be polite while he was robbing you blind. She was intrigued and frightened at the same time. The song ended and he reached down, lifted her hand and kissed it.

"Thank you, Nubian queen," he said with a bow.

'Okay, he didn't mean any harm,' Crystal thought. She felt somewhat foolish for over reacting. She curtsied back at him and thanked him for the dance. He broke out in a broad smile showing all his teeth.

A slow song began to play and he indicated to her that he'd like to keep dancing with her by spinning around and stopping in a Bob Fosse jazz pose. She was beginning to understand his way of requesting a dance but shook her head and declined. Alas, she was not here to enjoy herself tonight. She had a sick friend to tend to. Plus she definitely didn't want to get her hopes up regarding yet another man. She curtsied for him again and walked back to the bar to see about Brenda. The semi-hooligan smiled, marveling at her polite gestures. He thought they were the cutest thing he had ever seen. Crystal nodded not knowing what to think about the bedazzled way he was staring at her.

When Crystal returned to the bar, Brenda and her stranger had their heads, not to mention their knees, tightly locked and pressed together. Crystal stood directly behind them and cleared her throat loudly to get their attention but that didn't work in prying them apart. Crystal surveyed the room and found her dancing partner with another woman. The woman wasn't shy about getting closer to him and now that the shoe was on the other foot he was backing away and keeping her at arm's length. She had Brenda to thank for missing the opportunity to slow dance with what now seemed like a really nice guy and she was going to make sure Brenda paid dearly for that. Brenda looked up and tapped the stool beside her for Crystal to sit down. She thought that Crystal's hovering might cause her stranger to run away. The stranger extended his arm across Brenda's breast and took Crystal's hand.

"Hi, I'm John."

Crystal didn't take his hand but pretended to search for something in her purse instead. She already didn't trust him.

"Nice ta' meet cha', John. I'm Crystal and by da' way the woman next to you is my freen', Brenda," Crystal boar her eyes into Brenda's face equipped with raised eyebrows and knowing glances.

Crystal was trying to send a telepathic message telling Brenda to ditch the stranger and join her again in discussing her impending motherhood. John leaned over and whispered something into Brenda's ear. Crystal couldn't hear him even after draping herself across Brenda's lap.

"Want to get lost?" John suggested to Brenda.

"That's sounds like a great idea," Brenda said enthusiastically to both John and Crystal. Apparently, she had needed Crystal's nurturing nature earlier in the day but the scene had changed. They were out. And Brenda wanted to play a little while longer. The thought of becoming a mother brought forth images of being a caged animal. She had trouble reconciling with the changes she would have to make in her lifestyle to accommodate a child. Crystal insisted that she move forward in her life and take on this responsibility bravely. While John, her new found friend, embodied what she would have to give up, adventure, new possibilities — men.

"Crystal, I'm going to be leaving with John."

"Well, alright. If we're leavin', let mey go and use sah' bathroom first. What ever yu' do, don't leave without mey, okay?" said Crystal.

"Okay," Brenda said to both Crystal and John.

Crystal trotted off to the bathroom with one eye forward and the other fixed on Brenda and John, a name too appropriate of the function for which Brenda had in mind for him. Crystal wondered if he really knew what he was getting himself into. She forgave Brenda her appetites and knew that in the morning Brenda would call her up to finish their talk. She was all too ready to leave. Then as she approached the ladies room she felt even less enthused with the place. There was a line that stretched all the way around the perimeter. Twenty-two steps later, she counted, and finally inside, where cigarette smoke overpowered her. Women were lounging all over the counter tops puffing away and reapplying lipstick already ten layers thick. Crystal cupped her hands over her nose and gasped for air to no avail in the windowless hovel. Clearly a fire hazard; clearly no one minded except Crystal. Now she had one more reason to run out of *the club* and never look back.

Moments later, she scuttled out and over to the bar for what she hoped was the last time she would have to see it. She needed air and possibly something to flush her lungs and to refresh her clothes. If she could have ordered an oxygen tank to go, she would have. However, as she approached the rim of the bar, which took some doing with so many people congregating about, she immediately sensed something was wrong. She had gotten slightly disoriented by the movement of the crowd but she could still see the barely touched glass of soda that Brenda was nursing but neither Brenda or John were standing near it. She looked around the dance floor to see if maybe they decided to dance before rushing off. She didn't see them amongst the hazy swell of faces so she asked the bartender if he knew where they went, praying that he had excellent people recall skills. He gave her an 'I don't know' pose, thought about her question, then pointed towards the door.

Crystal froze but she hadn't begun to fully panic yet. She mentally counted the money in her purse to see if she had enough to get home, made her way over to the door and peered out. There was a small group of people meandering by a parking meter but no sign of Brenda or John. Crystal went back inside the club and searched every inch of it. She squeezed between couple after couple and came up with not one familiar face. It was so frustrating for her small five foot two frame to see over so many heads.

'Brenda dumped meh' fo'r a bar buuuummmm,' she thought, 'That is the worst possible rai-son to leave a friend stranded in the midda' of da' night,' she thought, 'A friend that yu' *promised* yu' would take home after havin' one drink and one particular conversation!' Neither of which were fulfilled. Crystal knew she'd be on her knees all night trying to forgive her this one. The Bible says forgive seventy times seven times. Crystal knew that that wouldn't be enough tonight.

She found herself back at the bar and hoped that they had returned from wherever they had gone. She didn't see them there. So, she rested her head on the mahogany wood. She wanted to cry. She figured no one would bother her because they would assume she was passed out until she got a tap on the shoulder. She spun around to disappointedly find the guy she was dancing with earlier standing over her and smiling.

"I hope we're not keeping you up," he joked sensitively.

He could see right off though that she was in no joking mood. Despite Crystal's effort to cover up her irritability, her bottom lip quivered like Jell-O.

"Ma' ride home 'pparently left w'out me," Crystal said rather matter-of-factly figuring she'd just have to take the train.

"Is that all? I can drive you home," he responded assertively.

Crystal lifted her head and gave him a wide-eyed gawk.

"Wh'ut?" she asked.

They were strangers. Unlike Brenda, Crystal had strict rules about getting into unfamiliar cars with unfamiliar men.

"Look it's no problem, really. Actually it's what I do for a living, driving people around, I mean," he pulls in closer to her, "I've got the limousine I drive for work parked out front."

Crystal tilted her head to the side making every effort to politely decline his offer but the words wouldn't come out.

"Look a here, you don't have to answer right now. We're here to have a good time, right? Why don't we just dance a little bit more and then you tell me what you want to do. 'kay?" he suggested, again sure of himself without putting any pressure on her.

He liked her and could tell that she didn't want him to push the issue. Crystal couldn't argue with his logic. She could have kicked herself for only having enough money on her to take the subway home and not a taxi. Brenda had totally ruined her plans for the evening and she had to admit that she wanted to get out of the funk she was falling into, or rather the valley as she called it.

"Make the best of a bad situation," she agreed.

"That's right. Let's go," he agreed and escorted her onto the only part of the dance floor that wasn't occupied.

They each took every opportunity to steal a good look at the other. He liked what he saw. He thought it was sweet that she had on a ruffled collared dress. It reminded him of the western movies he used to watch with southern girls who wore frilly little frocks. Crystal too was more impressed with him. He had a gentle way about him despite his appearance leading one towards the contrary. Crystal kept thinking of the saying 'Yua' can't judge aah book by its cover.' Her intriguing stranger, dancer, savior was a perfect example of that.

The floor became denser as the bartender played the electric boogie song and everyone tried to shuffle along in unison. Crystal and her new friend were forced into a tight squeeze. Crystal tried to make herself smaller as not to get too close to him. He noticed how uncomfortable she was, and immediately whisked her off to the bar. Then that record faded out and the crowd cheered for another. But, the bartender politely announced that the next song would be the last. He reiterated that it was four in the morning and that the restaurant next door served breakfast.

"You can dance," her cute dancing friend said trying to extend the evening a little longer.

"You too," Crystal said fanning herself and taking a napkin to wipe her brow.

"Woo, it's hot in h'ere," she declared.

Her kind stranger nodded in agreement while watching the proficient bartender mixing five of the last drinks to be served for the night.

"Woo! Ah can't remember when Ah've had so much fawn," Crystal continued.

She wanted him to jump right in and join her but he was preoccupied with the goings on of the room as people tried to sneak in one last dance or one last nip.

"Thai-nks," Crystal went on determined. "This dancin' even made mey' forget about my so called friend, Brenda."

After a couple of seconds passed, and a dejected Crystal saw that he wasn't listening, she looked in her purse for her subway token.

"You know, my offer still stands," the stranger said politely, "But I don't want you to feel uncomfortable. If you do feel uncomfortable I'll give you cab fare to get home, how's that? And you don't even have to pay me back," he said in the most casual way.

He wanted to make it clear that even though he liked her and would thank the devil for her number, his main concern was that she made it home safely. Crystal was touched.

"Y'u know, Ah' don't even know yo'a name," she said.

"My friends call me Rob," he said with a smile brandishing even his back teeth.

"Whu't should Ah' call ya'?" Crystal asked.

He paused, "A-n-y-thing-you like."

Then he raised her hand up and gently kissed it.

"Pleased to meet you…huh…?" he said.

"Ah, Crystal. My name's Crystal," she said.

"Pleased to meet you, Cryst'all."

Sarah's apartment

Matthew took his time putting his van in park. Sarah, his passenger, was in no hurry to leave. He was sure of that because she hadn't even woken up. She had her head resting awkwardly against the car door and the cushioned leather seat. Prior to passing out, she had told Matthew all about her little disagreement with Karen in a performance given to the whole restaurant or at least that's what he thought he heard her say. Between the tears and obscure references to their school days and joint vacations in their twenties, he made out some of what happened but he was quite sure he hadn't heard the whole story. He wasn't shocked by her call to be picked up in the middle of the night. He had high hopes that she would one day take him up on his driving offer but he thought it would be later rather than sooner. But, now that he was face to face with her, he wasn't sure what to do next.

Moments later, he swung her front door open and shouldered her into the living room, propping her up against the hallway wall as he opened each of her three inner doors. Sarah, dozing in and out of sleep, was remarkably steady once she saw her sofa. She marched right over to it and hurled herself down onto the soft throw pillows. Matthew closed up and locked the doors behind him then came over to check on her. Sarah couldn't wait to take off her shoes and flipped them across the room with her toes as she stretched out on the couch all with her eyes shut. Matthew knew all too well what she was going through from his many over indulgent days with wine and went into her kitchen to put on a pot of coffee. He was unusually at ease in her home, he thought, and had no trouble poking around her kitchen cabinets or looking in her refrigerator. He had dated women for months and was reluctant to go anywhere in their place besides the bedroom and bath. He would always maintain safe, practically stranger-like formality, making sure not to cross the acceptable date parameters. Oddly enough, Matthew found Sarah's general distrust of him refreshing. He for once didn't have to live up to some macho male image or carry on as though he were the consummate gentlemen. It was as if she knew him better than he knew himself.

The water heated up quickly and he took down two cups and placed them on a tray. As he turned to find some sugar and cream, Sarah appeared next to him, opened a cabinet drawer and tossed two spoons on the counter. Matthew chuckled at how precise she was even with her eyes closed. She groped her way back into the living room and plopped once again on the sofa. Matthew followed her out of the kitchen and laid the now much needed remedy on the coffee table. He took off his jacket and watched Sarah groggily lift one of the cups and sip from it. He preferred tea but he was more concerned about her desire to regain consciousness.

"Are you too tired for company tonight?" he asked politely.

Sarah waved his question away with her finger, while her hand wrapped around the coffee mug and she 'mmm'd' and 'awed' at the taste of the special blend. Matthew noticed how erotic it was to see her tilting her head back and allowing the hot liquid to slip into her parched mouth and roll down her insides. Sarah came to life right before his eyes after only one long gulp of the black gold. Matthew reached down and poured the rest of the cream from the container into his cup. He didn't anticipate the same experience as Sarah. He took one of the spoons and stirred vigorously until he looked as though he were only drinking milk.

Sarah lifted her head and smiled at him.

"Thank's again for rescuing mey'," she said resolutely.

Matthew grimaced at the bitterness of the ground roasted wonder and nodded *you're welcome* to her.

"Do they have Boy Scouts in London?" she inquired humorously.

"Not that I'd like to bring this up again but I did interrupt the normal flow of your traveling arrangements," Matthew responded with a tinge of guilt and an air of not wanting to shed too much light on their accident.

"What if I said you're off the hook," she mused.

"I'd say. Cheers," he tapped his cup to hers and tried to swallow some more of his watery concoction.

"I'm surprised you didn't have a date tonight," Sarah posed more as a question than a statement of fact. Matthew sat up and weighed how he should respond. He had broken up with Debbie over the telephone a day ago and didn't want to revisit the drama that followed thereafter. Debbie called him every hour on the hour at his studio as well as at his home to ensure that she was the one who had the last word on the matter. She called him immature in every possible way that she could think of. She apparently was quite prolific on the subject and several times Matthew agreed with her findings.

"Well, let's just say that I'm not seeing anyone at the moment," he conveyed as if he had been dragged through a meat grinder.

"Sounds intriguing," Sarah said making certain that it didn't sound in any way like she wanted to hear all the details.

She could tell that he wasn't ready to spell out whatever transpired.

"For the record," he began to Sarah's surprise, "she and I didn't see eye to eye on quite a few issues."

"Boy, can I relate to that," she blurted out between slurps.

"I thought you might," Matthew said with a knowing glance.

It was true Sarah had found herself more times than she cared to mention in the midst of arguments with people who were misreading her words or not seeing things she thought to be obvious. The piece of this puzzle that disturbed her the most was the fact that her friends were on the other end of the quarrel; friends that she had always been able to count on to recognize what she saw and stand on the same side of an issue with her. Matthew watched Sarah's face distort as she thought about her friends.

"You know I've been thinking about you and your friend Karen," Matthew offered up for discussion.

He was careful not to plunge right in with his opinion.

"Have you now?" Sarah was more than a little bit curious to hear a man's point of view on the subject.

Matthew had actually been there with her as a witness and up until now it hadn't occurred to her that he too might have some reflection on the subject of his own.

"Yes, I have," Matthew replied.

Sarah wiggled herself into a more comfortable position and waited without expectation, way too tired for assumptions.

"Well, I'll just get right to it then," he paused more to find the right words than for effect, "I take it that you two have been friends for a long time and with that comes certain unwritten obligations, right?" he said rhetorically.

Sarah's ears perked up at the hint of his synopsis revealing some depth and incite.

"One thing I know in life is that things change. I know there's nothing remarkable about that statement. I'm not telling you anything you don't already know. You and she are just not the same people you used to be."

Sarah shook her head up and down vigorously. She was all

too well aware of the changes that had taken place in their friendship over the years.

"This may come as a surprise to you," he joked, "But I used to be a bit of a screw-up in grade school. So much so, that my father had a longstanding monthly appointment with the Head Master. And there was never an occasion when his visit was in vain. I admit it. I was a hooligan. Anyway, here I am all the way across the Atlantic, making it in the States, a grown man, a photographer of models for Christ's sake, no longer the wicked lad of my youth and my Dad still at times treats me as if I've accomplished nothing with my life."

Sarah got the analogy immediately both for her relationship with Karen and for the one she had with her mother. She held herself steady as not to become too introspective.

"I don't blame my Dad for not seeing who I am today. It's not his fault. He wasn't with me when I took each baby step towards manhood. How could he have been? He was busy living his own life," he paused letting that notion take on the full weight of its implications, "I really do believe that our job as children is to re-educate our parents, redefine their definition of us, you know?"

With each word, Sarah felt deep in her soul that he was connecting with her soul. She had all too often told herself the exact same thing. She had an image of a giant bulldozer crushing her most treasured memories and mementos leaving her with a bunch of yellowing photos and stained keepsakes. Karen was an adult now having the right to change and direct their youthful jointly planned dreams and run her life anyway she saw fit, even if that meant without Sarah.

Sarah rocked forward and stood up. She placed her coffee cup down on the table and walked over to Matthew. Later she would tell herself that she had only intended to kiss him on the cheek to say thank you for a great conversation and that she was caught up in nostalgia. His breath was sweet from having drunk so much sugary cream. Before she thought of pulling herself away from him, his arms were already around her waist leading her gently down onto the rug. He placed her between his knees and allowed her to rest her body against his legs. His kisses were intimate and passionate. She could feel his heart beating through the sound of her own in a rhythm that made her respond as though she were in familiar territory. Her entire body buckled underneath the soft tender touch of his mouth. Each kiss lingered like an imprint of a sweaty palm against a window. She wanted to explore more of this warmth, this tantalizing sensuality, and with that unbuttoned his shirt. He let her face rest on his chest and watched her nibble there for time to pass into tomorrow. He too was caught up in the moment at seeing Sarah wanton and sensual. He loved that she took control for both of them. She knew what she wanted and was not at all bashful or shy like a little girl watching herself and editing her every move. Sarah reached up and pulled Matthew to her. She desired him and he her. She leaned down on the rug and lowered him down there with her by interlocking her arms about his neck. He was certain that he was falling for her literally as well as figuratively. They chortled together as their bodies bounced against the fluffy fibers of the shag. He rolled them both away from the coffee table and they stretched out on the floor along the foot of the couch. Sarah pressed her body tightly against his and ran her leg slowly up his thigh. He shook from the pleasurable sensation of her playful wrestling. She nibbled at his neck and earlobes as he caressed her back and shoulders working his fingers up and down her spine. He closed his eyes and let his body rock back and forth with hers. An ocean of feelings swept over each of them and yanked and tugged at their racing hearts. She cupped her hand around his chin and gently guided his face upon her chest. He kissed her breasts, her neck, and her entire face. Sarah shivered and moaned each time his lips came in contact with her flesh.

Then Matthew paused.

He looked up from their rather steamy embrace and abruptly straightened up. Then he delicately lifted Sarah's arms and legs from around him. Sarah thought he was coming up for air as their intensity overwhelmed them both. This filled her even more with intense longing and anticipation. Instead he just sat up and gave her a long penetrating stare. His mood had shifted brusquely but his smile was continually warm and inviting. Still it made Sarah anxious and self-conscience. She rose from the floor and sat on the couch and waited to see what his next move would be. She couldn't help herself from wondering what he thought of a woman who claimed she hated him then brought him over to her house and ravaged him down to the floor.

"You didn't like what we were doing?" she asked hesitantly.

Matthew blushed and while buttoning his shirt back up leaned against the sofa.

"No, yes…Yes, I did. I just didn't want it to go like this," he admitted.

Sarah dejectedly lowered her head and tried to disappear.

"Don't get me wrong, I like you," he said turning rather lovingly taking her hands within his own.

'Oh God, Oh God, Oh God!, she thought.

"But?" Sarah asked taking her hand away and sweeping her hair back into place.

"No buts," he said solemnly as if taking an oath.

He leaned over her and stroked her hair out of her face. He took his palms and pressed them to her cheeks. He raised her head and simply touched his lips to hers.

"I want to do this right. I like you too much to take advantage of you. There *are* boy-scouts in London too."

Sarah fell back onto the cushions and stared at the ceiling wishing it would cave in on her head. At least then she wouldn't have to hear Matthew's lame excuse for not wanting to be with her, she thought. He seemed sincere enough, she admitted, but not convincing. She turned ever so slowly and addressed him dogmatically.

"Get out," she said presenting the front door with a fanfare motion.

Matthew was sure that she didn't understand what he was trying to convey and continued to explain himself.

"I've been in this situation too many times and it never leads to anything except sex. I want to get to know you better and..." he went on.

"Get out," Sarah exclaimed again.

As she suspected, he did consider her to be one of a whole chorale full of women and she wasn't going to be made a fool. Matthew took her hand once more but this time she jumped up from the couch and briskly headed towards the front door.

She opened all three, impatiently tapped her fingernails against the wood frame and soothingly lowered her head. Matthew rose uneasily and stepped through the first one persistently holding out his hands in a pleading movement towards her. He was at a loss.

"Sarah, I really like you. Can't you see that I'm trying to be a proper gentleman for once," he pleaded.

She looked at him then nodded her head in the direction of the great outdoors. He read her body language loud and clear while fighting to uncover exactly which words uttered had so altered her.

"Please leave," it came out meaner than she intended.

She was hurt. He stood in the frame of the front door and tried hopelessly to turn back the clock.

"Can't we at least talk about this? I didn't mean you any disrespect. I like you! I don't think you understand just how much."

"Night," she said.

"Come on, don't be like that," he tried.

Sarah slammed the door prompting Matthew to jump away from its swing.

"Sarah, Sarah? Please! Please! just want to talk to you. Please? I don't know what I said that made you so angry but believe me, I didn't mean anything by it."

Sarah turned off the light and walked away from the door. Matthew pounded on the door a few times.

"Don't walk away, please? I feel really bad. I thought I was doing the right thing. I didn't mean to insult you. Please come back and open the door. Come on, Sarah. Sarah? Sarah?"

CHAPTER TWENTY-FIVE

"We're all sensitive people with so much to give
Understand each other
Since we've got this feeling let's live
I love you
There's nothing wrong with me loving you
Baby nah uh uh
And giving yourself to me could never be wrong
If your love is true…"

Once upon a time, they had squeezed snuggly into their dance threads. They were twenty. Five decades later, their wives are looking on at them unimpressed. There men are now on the dance floor trying to out dance each other. In vague detachment, they're shuffling alongside, simply happy to be out of the house. The wives try not to laugh as one of the men begins to rotate his hips as fast as he can while his combatant does a sort of African kiba move. Both have abandoned the idea of rhythm and beat. A smattering of nervous applause from the crowd gives them the encouragement to escalate into a full-blown competition. Much to the dismay of their wives, who have stepped aside to give their husbands room to make further fools of themselves. The volume goes up a notch on the music. The crowd too, widens the area around them. The DJ yells out, "Don't hurt yourselves now," and he meant it. He paid careful attention as one man lowered his body all the way down to the floor. When his knees touched the tile, he started mouthing the words of the song.

"You don't have to worry that it's wrong
If the feeling moves you let me grove
Let your love come down…"

The crowd cheers a chant in his honor. Then he prances around his combatant with his head moving in and out and his arms flapping like a chicken. He solicits additional applause from the crowd. They follow his instructions and begin to clap in unison. As they offer homage to him, he slowly begins taking off his imitation silk ruffled shirt. The buttons were already strained against his belly, popping out as he loosens each one, where then his stomach lurched out over his purple pastel gabardine knit pants. His wife steadied herself as he slowly stripped down to his boxer shorts. The crowd bellowed in such frenzy of both amazement and hilarity that his opponent bowed in defeat. The winner turned around permitting some of the women to rub his tummy before his wife grabbed him by the ear and dragged him back to their table. He jokingly followed her. This too received applause.

Not too far away sat Sarah and Brenda. Neither was enjoying the goings on, each pretended to be present while their minds lay elsewhere. Sarah sipped a mixed drink and kept a steady gaze on the people dancing. Brenda was unaware that Sarah vowed never to speak to her again.

"Huh?" Sarah grimaced defiantly turning her chair away from Brenda.

If Brenda didn't understand her curt answers, Sarah was not about to explain.

"Is it really such a big deal?" Brenda said while sucking air through her teeth.

'The audacity,' Sarah thinks.

"You're really a piece of work, aren't you?" Sarah tells her.

"What?" Brenda questions as if to say that Sarah's just being dramatic.

"What?" Sarah mimics Brenda and the absurdity of it all.

"Brenda, it doesn't take a genius to know that you don't just set one of your girlfriends up with a married man! And then expect her to be happy about it."

Crystal and Rob walk over to the table hand in hand. They both heard what Sarah just said.

"Rob, baby, could ya' please go and get mey' somethin' to dra'nk," Crystal gives Rob a head nod signal indicating that he should disappear for a few minutes.

He obeys without hesitation. However, before going to the bar, he takes her hand and kisses it gently. Then he addresses Sarah and Brenda.

"Would either of you ladies care for something else to drank?"

"No, thank you," Brenda replies wondering if he meant drink.

Rob politely nods and walks off to the bar.

"He's nice, Crystal," Sarah says then quickly puts back on her sour face.

Crystal gushed with pride, "Thanks."

Then they all sit in silence.

Brenda stared at Sarah. Sarah stared at the dance floor. Meanwhile, Crystal focused on Brenda then turned her head and eyed Sarah. Sarah wanted to let Brenda suffer a while longer. In truth, she wasn't even that upset with her anymore. Her thoughts were resting on Karen and Norman interspersed with uncertain feelings about Matthew. She decidedly didn't know which was more vexing, Karen cursing her out in her favorite restaurant or Matthew refusing her romantic advances.

Crystal was excited that a dialog was beginning, "What's

going on," she asked. Brenda was reluctant to answer Crystal for fear of incrimination. Therefore, Crystal turned to Sarah. Sarah was more than willing to recant her allegations against Brenda.

"Our little friend here fixed me up with a married man," she said bluntly, "And she doesn't seem to think she did anything wrong," Sarah explained.

Crystal pivoted her entire body toward Brenda, deluging her with the meanest look she could muster. Sarah continually shook her head up and down as if she had to assure Crystal that it did indeed happen. Crystal didn't need any convincing. She had a bombshell to drop of her own.

"Well," Crystal began with her Southern accent being twangier than usual, "Our lil' friend here lef' me at de' disco-teck' the au'ther nieght' with no money and no way home," Crystal relayed bluntly.

"Daammmmmnnnn! I'm sorry, all-right," Brenda apologized quickly through tightly pinched lips.

Brenda seemed more preoccupied than repentant. In fact, she looked like she was about to cry. Then she rose from her seat abruptly and sprinted toward the bathroom. She had an expression on her face that beckoned she wanted Sarah to follow her. Rob returned with the drinks and sat down beside Crystal.

"And, she's preg'nt," Crystal told Sarah.

Then she gave a grand smile to Rob as he stretched his arm around her shoulders and handed her a glass of Coca Cola.

"Thanks, baby," was all Crystal could say through her huge display of teeth.

"And she had an abortion?" Sarah asked Crystal.

"God no," Crystal said proudly aware of her involvement in Brenda's decision.

Sarah curiously stared at Crystal. Rob became aware of the fact that his presence wasn't required once again and walked over to the dance floor to watch people attempting to execute a conga line.

"Ah' convinced ha' ta' have it, the bey-by, that is," Crystal said with a cool shrug of her shoulders while taking a sip of her soda.

Sarah was stunned. She gave Crystal a wide-eyed gape and chuckled at the thought of how absurd that conversation must have been. They both knew that Brenda wouldn't have taken advice from Crystal to move out of the way if an airplane was flying towards her head.

"And, believe it or not, betwain yu' n' mey, Ah' thanked Brenda for leaving mey' stranded in that dis'co," Crystal added, again uncharacteristically calm while describing an incident involving Brenda.

"You thanked her?" Sarah found herself gently lulled into yet another peculiar conversation.

It was only fitting that it was Crystal's go-around. She started with Brenda and her date with the much-married Michael. Then there was her embarrassing encounter with Karen later that week amongst the elegantly posh. Now it was Crystal's turn. If she threw in her equally thwarting get together with Matthew, she would have a complete set of madness to draw from.

"Well, see that's just it. When she left mey' like that, Ah'm not gonna to lie to ya', Ah' was angry 'nough ta' spit. But ah' had ta' make da' best of it. Didn't have 'nough money ta' get home but what was ah' ta' do? Then wit'out ev'n lookin' for romance, ah' met Rob."

"So you met him there?" Sarah asked.

"Ah' guess that's what the sayin' means that we should be patient and wait on the Lawd 'cause he can werk it out betta' than we ever could. And it's funny, au' didn't ev'n like him at first. He seemed sort of like a homeboy. Did ya' notice dat?" Crystal asked batting her eyelids and titling her head to one side like a Cocker

Spaniel.

Sarah took a moment to give Rob the once over. She saw Crystal gazing at him as if he wore a suit of armor. His party style was a pair of belt-less, baggy jeans, hanging off his butt, of course, underwear underneath showing, of course, matching a perfectly pressed bandana dangling from his back pocket, of course. His hair was most impressive for although clean, it looked like it had never seen a comb or brush.

"Well, I wouldn't go as far as to say homeboy, but…huh.. I know what you mean."

"Well, ah' did. And that's exactly what ah' didn't want. But then we started dancing and he was looking at me. Ya' know, da' way a real man looks at a woman not lustful or dirty but like he wants ta' do thangs for ya', nice thangs. And before ah' knew it, we were making plans for da' future."

Ever since she moved up to New York she had relied on Sarah to help her get more acclimated into the pace of the city. Sarah hadn't even noticed that Crystal no longer needed her help. In fact, Crystal had things so together that Sarah had no choice but to sit back and admire her. She smiled and hugged her congratulating her on her successful budding romance.

"You two look good together," Sarah said.

Crystal was so tickled she raised her eyebrows in excitement. Rob walked back just then and kissed Crystal on the cheek.

"Hey Baby, we were jus' talkin' 'bout yu'."

"All good things, right?" asked Rob.

Crystal and Sarah both nodded, yes. Sarah began to feel out of place as Rob and Crystal warmly gazed into each other's eyes. Rob caught Sarah's expression out of the corner of his eye, nudged Crystal and began to survey the room for a vacant table. They didn't find one but Rob saw a photographer taking pictures of other guests and got an idea. He turned to Crystal, "Dance with me, baby, and then I'm gonna' take you to have your picture taken. You look so good tonight," Rob suggested.

Crystal was all a blush as Rob put his arm around her waist and led her onto the dance floor. She glanced back at Sarah while she was leaving and nodded her head towards the bathrooms, indicating her desire for Sarah to go and talk to Brenda. Sarah waved back at her not sure she liked the new more mature Crystal. She waited until they were half way across the room before mouthing, "I'm going. I'm going."

"Those women have counted that money at least ten times already," Millie muttered underneath her breath.

Mrs. Rivers and Mrs. Yates, two of her club associates, were by the front door going over the money collected in the cash tin again. A bouncer stood apathetically on watch for the fourth time. Sarah could read her mother's lips from all the way from her table. So, she journeyed over to catch her before she exploded. Jacob walked over to her also with a drink in his hand.

"For you, sweetheart," he said handing it to her.

Millie drank whilst never taking her eyes off Mrs. Rivers and Mrs. Yates.

"Thank you, honey," Millie patted Jacob on the arm.

He reached over and kissed her on the forehead, as Sarah approached.

"If I knew you were coming over here, Sarah, I would have gotten you one too," Jacob told her.

Sarah got one whiff of the alcohol and stepped backwards in a nauseous stagger.

"That's okay, Daddy," Sarah said.

She placed her hands on her stomach and head and rocked from side to side to find balance.

"Are you okay?" Millie asked her.

"Yeah, yeah," she lied swallowing hard a few times before turning and sprinting into the ladies' room.

"I'll be in, in a minute," Millie told her while eyeballing Mrs. Rivers and Mrs. Yates again.

Sarah ran into the bathroom and quickly ducked into a stall. She was still hung over from the Tequilas and felt as if her insides wanted to escape. Nothing. It was more of a precaution than anything else was. She thanked God for that. When she poked her head out feeling rather foolish, she saw Brenda sitting in front of the mirrors. Brenda was staring blankly at her own reflection. Sarah hesitantly walked over and reluctantly she sat down beside her.

"Women do it all the time," she started right off no introduction.

Brenda began to cry, "I can't tell Crystal anything without her telling everybody my business."

Sarah slowly reached out and hugged her, "So, you can't sleep with everything in sight anymore. In addition, you're really going to have to stay in for a change. Get to know your baby and yourself, you know? So, you'll stick to one man in your life for a change. It's not so bad to have a steady, someone you can count on..."

Sarah's voice trailed off lost in her own thoughts and unable to continue her own sentence.

Brenda picked her head up, "What?"

"I'll be there too," Sarah says, picking up where she left off.

"Thanks, Sarah," Brenda pauses, "We can get those mother and daughter outfits if it's a girl, right?"

"In African print," Sarah said grinning, fascinated at how Brenda can so easily look on the bright side.

She hopes that Brenda is not just putting on a brave face for her sake.

"Why did this happen to me? Why didn't it happen to you or Crystal?" Brenda blurted.

They both knew the answer to that question.

"Brenda, don't make me answer that. We're having a moment here. 'Cause I can talk 'bout yu' if I have to," Sarah says delicately.

Brenda laughed.

Karen put a safety pin on Yolanda's dress to hold the lace collar in place. Norman was seated at the bar having his third straight whiskey. Karen prayed that he wouldn't come back over to the table desiring to get friendly with her. She couldn't bear the scent of the alcohol he would leave all around her mouth after his sloppy kisses.

"That ought to do it," Karen said warmly, pecking Yolanda on the cheek.

As she lifted her head, she saw Sarah and Brenda coming out of the bathroom arm in arm. She noted that they were smiling as they returned to the table. She thought about how good it was that they had reconciled.

"You stay right here," she told Yolanda, "I'll be right back."

Then she nudged her way through the rows of tables. She wanted to catch them before they got to theirs. She wanted the greeting to seem casual, not forced. Though by the time she made it over to them, they had already sat back down. Karen hesitated for a moment as she approached. She wanted to put on a face that showed everything was forgiven and forgotten. She was thrown off track when she saw that Brenda looked like she had tears in her eyes.

"What's wrong with her?" Karen asked Sarah.

She was worried that Sarah might have already told Brenda

everything. She immediately felt embarrassed.

Sarah looked at Brenda, "Brenda!" she asked. She wanted Brenda to be the one to answer. Karen sat down and put her arm around her, "What's wrong with her?" she asked again.

Sarah drew an arch in the air from her chin to her stomach with her hand cupped.

"Oh, Brenda, I'm so sorry. I know this was the last thing on your mind," Karen told her.

"I'll be all-right. It just takes some getting used to," Brenda tried to sound calm.

"You can believe that," Karen joked.

Sarah and Karen sat in silence while Brenda lowered her head and waved her hand indicating she'd like to change the subject. She lifted her head back up when she didn't hear any talking going on between Sarah and Karen.

"Okay, what happened?" she asked Sarah and Karen astutely.

"Nothing," they responded quickly in unison.

"Well, I may be in a family way but I haven't lost my mind," Brenda said searching each of them for clues.

Karen sat looking in one direction while Sarah stared off in another.

"Look, Sarah, uh, can I talk to you?" Karen cautiously asked her.

"Well…" Sarah began wondering what to say next.

She was about to say yes when Karen suddenly cut her off.

"Look, if you don't want to talk, we don't have to," Karen said trying to keep it light hearted but with that statement, she stood up.

Her actions made it clear that she did not wish to start a conversation but to finish one.

"See, I knew it. Something happened," Brenda said staring at Sarah then Karen, "What is this all about? Come on. Talk to me."

"Sorry, Brenda..." Karen offered meagerly.

Then she walked back to her table. She was disappointed at not getting the chance to say what was on her mind. Firstly, she wanted to make sure Sarah would not go around telling everyone what she observed. Try as she might she knew she couldn't turn back the hands of time. If she could, she would have closed the shutters more tightly around her living room windows. 'Then maybe she wouldn't be in this state of affairs,' she told herself. She had no one to turn to now. Sarah, Brenda and Crystal were the ones she called when things weren't going well. Now, whom was she supposed to turn to? She felt trapped. She feared that it was only a matter of time before all of her hidden secrets would seep out of every crack.

"Sarah?" Brenda asked holding up her hands signifying her total bafflement.

Sarah didn't answer her. Instead she got up and started walking toward the bar.

"Not now, Brenda. Not now," was all she said as she left the table.

She knew that both Karen's and her behavior seemed rude and peculiar. After all, they were all supposed to be best friends, right? Deep down though, she didn't think it was necessarily her place to give Brenda a blow-by-blow description on anything. Besides, she knew that it would just be gossip to Brenda and wouldn't bring them any closer to a resolution. Brenda pointed to her stomach, "Can you bring me some milk?" Brenda asked Sarah as she was walking off to the bar, "And when you come back I want to hear all the dirty details, okay?"

Brenda was not used to being in the dark about her friends' personal business. She had a difficult time being the last one to know.

"Yeah, sure," Sarah half-heartedly agreed.

She walked over to the bar, sat down and placed her hands over her face. She wasn't concerned at how she must have looked to others. She peaked through her fingers and saw the bartender at the other end with a huge crowd in front of him. Just as well, she didn't come over to have a drink in the first place. It was just a ploy to get away from having to have yet another intense anything. She turned for a while and watched people swaying to *Boogie Nights*, or something that sounded like it. She could see her parents in the distance doing the one-two step, the one they did to every song. She smiled remembering how they used to throw parties at home and dance together like that all night long. Not too far from them was Rob and Crystal doing their modern version of the hustle. Sarah marveled at how wonderfully they danced together. She thought that that must be one of the signs of compatibility, how well a couple danced together. If the premise had any merit, Crystal would marry Rob and be together at least as long as Sarah's father and mother.   Sarah admired Rob and Crystal a while longer and saw that they were off to a great start. Then she shifted her weight a little to see if the theory applied to anyone else on the dance floor. She was pleased to see that there were many destined for greatness. It was then that she noticed beyond the crowd that Karen was staring directly at her. She paused, tried to crack a smile, but she knew it wasn't genuine. So, she turned back around on the stool and waited for the overworked bartender to make his way over. As fate would have it, just as she was quieting her mind of any unpleasant thoughts, a man stepped up behind her and tapped her on the shoulder.

"Fancy meeting you here," Matthew said, slightly startling Sarah.

"What?" Sarah stammered thinking, 'What are you doing here?'

Matthew sat beside her and held up his camera. Sarah adjusted herself once more on the stool trying to avoid his lens. She made it seem as if she were flagging the bartender again.

"Hi," Sarah said casually trying desperately to appear aloof.

"I'm glad you came tonight," Matthew said sweetly.

Sarah waved at the bartender one final time. If he didn't come along, she was going to get up and go back to her table as quickly as possible.

"Really? It is my mother's party," Sarah couldn't resist having that word come out sounding like a question.

It was difficult for her to feign disinterest when her whole body lit up like a Christmas tree at the sight of him. She knew that she had become like all of his other women, in love with a man who was only in love with the conquest. She wasn't about to humiliate herself any further. As she spun herself around and leaped off the stool, the bartender walked over to her.

"What will it be?" he asked.

She thought that she might as well order something.

"Ah, Ginger ale, please," she answered. The bartender scurried away to get it.

"And some milk," she shouted at his back suddenly remembering pregnant Brenda.

The bartender grimaced and signaled that he heard her request. Sarah saw that he was taking other's orders all the way to the opposite end and that it might be a while before he returned. So, she sat back down.

"Are you working?" Sarah asked seeing that he had more than one camera hanging from his neck.

"Ah, well, your friend...Brenda got me the job," Matthew answered.

"Good ole, Brenda," Sarah smirked.

"She's really something else," Matthew continued in an effort to keep the conversation going.

"Quite," Sarah responded.

Matthew hoped the bartender would take a good long time returning with the drinks but no sooner did he have that thought, the bartender came right over. Sarah reached in her purse to pay but before she could get her money out, Matthew tossed a couple of bills on the bar.

"It's a free bar, man," the bartender said to Matthew handing him back his money.

"That's a tip," Matthew replied never taking his eyes off Sarah.

Sarah tried not to feel flattered or anything else for that matter. She looked elsewhere.

"Aren't you supposed to be taking shots or something?" she finally said demanding he look anywhere other than at her.

She took a sip of her drink and prayed that someone would walk over and ask to have their picture taken. Instead Matthew put his camera up to his eye and starting taking pictures of her. Sarah swallowed and coughed.

"Oh, my God, there's milk in my ginger ale," she exclaimed just as Matthew took his first shot.

The bartender was still in earshot and walked back over.

"Isn't that what you asked for?" he asked rather confidently and ready to defend his sense of hearing.

Matthew continued snapping away and smiling at the exchange between Sarah and the bartender.

"You're right... sorry. What I meant to say was that I wanted two separate drinks. Sorry," Sarah said realizing that he was right.

The bartender shuffled away accepting her apology and went about the business of completing her order. Sarah could hear the shutter of Matthew's camera opening and closing rapidly in succession. She placed her hand over the lens.

"Ohhhhhhhhh, I'm used to dealing with uncooperative models," Matthew joked and simply lifted his other camera.

He looked in her eyes and could see that she wasn't amused. Finally he lowered the camera and placed her hand in his own. They sat face-to-face for a few moments. Matthew stroked her hand and let his eyes roam around her. He thought, 'What a beautiful face.'

"I confess. I really came here to see you," he said so directly and passionately that Sarah momentarily believed him.

Matthew could see that this was making some headway so he continued holding her hand. But Sarah let go of his hand and turned to face the dance floor. She was relieved that there was something else to look at besides him. She let her eyes sweep across the room. Her parents were seated at their table now talking to some of their friends, while Crystal and Rob were still out there holding hands and now blowing kisses at one another. She was reluctant to sneak a peak at Karen's table. She didn't want to have another weird exchange or awkward moment but her curiosity got the better of her and she looked over anyway. Yolanda was hanging backwards in her chair. Norman was gone, no doubt still at the free bar.

"Yolanda, behave now. Sit down before you hurt yourself," Karen warned her.

"Yes, Mama," Yolanda replied and sat up in her seat.

Karen looked bored or frustrated or both. She kept referring to her watch every couple of seconds and changing her position in her chair. She had almost a whole plate of food in front of her and a full glass of dinner wine. Sarah longed to go over and talk some sense into her. They never went to one of Millie's parties where Karen sat clear across at the opposite end of the room. The whole thing infuriated Sarah.

"What do you want from me?" Sarah asked Matthew tersely as she spun back around on the stool.

It came out harshly. Even she knew it was partly due to Karen. She wanted to fix it, but then he calmly replied, "Just a dance."

She felt obligated to oblige him. He stepped down and held out his hand for her to join him. Then he ushered her deep into the crowd right in middle of the floor. He wanted to continue to hold her hand but Sarah gently pulled away. She was still self-conscious about their last encounter. He didn't seem as if he remembered it at all. 'Men,' she thought, 'Maybe it's a typical male tactic to drive a women insane.' She straightened herself up a bit and when they initially started dancing she treated him like a complete stranger. While he gauged her every move as if there was nothing else worth seeing in the entire universe. She was the lone star in the firmament. He was so engaged that if she moved left or right he followed and mirrored her every step. Sarah became intrigued with this and started changing her steps on purpose to see if he could keep up. He was an apt partner with a certain flair and he played along for as long as he thought it amused her. It didn't last long. The music went from Janet Jackson, "Miss You Much" to the seventies hit, "Break For Love" and Sarah's attention began to wane. Again starting with Millie and Jacob, Sarah surveyed the room and finally ending with Karen and Norman. Norman had come back to the table, acting weird. No surprise. He was circling it like he was stalking Karen. He was loud too. Sarah could clearly hear some of what he was saying over the music.

"Tell your mama I'm going out to get a real drink now," he said loudly.

"She's right there, Daddy," Yolanda innocently pointed to Karen.

Karen gently waved Yolanda's hand away.

"It's not polite to point," she instructed Yolanda while shaking her head at Norman, who she knew already had too much to drink.

"Norman, there's a full, bar over there. Why don't you just go back over there to get yourself another one? I thought that's why you wanted to come here tonight in the first place." Karen didn't want him to think that she thought he was being silly.

'Goodness gracious,' she thought.

She knew she never should have told him about the dance.

"I want a *pacific* type to drink from a *pacific* place, if you don't mind," he roared.

His voice traveled throughout the hall causing practically everyone to lift an eye in his direction. Jacob noticed the trouble had a name earlier on and knew it was Norman. He had seen him sitting at the bar since he walked in. It didn't take a genius to know that Norman didn't come for the camaraderie or the decorations.

"What's wrong with that boy?" Millie asked Jacob.

She shook her head from side to side and motioned for the bouncer to go over to Karen's table. Karen felt all eyes on them and stood up and held onto Norman's arm.

"Norman, Norman, please don't," she implored.

"Don't what?" he replied nastily pulling his arm out from in between hers.

"Just please don't start. Not here," Karen begged.

She felt perilous. Things were unraveling right before her eyes. Norman didn't care. It was all about the liquor. He'd sleep this off and never have to see these people again. Karen left Arizona not just because he lost his job but also because she genuinely missed being with her childhood friends, her surrogate sisters. She had to distract him. She was desperate to calm him down so she kissed him. That always seemed to work before.

"Baby, why don't we have a drink together first?" Karen lowered him into the seat next to her and poured two fresh glasses of wine.

When the bouncer saw Norman sitting down, he backed off and waved to Millie that everything would be all right. Millie wasn't convinced but accepted his opinion for the moment. Once Jacob and Millie turned away everyone else followed suit.

Matthew moved in a little closer to Sarah as soon as she began to dance again. He was pleased that the small commotion had not put a damper on the whole evening. This might be his only opportunity. Delroy told him earlier that her car was ready and that he had already called Sarah and asked her to pick it up.

"Debbie's gone," Matthew divulged as if Sarah had asked him.

"I don't believe I asked," she stated like a question.

"I just wanted you to know," Matthew said sincerely.

"Why?" Sarah asked.

"Well, I kissed you last night and..." Matthew began in a whisper.

"And?" she shrugged.

"And, contrary to what you may think of me, I don't go around kissing every woman I meet," he replied, "But with you..."

"But with me, what?" Sarah interrupted.

"It's like I couldn't help myself," he said as if Sarah was a delightful surprise.

She wasn't sure if she believed him or not but she had to admit that that was a nice line if it was just a line.

"I've heard that before," Sarah said snidely but she hoped that wouldn't stop him.

"See that's what I mean," he said referring to her response.

Then he took another step towards her, "But *I* mean it."

Sarah found herself believing him a little more.

"If I weren't such a gentleman last night, I'd still be wrapped in your arms," he said kissing her hand and holding it to his chest.

Sarah could feel the fiery pace of his heartbeat and the warmth of his skin against her fingers. Then he leaned in and gently pressed his lips against hers. For a brief second she had forgotten where she was and whom she was with. Sarah saw herself walking down the aisle with Matthew standing at the altar waiting for her.

Then, poof, it was gone, abruptly curtailed by sounds of Norman ranting and raving at the top of his lungs - again. This time around, the dance floor emptied out completely. Apparently, nothing could go on as long as Norman was upset. So everyone went back to their table and sat and stared at him.

"Am I embarrassing you in front of your sissy friends?" was his witty repartee.

"I don't have any friends at this here place and I would feel mo' comfortable with some of my own kind," he went on and on.

Everyone was captive, in the school detention sort of way.

"They're not stuck up like yor'es," said Norman specifically in the direction of Sarah, Brenda and Crystal who had now banded together close by.

Karen fixed her eyes on Sarah, who was now in her immediate line of sight. The bouncer walked briskly over to Norman determined to put an end to this nonsense once and for all.

"Look at them," Norman said pointing to Karen's friends.

He boar his beady eyes into them.

"Got their noses all turned up like somebody got a problem or something. What you looking at? Just like those damn white people at my job always nosing into other people's conversation. I'm talking to my wife, if you don't mind!" he yelled.

The bouncer walked up to him, and stood chest to chest as Norman waged his finger in his face.

"Look man, you got to chill," the bouncer demanded while making sure Norman recognized that he had to look up in order to be at eye level.

"I'm talking to my got' damn wife! I've got a right to talk to my own got' damn wife, you motherfucker?" Norman responded in a way that showed he was not intimidated.

Karen knew better. It was the liquor talking.

"Who you calling a motherfucker," the bouncer said clinching his fists, prepared to deliver to Norman a little naptime.

Millie signaled him to stand down.

"Look man, you're drunk and I don't want to hurt you. So, you got to leave, simple as that," the bouncer held out his hand to usher Norman to the door.

"I'll leave when I'm good and got' damn ready to leave. You're not my god damn brother's keeper," Norman could barely stand up but even that didn't stop him from mouthing off to a guy two times his size.

Karen didn't want to see him get hurt, so she stood up and walked in between Norman and the bouncer.

"Honey, please," she pleaded.

Norman pushed her out of his way and she fell back into her chair. Crystal rushed over to see if she was hurt. Rob followed.

"Are you all-right?" Crystal asked hugging her and checking her for bruises.

Karen didn't answer.

"Yu' o-k?" Crystal asked again.

Karen turned and stared at Sarah again unable to forget some of the words that were said at the restaurant. Her worst fears were coming true.

"I'm fine," Karen managed to say without crying.

"Norman…" she began again, "Norman, let's go."

Millie and Jacob had now walked over to Karen also, more so to assure the other guests that everything was fine. The bouncer quickly grabbed Norman's arm and shoved him to the door.

"You've got to go, man. Now! This is not that kind of party. Let's go. I don't want any trouble," the bouncer said operating efficiently and with total control.

In truth, he wanted to take him away from prying eyes so he could teach him some streetwise respect. So, he forcefully pushed Norman out of the ballroom's main door and into the hallway.

"Damn people here treat you like you've got a problem! I'm leavin'. I'm leavin'," Norman shouted as if he had a choice.

The bouncer then released his arm.

"Woman, you comin'?" Norman slurred while making his way towards the outer door.

"In a minute. I want to say…good-bye," said Karen quickly turning to see the pained expression on Millie's face.

"Say good-bye to your got' damn pussy friends and let's go!"

Then Norman waved his hand in the air at the bouncer and exited through the double doors. The bouncer followed him out to make sure he exited all the way out of the building. Jacob and a few other men followed. Karen lifted her head to see Sarah and Brenda giving her puzzled stares. Crystal had tears in her eyes. Karen didn't want to let this go on another minute.

"Thank you," she mouthed inaudibly to Millie.

Crystal and Millie gave her a hug.

"Karen, you don't have to leave, baby," Millie said lovingly.

She was concerned about the ride home. She thought it might be best for Karen to stay while Norman went and slept off his liquor. Karen didn't seem to hear Millie's suggestion. She was too busy trying to run out of there as quickly as she could.

"Yolanda, let's go, honey," Karen said as steadily as she could.

Then she and Yolanda took the long walk through the parted crowd and went out through the double doors of the dance hall. Sarah bowed her head as they went pass. Although this confirmed what she already knew, she still didn't want it to be exposed this way.

Once outside, Karen and Yolanda walked over to the parking lot directly adjacent to the hall. It was drizzling and the temperature had dropped considerably from earlier that day. Norman stood by the car jiggling the keys in his hands. He sulked and pouted as if he had been detained for hours when, in fact, it was only a matter of minutes.

"Got' damn weight lifting ass hole. That's the way they treat ya' when they're on the steroids. Who does he think he is, King Kong or something?" Norman recapped his tirade on the bouncer until Karen and Yolanda reached the car.

"Give me the keys, baby," Karen said reaching for them from Norman's slack fingers.

"I can drive!" Norman shouted, "I taught you how to drive remember?" he firmly clutched the keys to his chest and defiantly waited to be heard.

"Baby, I know you can drive. Of course you can," she placated him, "I just don't want you to drive in your condition."

She chose her words and more importantly her tone very carefully. Norman was already in a highly excitable state. She didn't want to anger him anymore than he already was.

"What con-dish-son? I taught you how to drive, woman! You wouldn't even be on the road if it weren't for mey'. And don't you forget that! You scare people half the death way you drive,"

Norman said boastfully.

In truth, Karen hated the way Norman drove. Drunk or sober she was not in the mood for having him speed up to tail gate every car on the highway. She wanted to drive as a means of avoiding the headache that inevitably ensued with Norman behind the wheel.

"Baby, I know you're the best driver, I know but…" Karen appeased and stroked.

"Don't touch these got' damn keys, woman. You hear me," he held them high over his head.

Something Karen had not seen him do since their days of courting. Back then it was done for fun. Karen stood impatiently in front of him now with her eyes rolling up to the sky. She figured she'd wait him out until he either gave her the keys or passed out. She guessed that the latter would occur sooner than the former. But her defiant stance annoyed him because he assumed that his word on the subject was the final word on the subject. He was furious. He couldn't believe that she would actually challenge his point. So, he grabbed her chin with the hand that held the keys and shoved her against the car hood. She had just enough time to prepare her body for the impact and managed to twist around so that only her shoulder hit the windshield. 'Lately, there wasn't anything funny in anything Norman did,' she thought to herself.

"Norman," Karen mouthed almost inaudibly as her eye brushed faintly against the cold metal trim of the glass.

She had a slight stinging sensation running down her arm from her collarbone slamming into the hard glass but she was more concerned about how her daughter was handling what she was seeing. Yolanda stood rigidly, startled by her father's seemingly unprovoked actions as were a few passersby heading to their cars. Norman went on as if nothing had happened. He flung the key chain round and tried to find the right one. He fumbled with several of them desperately jamming them into the lock. Finally frustrated and defeated, he accidentally dropped the entire ring on the ground. He was too drunk to maneuver himself down to get them without falling, so he leaned on the hood contemplating an alternative course of action. Yolanda stepped behind him and picked up the ring. She gently touched his back to make sure that he was steady then she went around the car and opened the passenger door for him. He groped about to the door holding onto the car as if it were a crutch. Yolanda had to meet him half way round to support him the rest of the way. She let him fall down in the bucket seat then she slid in behind him. Karen watched her daughter with a fused mix of both pride and shame. She knew that Yolanda was the peacemaker of her family, the adult, and that thought frightened her. How had her daughter grown up so quickly? Sooner or later she guessed Yolanda would be embittered by the immaturity of her parents. The price of their foolishness was her youth. Yolanda then reached over and opened the driver's side door for Karen, placing the keys into her palm.

CHAPTER TWENTY-SIX

T he three friends were hiding, intent on not showing their faces outside for a while. Crystal picked through all the free make-up at the counter, taking several selections and testing them one by one on the back of her hand, while, Sarah and Brenda searched the mirrors for imperfections on their faces. The crowd was naturally curious about their take on the evening's events. Sarah, Brenda and Crystal waited it out just long enough for the attention to shift in another direction, any other direction.

"Ah' jus' love the wey' they have all of this free stuff in here. Ah' wonder if they have cologne in the men's room. Ah'll have to ask Rob," she stated, over emphasizing Rob's name.

Brenda followed behind her from time to time when she saw something in her shade.

"I saw you with Mr. Reckless," Brenda stated to Sarah.

She enjoyed any opportunity to bring up a conversation about men.

"How'd you convince my mother to give him the job?" she asked.

"Your mom needed a photographer," Brenda replied, "...simple."

Since Brenda was seldom motivated by pure altruism, Sarah and Crystal waited for the real reason.

"All right, all right, he's a good looking man," she divulged, "It gives us something to look at, okay," Brenda further admitted humorously, "Besides, if you don't have any use for him, I'm sure

I could find the time to take him off your hands."

Crystal leaned over Sarah and tried on another one of the free lipsticks.

"Ah' hate to sey' it but she's right, ya' know." Crystal agreed with Brenda.

Both Sarah and Brenda were left speechless, awaiting her homespun explanation.

"Well, ya' did sey' he was too much of a playboy for y'u," she went on, "He don't seem like such a playboy to mey', not ta'night, anywey. Ah' just can't believe he wrecked your car though, is all," she concluded leaving Sarah and Brenda with their foreheads scrunching in slight confusion.

"What do you mean by that?" Sarah sat up and asked, though she was bothered by the fact that she was now the topic of discussion.

She came to her mother's party to drown out the complications of her week, figuring a little music and a friendly atmosphere might pull her out of her funk. She was wrong. It was apparent that no one wished to discuss Norman and Karen.

"Well..." Crystal began by clearing her throat as if she were the keynote speaker at a symposium, "...most guys like him drive really, really well," Crystal replied authoritatively bringing the momentum of the conversation to a dead halt.

Brenda glanced at Crystal with one eyebrow raised and the other searching her expression for intelligent life. It didn't help Crystal's case that she now had several shades of lipstick on her mouth, cheeks and all over both of her hands.

"Where did you learn that nonsense from, on the farm?" Brenda asked laughing excitedly at her own joke.

"Funny, funny, funny from a pregnant lady wit' no daddy for da' baby," Crystal served back without regard to insensitivity.

Sarah searched Crystal's eyes. There was no sign of her

retracting a single word. Brenda was staring at a completely new Crystal. The old Crystal would have apologized immediately and profusely. Brenda stopped laughing abruptly and went back to finding the right shade of blush from the pile of used cosmetics.

"He duz' seem sincere. And he duz' like you. Ah' can tell," Crystal said to Sarah now that she had no farther interruptions from Brenda.

Brenda was pretending that she wasn't listening. All eyes were on Sarah. She looked blankly into the mirror and waited for them to turn back around. Brenda tossed the make-up back into the baskets and stood up. Then she reached down and took Sarah's arm and pulled her to her feet.

"She's a grown woman, Sarah. She can take care of herself. Heaven help Norman when she comes to her senses," Brenda told them both, "In the mean time," she went on, "you're coming with me."

Sarah just nodded and labored at getting up. She was tired of being sociable.

"You already knew about Norman, didn't you?" Brenda asked her.

Sarah simply nodded, yes.

"So, *that* is what all of *that* was all about earlier?"

Sarah nodded again but this time hoisted herself up out of the chair. If there was a choice between her talking to Matthew or recapping what she saw at Karen's house, her choice was clear.

"Lord, if there's anyone who can take care of themselves, it's Karen. Now, if it were mey, ya'll know 'ah couldn't deal with it. Nah, nah. Ah'd need the full armor or God to be real armor," said Crystal.

"Right. I'm telling you, girlfriend. They'd have to scrape me off the ceiling," Brenda said with a huh huh.

"I hope you two don't mind but I think I should just go home.

I'm just not feeling very well tonight, just not quite myself,"
Sarah politely interrupted.

They ended their little bathroom social having determined that
there wasn't much they could do. Karen apparently wanted to be
left alone.

They exited the serenity of the bathroom to the sounds of a
roaring party. It swelled with laughter and life, not a trace of the
raucous Norman. Matthew noticed them right off. He walked
over to Sarah desiring another chance to make up for last night.

"I was just looking for you," he told her, "I think I'm gonna'
be heading out now," he lied hoping she'd persuade him
otherwise, "I think I've taken enough pictures already. And I'm
sure you're a little bummed out about what happened here
tonight...So...Well, if you all need a lift..." Matthew said looking
squarely at Sarah,"...I can take you..."

Crystal and Brenda grimaced at each other.

"...and...I was wondering if you didn't mind, that is...would
you like to have one last dance with me before we go?" he was
emphatically direct.

He didn't want Sarah to think for one moment more that he
was not interested in her. Sarah didn't move, "I don't know," she
hemmed and hawed.

Brenda grabbed her hand and clasped it firmly into Matthew's.

"Ah and I...uh...well we...we need to get lost," stuttered both
Brenda ad Crystal in unison.

Then they walked away all the while looking over their
shoulder giggling.

An upbeat song spun round and energetic, spirited people
adorned the hall. Matthew and Sarah faced one another on the
dance floor. Matthew forced himself to move back and forth to
the music, as did Sarah. He would have preferred a mellower

tune, one that allowed him to snuggle close to her. He longed to press his check up against hers like they were last night. Sarah looked around the room, pensive. Matthew's eyes never left her.

"You're beautiful," he said almost in a whisper.

Despite her sad disposition she broke into a smile. It faded quickly though as thoughts of Karen drifted back into the forefront of her consciousness. She didn't care much for entertaining any other emotion. Matthew recognized a nod that could have been interpreted as thank you. He wasn't certain but accepted it none-the-less. "When Was The Last Time Music Made You Cry" by James Ingram gently seeped in underneath the drums of a song neither of them were listening to. The mood of his voice and the smooth melody leant itself to a slow dance. So, they moved in a little closer to each other, Sarah still maintaining a rather hearty distance.

Across the floor, Millie sat with Mrs. Rivers and Mrs. Yates.

"How much money we done made tonight?" Mrs. Rivers asked.

"I didn't count it yet. I don't know. A lot, I reckon. I'll go count it," suggested Mrs. Yates.

"I'll go with you," followed Mrs. Rivers. She then turned to Millie, "You comin'?"

"No, you two go count it without me." Millie rolled her eyes around and looked at them as if they were insane.

Mrs. Rivers and Mrs. Yates rushed over to the front door to check the accounts. Millie watched them as they left, then looked elsewhere. She spotted Matthew and Sarah, and welcomed the distraction.

"The kids look good, don't they?" she said to Jacob.

"Hum," he nodded.

"Remember when we were their age? We could really cut a rug, couldn't we?

"Yeah, we really knew how to have a good time."

Jacob stood up and took her into his arms.

"Would you like to dance?" he asked whisking her around.

Millie cleaved to him and let him glide her into a waltz. Jacob held her tenderly. They glided across the floor like two seasoned professionals. Other couples marveled at their simplicity and ease. Matthew looked over and followed suit putting his arms around Sarah. Still she danced about three feet away.

"Do you feel a draft?" he joked.

Sarah stepped only slightly nearer.

Silence.

"When was the last time you danced like this?" Matthew asked.

"The last time I danced like this?" she mused throwing her head back in thought.

Matthew searched the curves of her neck and how he had placed his lips upon it mere hours ago.

"You would ask me a question like that," she said still thinking of an answer.

"I want to get to know the person I'm dancing with," he told her.

"Well...I remember...being twelve years old at the time," she said.

Matthew looked at her questioningly.

"Really, I danced with my father.'

She paused.

"Go on."

She smiled, "I know, I know it doesn't seem like much but to me, at that time, it was everything."

Matthew motions for her to continue.

"You see, I got stood up at my junior prom."

"You?"

"Yes. My father and his friends were acting as chaperons at the time. Well, anyway, I went to the prom by myself. I was standing at the door and people were actually laughing at me...as I walked in. News of this nature, embarrassing news, travels quickly. My date was already there having taken a girl who, well, she and I didn't get along."

"What happened?" he asked, listening intently.

"I looked over and saw that it was some of my father's friends; his macho, obviously immature friends doing most of the laughing. They always told my father and mother that I should have been a boy. And they treated me like I was a boy when I was growing up."

"No wonder you're so independent," Matthew observed.

'In-de-pen-dent,' she thought, 'Where have I heard that word before?' Sarah let the word sink in. 'Here it comes,' she thought. This is when her dates usually say that she's too strong to need anyone in her life.

"I like that about you," he said easily.

"A...n..ny...way..." Sarah stumbled, surprised, "my father walked over to me with this look on his face. I thought he was mad at me or something because I embarrassed him in front of his friends or something but instead he grabbed my hand and escorted me onto the wooden platform floor. He danced with me until my feet hurt. I felt so lucky to have a dad like him."

"It sounds like he knows what's important."

"Yes...yes...he does, doesn't he?" she never really thought of it that way, "When was the last time you danced like this?" she returned the question to Matthew.

He took a moment. They were finally talking and it was nice.

"Last night with you," he winked.

It was something in the way he said it, so smooth and with a hint of vulnerability. She softened at the sound of it. Matthew gently tugged her towards him. She allowed him to do so this time. Maybe it was the way he listened to her that ultimately melted her. Her knees buckled a bit and her head angled to him. She grew more comfortable in his arms as he manipulated her body to the music. 'This is nice,' Sarah thought. Matthew lowered his head onto her shoulder. Sarah nudged his head so that he'd straighten it again. He pretended not to notice then he lowered it again in another attempt at getting closer to her. They were now dancing cheek to cheek. He leaned his head on her shoulder and enjoyed the flowery aroma of her perfume.

"I love...I love what you're wearing. It's intoxicating," he said letting himself sink into the scent of it.

"Is that what it is?" she hazily replied.

Meanwhile she didn't know what he just said. She just knew that she felt an odd sensation. She was weak and electrified all at the same time. She had a similar feeling last night towards him but it differed now sober. At her place, she wanted him because he was male and available. Now she wanted Matthew, this charming Englishman whose singular desire was to apparently be with her. They turned and looked into each other's eyes. They leaned into one another and tried to find the best way to kiss. Sarah moved her head to the right and Matthew leaned his head to the right. Then she leaned left and he leaned left also. Then they stared at each other once more. Finally Sarah leaned left and then Matthew leaned right and they simultaneously embraced. Their hearts intertwined and laced through one another's, clothing them in a blanket of passion. An up-tempo song came trampling in, colliding with the slow music, which increased their already rapid heartbeats. Sarah yielded finally to her own desires, abandoning her normal stiff back and solid distrust of Matthew. The crowd started leaving the dance floor, save Sarah and Matthew who were locked tight together in the middle of it. He was nothing at all like she imagined. He was better.

CHAPTER TWENTY-SEVEN

K aren bore too far right and ended up having to get off the expressway. Now she was squeezed between two trucks and couldn't see the upcoming divide in the road. Norman snorted and sucked his teeth as Karen tried to find another entrance up ahead.

"Where are you going? You're going to get us lost again," he complained.

"Home, Daddy, home," Yolanda said with her thumb in her mouth.

"Hush, Yolanda. It's hard to see out here tonight. And, Yolanda, you're too old to suck your thumb," Karen sternly reprimanded her.

Karen hated the fact that she had to do it. For it was the only thing Yolanda did that showed she was still a child. Norman turned his head around and smiled at Yolanda.

"She can suck whatever she likes, right honey?" he twisted his lips and chuckled until he coughed.

Yolanda nodded her head up and down in agreement.

"Yolanda! Yolanda!" Karen shouted whilst looking through the rear view mirror.

Yolanda ignored Karen defiantly.

"Stop pickin' on her and watch where you're going," he groaned.

"I'm not picking on anybody. Let's just stop screaming at each other, please. It's too slick out here. I need to concentrate."

"That's because you still can't drive. I tried to teach you but you just too stupid. Stupid," he said, very pleased with himself.

Karen paid him no mind and referred all of her comments to Yolanda instead.

"Baby put your seat belt on. It's slick out here," she told her.

"Daddy said I don't have to if I don't want to," she was impish.

Karen decided to let that one slide. She guessed that Yolanda deserved some childlike behavior. Rebellion at least felt normal.

"That's right. Shut up woman!" Norman growled.

Karen had difficulty staying at a steady pace. She constantly found herself behind motorists who were either driving at a snail's pace or weaving in and out of cars at overly accelerated speeds.

"These people don't know what they want to do tonight," Karen stammered, maneuvering the car through the dense traffic and rain fog.

"You're the one who don't know how to drive in the rain or anywhere else for that matter," Norman grumbled and huffed.

Karen did her best to let his childlike behavior slide as well. It was difficult though after the evening she had just spent with him. She always thought she had a good handle on things but tonight her nerves were at the peak of being completely frazzled. Her head was still reeling from the performance Norman put on at the dance. She and Norman had gone to practically all of Millie's dances before they moved to Phoenix. Millie and Jacob treated Norman like a son and her as a daughter. She felt ashamed more than anything else. It was one thing to have Norman act his nature at home. She was overcome by shame to witness his antics in public. She knew that no matter what Norman did or did not do everyone was watching them both. She couldn't separate herself from how badly his actions reflected upon the whole family. The head of the household set the tone and Norman proved over and over just how out of tune they were. She looked in his blood shot eyes as he was pushing his chest out and strutting around like a proud peacock. She was sure that she did not recognize him. It was as if she were seeing him for the first time, the man inside of the man, his inner soul, the man that he had become, over their so many years of marriage. Not to mention the experience of watching Norman through other people's eyes. It sickened her. Their faces were distorted and rumbled up as if they were all watching someone lose their lunch. The stench alone, and then all eyes turned towards her. They pitied her. She knew that it would take every ounce of energy that she had in order to deal with that realization. Their status as being the most envied couple was now officially long gone and forgotten.

"Where the hell are we now? Are you going to get us lost again?" he barked in her ear.

She turned and could have sworn she saw him foaming at the mouth.

"I just made one wrong turn," she laughed on the inside at the irony, "We're going in the right direction now."

She lowered her voice when she spoke. She thought that if she really let out what she was feeling, the scream would have shattered the windshield.

She would recount later that it all happened so fast. That she obviously wasn't thinking clearly, her thoughts manipulated by years of error, and indescribable weakness. It would be her own shortcomings that she'd now face as she explained about the longest two minutes of her entire life. They came upon a traffic light, the story would begin. Karen would recall that although the stoplight was directly in front of her, she could barely see the red light through the steamy mist. Her side windows were completely clouded with condensation despite the fact that she had opened them a bit to allow the staleness of Norman's drunken breath escape into the night air.

"Stop! Stop the damn car! It's red!" he yelped.

"Please stop screaming at me. I am stopping. Can't you see that the roads are slip...that the roads are very slippery? It's hard enough just trying to get us home safely. I don't need you yelling at me every other minute," Karen did her best to allow the words to come out without quivering.

She needed them to sound nice and even with as much patience as she could pretend to have. Truth was, were it not for the lights from the car in front of her, she wouldn't be able to stay on the road at all. She said a silent prayer throughout every inch of their journey home. She hated to drive at night. She always had difficulty seeing in the dark.

"You can go now," Norman instructed brusquely as the light changed from red to green.

"We know, Daddy," Yolanda said playfully.

Norman turned around slowly and eyed Yolanda, "Are you getting fresh with me?" he asked her reaching back and whacking her on the forearm.

At the sound of Norman's hand upon Yolanda's flesh, something inside of Karen snapped. Every muscle in her body tensed and her mind fixed itself on only one objective and that was to protect her daughter. As she turned quickly to get a glimpse of Yolanda all she could see was the red weld imprint from where Norman's hand had just been.

"You..." came out of her lips softly, a small whisper but nothing more.

Norman shifted against the leather interior ever so deft in his devastation.

"...bastard," swelled out of Karen's mouth and her spit hit the dashboard.

Norman's head rolled under and up. His eyes practically flung out of their sockets as he looked at his wife.

"Don't you dare hit my baby you son-of-a-bitch! Bastard! Bastard!" she began screaming over and over again while flinging her free hand on his shoulders and head.

Norman reared his body back against the seat and tried his hardest to block Karen's slaps.

"Who you calling a son-of-a-bitch, bitch?" Norman asked indignantly.

Then he pushed Karen to the side of the car and took another swing at Yolanda. Yolanda raised her little hand up over her face in order to block Norman's descending blow. Karen thought her shoulder was being dislocated as it banged into the wheel. She gathered all her courage and managed to hurl her body around just in time to catch Norman's hand in mid air. She gripped it and held fast to it, which took some doing for her. Norman was a strong man even in his inebriated state and Karen was holding the wheel with her other hand. All she could think of was how many times she had ended up in the hospital behind Norman's misdirected anger. She didn't want that type of pain inflicted on her daughter.

It would be days later before she could remember how she suddenly began to lose the grip she had of Norman's jacket. Every painted fingernail was torn off or broken. It was only after the puffiness of her fingers wore off that the clarity of those moments would resurface into her consciousness. Then, and only then, would she see in her minds-eye the moment that she had turned and faced Norman, placing both her hands around his sweaty thick neck. Everything would come flooding back to her then. How she pressed the weight of her body atop of his and pummeled him with her bare fists. How she screamed, kicked and punched and swore at the man whose very essence she no longer believed to be the man she married. The great love for her daughter over powered her. The desire for freedom engulfed her.

It awakened in her a resurgence of her old life, which had been buried and long forgotten. All at once a burden had been lifted off her chest. A fountain of emotion gushed forth filling her limbs with incredible strength, enough to pin Norman down to his seat and begin to strangle the breath from his body. At that moment she hated the sight of him and would recall much later thrusting her fists into his jawbone while her other hand held tightly to his windpipe. Norman struggled and thrashed about trying to hoist her off of him but his efforts were in vain as he steadily started losing consciousness. He managed to place his body in a sloped position and spun himself out from underneath Karen's arms but that proved useless as well, for she increased her grip on his neck. His eyelids were becoming heavy and he began to feel light-headed and woozy. Karen wasn't satisfied though until Norman's body no longer shook under her fingers. Rage was like a drug pumping through her veins. She wouldn't remember any of her actions until many hours after and then she wouldn't forgive herself. The anger that she had bottled up exploded out of every pore to a point where she couldn't even control herself.

At that moment she couldn't hear Yolanda's screams asking her to stop hurting her Daddy. She couldn't see her little hands covering her little face and sobbing uncontrollably. She couldn't feel the friction from the hard plastic coil of the steering wheel rubbing against the side of her thigh or the rocking of the car as it spun and skidded alongside the cement partition in the middle of the road. In some hollow corner way deep in the back of her mind she gathered that something was spinning into the black night. She was so focused on the wrinkles that formed on her hands as she strained to maintain hold of Norman's neck. By some miracle, other motorists swerved in time to clear a path...save one lone truck.

CHAPTER TWENTY-EIGHT

A smattering of people were huddled together underneath the thick cement awning barely able to remain dry from the spray. They're awaiting an opportunity to sprint to their several destinations between down pours. Many try hovering inside the waiting area but there isn't enough room. It had been steadily raining since they had arrived that morning. *'The City that never sleeps,'* Crystal thought as she supportively rubbed Karen's shoulders. She never regarded that saying as necessarily a good thing but somehow now at the crack of dawn she liked the fact that she wasn't the only one up. In fact, it looked like the whole world was wide awake. Hospital employees and EMS workers darted quickly and quietly away from anyone who didn't work there. While Sarah, Matthew and Rob sat a few seats away observing people, especially Brenda who was on the telephone with an all night diner.

"..and some potato salad..." she said exasperatedly to the woman on the other end, almost certain that she was hard of hearing.

Crystal turned towards her and yelled for her not to forget something to drink. After all the dancing she had done with Rob, she was "plenty parched," she told her.

"...Yes, a turkey and collard green sandwich," Brenda repeated from her list.

"Oh, Brenda, yuk," Crystal yelped confirming the sentiment of everyone save Karen.

Karen had her eyes fixed on the large white Formica front

desk. When she finally saw a figure making an appearance there, a receptionist, she got up and quickly made her way over before anyone else beat her to it.

"I'm pregnant, what do you want from me!" Brenda screamed into the receiver.

The receptionist strained to make out Karen's low hoarse voice over the clamor Brenda was making.

"It may sound disgusting to you but that's what I want! And a two-liter bottle of Diet Coke, please. Thank you," Brenda declared as she hung up the receiver with an attitude of indignation before marching back to her seat.

All eyes fixed on her as she sat.

"Huh, Brenda, when yo'r sandwich cume's, y'u go sit over the-re..." Crystal said pointing to the other side of the room, "...and eat it. Au'heard ov' some pretty country thangs to eat but au' ain't never heard nothin' like that. Good lawd."

Matthew and Rob tried not to crack a smile but it was hard. There was a lot of tension in the air and they needed any excuse to let off steam. They had no reason to worry about Karen. She was lost in her own thoughts. When she walked back to her chair, no one needed to ask what she and the receptionist spoke about. It was clear. Anyone could have read the solemnity of her face. She lowered herself into a seat as if her legs were too heavy and her hands shook as she rested them on her thighs. It was cold and damp in the waiting area yet sweat moistened Karen's cheeks. Sarah looked on at her from time to time worried that she might collapse. Each time she did, she caught Karen staring blankly at the walls. For Karen the events of the last two and a half hours replayed over and over again like a scratched record. The fear, remorse and numbing pain that she was experiencing choked the flow of blood to her heart. She was certain that it had stopped beating altogether. She found herself praying that it would. What was she thinking, was the operative question pressing on her, nagging her. It gradually bulged in her head like an aneurysm. As misfortune usually produces, she wasn't just thinking about her deplorable driving that evening. She thought of all the stupid things she had done since birth. She admitted secretly in her inner most self that nothing seemed to have turned out right. Failure. Every move she ever made grieved her. Crystal's efforts to relieve the stiffness in her neck only brought more attention to the aching that coursed through her entire body. When Crystal started up again, Karen grabbed her arm and gently pulled her into an adjacent seat. Crystal nodded her head as if to say she understood, but Karen was sure that she could not.

"This guy I'm pregnant by..." Brenda began addressing anyone within earshot including those she didn't even know.

It was painfully obvious that she craved an audience. Rob gingerly eased himself out of his seat and walked away pretending he saw something of interest on the other side of the lobby.

"...is not the fatherly type either.." she continued without taking a breath, a moment to consider - nothing.

"...I can't really see him changing diapers or making bottles, if you know what I mean..." Brenda postulated as she sucked down her last piece of chewing gum, "...And God forbid I asked him to get up in the middle of the night for three o'clock feedings..."

In all honesty, each one of them, Sarah, Crystal and even Matthew had a word or two to say about good old Norm but they had the good sense to shut-up.

"Brenda, huney," Crystal tried, "N'awt n'oaw, huney."

"I'm serious, he'd probably hit me too or something like

'*what'shisname*'!" Brenda exclaimed.

Sarah, Crystal and Matthew one by one peeked over at Karen. Karen was still lost in a self-made hell and numb to the rest of the world. It was a mixed blessing really because there was no stopping Brenda. At that time, Matthew decided to stroll over and join Rob.

"...That's why I really didn't want this baby..." Brenda said almost to herself.

At that, Crystal stopped listening. She assumed that whether to have the baby or not was already a non-issue. Surely she had prayed and preached enough, she thought. At that time, she too walked over and joined Rob and Matthew who were leaning against a flat top trashcan.

"...Anyway, I don't think I want to put the baby through such a lousy up-bringing, you know..." Brenda considered.

When Sarah lifted her eyelids, she found that she was the only one left entertaining Brenda.

"...You know, when we found out that I was pregnant, he just freaked out. He started throwing things around the apartment searching for his coat, no doubt, so he could make a quick escape. Can you imagine? And then he made it sound as if I was forcing him into marriage. Me, forcing him into marriage? Can you believe him accusing me of trying to lure him into *ever-after*? I don't think so," Brenda put her hands on her hips and presented her hand in a fanfare.

"I guess he just doesn't know me, now does he?" she shook her head back and forth haughtily.

Sarah just stared at her. What Sarah couldn't stand, at now three o'clock in the morning, was yet another idiotic conversation.

"Brenda!" Sarah snapped, jarring Brenda into silence.

"What?" Brenda jumped.

"No offense, but I can't listen to anymore of this crap!"

Then she placed her palm resolutely in front of Brenda's rather perplexed face.

"Gees, what's wrong with you?" Brenda asked gruffly.

"I was just talking about..." Brenda said.

"About you, you, and you!" Sarah said told her, "That's what you're always talking about, you. This..." Sarah illustrated by panning her arms out over the room, "...is not about you."

"Why are you saying all this? I really need your help right now," Brenda spoke earnestly.

"You really need my help?" Sarah mocked, "And why?"

"Because that's what friendship is all about. I'm always here for all of you, right?" Brenda asked in a pleading fashion.

Crystal's ears perked up.

"Oh, and you believe that?" Sarah questioned.

"Yes," Brenda answered glibly.

"Then yu' should practice whu't ya' preach," Crystal chimed in from half way across the room, "That is, if yu' believe what ya' se'y is true."

"Why do y'all have this attitude? I'm pregnant!" Brenda said sharply, shamelessly searching for sympathy.

"I suppose you think that makes everything all right?" Sarah asked rhetorically.

Both Sarah and Crystal knew that she was relying on commiseration from others present – an audience. Normally, that would have had some influence over their responses, but not tonight.

"Oh, and I suppose that means that, as a good friend, you're allowed to fix me up with a married man?" she asked pointedly, "Then leave Crystal here stranded on the other side of town whenever you get the *urge*? As long as Brenda is taken care of, forget about the rest of us?" Sarah asked.

Brenda sat back and stared up at Sarah, then Crystal. Brenda was beginning to see that this could not be swept up with a million *I'm sorries*. She had been down this road many times before with them and had always managed to get them to overlook her shortcomings.

"I care about you guys too. I do. I care a lot," Brenda tried, "I'm sorry, Crystal," Brenda said swallowing her words at the back of her throat, "I'm sorry, Sarah."

Crystal just nodded her head in acceptance. She knew that that was all she was going to get. Brenda wasn't big on humility and Crystal didn't expect much more. Sarah was less congenial.

"Look around you, Brenda," she barked, "We're in a hospital," she paused, "...waiting to hear about *Karen's* daughter. No offense, but this is not the time nor the place..."

Brenda gently waved at her in defeat. She couldn't believe that no one was interested in what she had to say. She blamed it all on the pregnancy. She hadn't been herself ever since she took the test.

The main door of the hospital opened gently and their attention was drawn to the damp air whipping pass. Beneath a torn umbrella and wet hood was a delivery boy, carrying two soggy plastic shopping bags.

"Yo'r chuck wagon's here," Crystal bellowed at Brenda.

Brenda immediately squealed with delight and made her way over to the door. By the time she got there Matthew, Rob and Crystal were already there pulling out their wallets.

"How much do we owe you?" Matthew asked the rain soaked boy.

"Nah, man. I got it," Rob reached for his wallet and pulled out a twenty-dollar bill.

"I've got it," Sarah interjected.

"Don't be silly," Crystal said to her and then under her breath, "Rob's got it," emphasizing the name, Rob.

"No, baby, I have this one," Matthew insisted, taking Sarah's hand in his.

'Ba-by,' she thought with a smile.

Meanwhile, Brenda stepped in between the adoring couples and paid the guy. Then she walked back to their little corner and sorted the food into piles. They eventually noticed what she'd done and joined her. Matthew gave Sarah two cups of coffee and he took one for himself.

"Is she going to be all-right?" Matthew said indicating Karen.

Sarah just shrugged her shoulders. Judging from Karen's secrecy about Norman, it was difficult to draw any conclusion. At least none of which Sarah wanted to mention. It was too embarrassing to have someone ask questions about a best friend and not be able to supply answers. It bothered Sarah that Matthew, a complete stranger to her circle of friends, was as up to date as she was.

"I hope so," was all she could muster.

She walked over to Karen thinking, 'It was a pat answer, sure, but sometimes a good acceptable evasive response is called for.'

"Here," she said to Karen handing her some coffee.

She didn't want to say much. She didn't want anything to ignite into a long drawn out argument. Talking to Karen of late was tantamount to walking blind folded in a minefield. The only reason they even knew she was in the hospital that night was because she put Sarah's name down on the in case of an emergency line the last time she was there. Even Crystal had a problem understanding how she could have been in the hospital so many times since her brief return to New York. It had only been a few weeks and according to her hospital record she had been in the emergency ward fourteen times. Then there was her description of the accident. There were loads of inconsistencies. It didn't coincide with any eyewitness accounts. Sarah was dying to hear the truth but was sure she'd have to wait for that. Karen went from being a friend who told her every detail of every day of her life to one who was now making up stuff. Karen smiled and accepted the cup from Sarah but she didn't bother to open it. She just held it in her hands and rolled it back and forth within her palms.

"I know I said some things that must have really hurt you and, that was never my intention, you know? I said to myself that I was trying to protect you. Isn't that a laugh, me protecting you..." Sarah started right in asking for forgiveness.

She was sorry that everything had turned out so badly. Never in her wildest dreams did she want things to unfold as they had.

"And you shouldn't apologize for it either," Karen looked up.

She finally took the lid off and drank some of the coffee.

"You know, it's funny, I've been acting like a battered wife. I have. And, I'm ashamed to admit it, but I have been for a long time. I don't know what happened. One minute I was married to the most valuable player. And the next minute, I'm in a hospital, waiting...waiting..." Karen trailed off.

Karen blamed herself. Sarah didn't want to upset her or pry but curiosity overwhelmed her better judgment and hospital etiquette.

"Karen, you're my best friend and I love you but I have to ask you this one question...how...how did this happen?" She asked hesitantly.

Karen took a long sip of coffee while mulling over Sarah's question.

"I don't know. I wish I knew," Karen shook her head from

side to side as she spoke.

Sarah waited patiently while Karen formulated her thoughts.

"We didn't start out this way," said Karen to Sarah with a smile, "Well, you know that."

"You two were the envy of everyone in school including me," Sarah admitted.

Karen laughed to herself.

"Some people have a way of breaking your will, you know? It starts off with a simple comment about your hair or your dress. 'What's wrong with your hair? Why don't you do it like so-and-so? Your make-up doesn't look right. Change it.' It's those little things that make all the difference in a marriage. Before I knew it, I began to believe what he said. I thought I was too fat, too ugly, too thin, too crazy, and too dumb. At one point, my hair wasn't long enough for him, so I got a weave. Then he actually had the nerve to say that my skin wasn't light enough. So I, like a fool, went out and bleached it."

Karen took a deep breath and a long pause. Sarah waited.

"I...uh...didn't want to come back here, you know? Not really," she confessed.

Sarah couldn't help but let her surprise show. It was the whole hoopla that Karen made upon her return. It threw Sarah off; obviously another performance.

"Well, how would you feel if you were envied in high school and then pitied for the rest of your life? I couldn't come home to that."

"No, girlfriend. Don't even go there," Sarah asked.

"What?" Karen asked unsure of Sarah's intent.

"I, we do not pity you. I cursed-out virtually all of my girlfriends this weekend and it had nothing to do with pitying them. If, I thought you couldn't take it, I would never speak my mind. What kind of friendship would we have then? No, I yell because I care, because I know you would do the same for me. That's what real friends do for one another. Please. When I scream, I want somebody to scream right back at me. Pity, huh," with that Sarah folded her arms and dared Karen to disagree.

Karen wanted to but she knew Sarah had a good point. Even with everything that had happened, Karen felt that there was a strength deep inside of her that was yearning to get out. She was always the strong one. Sarah had never ever seen her fall completely apart. They had always counted on her to pull them out of scrapes. This was the closest Sarah had witnessed of any vulnerability on her part at all. Karen leaned against Sarah's shoulder and smiled.

"Call me a stuck up bitch if they have to," Sarah said repeating her words, "Say I've never had a real relationship with a man, if that's what I need to hear. Pity. Girl, please."

Karen allowed Sarah's words to resound in her ear.

"Thank you," Karen said fighting back tears, "Thank you," she said, now sobbing.

Sarah lifted her eyes up for a moment from her embrace with Karen to see Matthew admiring her from a far. His gaze was so gentle and thoughtful. She couldn't help but marvel at how his eyes were able to penetrate so deep within. She no longer feared that she might be falling in love. She knew that she was. And now she could also say that she was finally getting her best friend back. It had been as if Karen had gone missing and was finally rescued and brought safely home. Crystal walked over and wrapped her arms around them both.

"Ain't this so bee-uta-ful. So, so totally bee-u-taful," Crystal cried.

CHAPTER TWENTY-NINE

T hen the main door opened abruptly again. Most of the people in the waiting area were asleep or glued to the overhead television set.

"Where is she!?" Norman came in and yelled from underneath a hooded parker.

Karen heard him but she did not turn around to face him right away. She hesitated, thinking of all the things she had always wanted to say to him. She knew that there wouldn't be time enough in the world to express how much she blamed him for their daughter's condition let alone hers.

While everyone else was watching Norman, Karen stared in the opposite direction for a good long time, thinking. As the clerk was being called away from the front desk something caught Karen's eye. She glanced over and could see the lone guard sitting at his post napping. His gun was protruding from his gun belt. The snap on the holster was loose and Karen stared down at the small piece of leather dangling wearily from its place.

"I said, where is she?" Norman yelled, stirring people from their sound sleep.

"Which she are you referring to?" Brenda asked sarcastically.

Norman pretended he didn't hear her and surveyed the room instead. He was hell bent on finding his wife. The doctors had kept him in the emergency ward for observation for two hours. They thought he had a concussion and feared he might pass out. Norman had had enough of their poking and prodding and snuck

out while they weren't looking. He still had on the hospital robe
and his behind was exposed to the elements and wayward eyes.
Everyone looked at him as if he were a nutcase. He finally saw
Karen, with her back turned, staring at the back wall.

"Woman! Woman, come here," he demanded.

Karen slowly turned but she did not move. All eyes were now
on her.

"Don't you hear me talking to you? I said, come here," he
stomped his foot on the floor like a disruptive child.

Karen walked slowly towards him staring through him.

"When I tell you to come here I mean come here," he
explained.

Then he raised his hand to her as if he would hit her but before
he could follow through, Karen shoved the guard's gun to his
temple.

Everyone froze.

The only sound heard was Norman forcing his breath into the
air. He was instantly obliging and Karen was deadly serious.

"Karen? Karen," almost in a whisper, he said, "Karen."

Sarah slowly walked towards them followed by Matthew.
Crystal and Rob moved out of the line of fire. Brenda dropped
her sandwich first on her lap then it teetered and eventually fell
to the floor.

"Karen? Put the gun down," Sarah pleads.

Matthew began to slowly maneuver his way around trying to
get behind Karen and Norman.

"Woman," Norman half shouted, half muffled.

Karen cocked the gun just as the guard stumbled out of his
stupor, taking a long while to focus on what was going on right
in front of him.

"Karen, please say something. Karen, please...it's not worth
it," Sarah advised.

"You got that right. You got that right," Karen laughed mischievously.

"K, k, Karen...Karen..." Norman stammered.

"Didn't you have something you wanted to say to me? You goddamn bastard - kneel! Kneel! I said, kneel," Karen demanded in a voice that sunk down to her lowest pitch.

She shakes her head and rolls her eyes like a sharpshooter aiming at a bulls-eye. Norman goes down on all fours, one loose leg at a time. He sweats, coughs and grunts but he doesn't say a word. Meanwhile, Matthew is almost fully behind Karen by this point hoping he can get at least close enough to knock the gun away. He's not sure what he can actually do but he wants to try and help.

"You almost killed my child you no good for nothing low down son of a bitch! You weren't happy just destroying me, no, you had to have her too! My child, my baby," Karen cries as she speaks.

The guard taps his side and nearly pees on himself when he doesn't feel his gun in the holster. He makes his way quickly over to what he determines as the crazy lady brandishing, what he now knows, is his revolver.

"Hey, what's going on here?" the guard asks groggily and so faint that no one even notices him.

"Say your prayers, you skank. I'm sending you straight to hell! My only regret is that this is a hospital but I'm gonna' make sure that they can't bring you back to life," with that statement, she pulls the trigger.

At the same time, Sarah, Crystal and Brenda scream, "No!" The gun makes a small popping noise. Norman drops down to the floor shaking and blocking his face. Matthew leaps over and grabs Karen's arm while the guard stretches his arm out for his gun. Matthew and the guard are off balance and Karen manages to somehow maintain her hold on the gun.

"No bullets? No god damn bullets?" Karen chides at the guard.

Everyone looks at Norman, who isn't hurt at all, except for his knees. He had jumped up when she fired then went crashing back down to the floor thinking he was hit.

No one moves as Karen holds the gun to his head again and for a second time pulls the trigger. She didn't even give him a warning. The entire waiting area holds their collective breaths in a panic, then everyone almost simultaneously start to yell for Karen to stop.

"No! No! No," they scream.

Again, the gun fires making a capping sound this time. Again, no bullets in the chamber. Karen, ever so slowly, turns and faces the guard.

"What the hell kind of guard are you anyway? You don't have any fucking bullets in this gun. I can't even shoot my own no-neck husband?" Karen asks.

Norman used this opportunity to jump up and run out of the hospital, his butt cheeks bouncing as he exits. Everyone stares at his privates bobbing up and down, protruding out from the hospital gown. People wanted to laugh but decided not to as they remember that Karen still has a gun. Loaded or not, no one wanted to anger her.

"You better run. You had better run as far as your skinny little legs will take you. 'Cause I'm gonna' kill you the next time I see you. I swear I will. Run, run, run!" Karen yelled after him hoisting the pistol over her head like a marks-man.

Once the electronic front doors firmly closed behind Norman,

Karen kneels down and brakes out hysterically crying. Sarah runs over first to comfort her, then Crystal, then Brenda. When Brenda approaches, Karen revealed that she was not crying at all but laughing so hard that she has tears rolling down her face.

"Girl, you pick a hell of a time to get your sense of humor back," Brenda holds her stomach and her chest.

"Give me that gun. Are you trying to scare us half to death?" Sarah asked her.

She immediately takes the gun from Karen and with a shy exchange of hands, gives it to Matthew.

"No, I was just trying to kill a rat" Karen laughs.

"Lawdy, Lawdy. Don't you know that that's a sin," Crystal offered.

"It's a sin to keep that man alive, honest to God," Karen said.

Then, Karen reveals to them only that she had the bullets folded up in her other hand the whole time. They all laugh just as a doctor pushes through the hospital doors leading into the lobby.

"Karen? Karen Montgomery?" he calls out.

The guard slyly motions to Matthew that he needs his gun back. Matthew slips it to him making sure that the doctor can't see what they're doing.

"Yes," Karen says rising up and dusting herself off.

The doctor walks her to the other end of the hall. She follows obediently.

"Be strong," Crystal tells her knowing that it's what Karen usually says to her.

"We're here for you," Sarah says.

Brenda runs over to her and holds her hands tightly. She wants to say something to her that would encourage too, but is sorely out of practice.

"Karen," she finally manages and hugs her.

"I know, I know," Karen whispers.

Karen knew she had done something right in her life. She had chosen a good group of friends. She turned and continued following the doctor down the hallway. Sarah and everyone else looked through the windows of the hospital doors as the doctor talked to her. Karen lowered her head when he was finished speaking. The doctor then brought her further into the hospital, out of view. Sarah, Crystal and Brenda remained standing and staring at one another. A few minutes later the interior doors swung back open. Karen came barreling abruptly through them again with her head down. She was sobbing uncontrollably. Sarah, Crystal and Brenda rushed over. Matthew and Rob joined them but tried to stay on the periphery.

"Karen," Brenda said.

"Ah'm so sorry," said Crystal.

"Honey, let it all out," Sarah told her.

"Is there anything we can do?" Brenda asked.

"Karen?" they asked.

Karen lifted her head up and eventually smiled.

"She's okay. She's going to be all right. I was so frightened. I was so frightened. I love her so much. She's all-right," Karen repeatedly told them.

Sarah, Crystal and Brenda encircle her. Rob and Matthew join them. It had been a long night for all of them and it was finally over.

CHAPTER THIRTY

"I can't see my feet!" Brenda shrieked, focusing with eyes cast down desperately trying to make out even the smallest portion of the red toe nail polish she insisted Crystal apply just yesterday.

"You're pregnant, woman! Quit complainin'," Sarah joked.

"How the hell did this happen to me anyway?" Brenda joked while rubbing her belly.

She had checked out all the books she could carry on parenthood from her local library. They were all strewn across the floor. She made a vow to herself that she would be the best mother she could be to her child. This intense studying, however, awakened a passion of sweets and breads soaked in butter. She gained enough weight to warrant a whole new wardrobe. For some, a recent conversation with Brenda could be a seemingly endless yawn on the miracle of proper nutrition, diet and exercise while pregnant, and it might have lulled some to sleep, but not Sarah. She was sure that this was time well spent. Sarah was proud of her in a way, if she could say that without sounding condescending. It was the only accurate way she could describe how she felt about the matter. Partly, it was a smidgen of guilt that kept her transfixed on Brenda's every word. She never thought for a moment that Brenda had the kind of strength that she was exhibiting lately. 'It was so out of character,' Sarah thought. Usually when faced with a serious problem Brenda's way was to go in any direction that involved her having a good damn time. It didn't seem to concern her which specific direction so long as the road had a watering hole nearby. Being social had always been such a source of life for her, what made Brenda, Brenda. Moreover, for as long as Sarah knew her she had always been the sexy one, the one that every man desired. She was still beautiful even with a few more pounds but it wasn't the outside change that made the difference. Brenda eventually thanked Crystal for all her prayers and told her that she had seen the light. Crystal shouted Hallelujah but didn't know what light Brenda was actually referring to. It could have been a stop light for all Crystal knew. However, Brenda admitted to Sarah that she had come to the terrifying realization that she might be a single parent and didn't like that idea not one bit. When Norman ran out of the hospital that night, all Brenda could see was Karen being left behind to raise their child. And, that broke her heart. Something about that image sunk deep into her very core. It scared her in a way as only a crisis can, when one is forced to throw out every previous notion and embrace the unknown. The kind of jolt to the system that insists a change is necessary or else suffer the grisly consequences. It was not how she saw herself, alone with a tiny mouth to feed. Brenda had nightmares of cooking full course meals and cleaning toilets for some well to do family after working at her other two full time jobs. She was the sexy one, right? She just knew that she wouldn't be the one who ended up single. After she awoke from fainting in the doctor's office at the reconfirmed news, she quickly assessed her situation and realized that these were the cards she was dealt. She was then determined to go into it fighting.

"I think I may sue Mike," Brenda stated like a woman on a mission.

"Get all your strength back first," Sarah advised her empowered friend.

"You're right. Wait until after my dance recital. Good idea.

I'll be ready by then," Brenda giggled triumphantly, while humming happily.

Brenda had just begun taking African dance classes for pregnant women at a neighborhood storefront. It was comical to watch and Sarah thoroughly enjoyed hearing the tales that Brenda would yarn about her classmates. "Of course, they dress in car covers," she'd say, "…and they complain non-stop about the size of their thighs." Sarah listened without judgment even though Brenda spoke endlessly about the condition of her thighs as well and wore housecoats out in public. Sarah was dutiful in her listening and even more so in her relaying every single detail to her mother, Millie. At Millie's request, Sarah was to assist Brenda in any way. There was absolutely nothing Millie would not do for Brenda. Daily she would cook and wrap up a plate for Brenda's lunch and her dinner. And, it was understood that Brenda's feet should not hit the pavement without a chariot awaiting her. As a consequence to which, Sarah became Brenda's chauffeur.

"Between you and me, though, I like this little condition I'm in," Brenda confessed one day to Sarah as if no one else could see that for themselves.

Brenda glowed and sparkled like a shiny, freshly minted penny. Her new outlook on life was refreshing and contagious. It changed their conversation. Sarah liked them much better than the ones they used to have. Lately Brenda spoke about her plans for the future. She vowed to take her time more when it came to relationships. Sarah reminded her that Brenda never had relationships but ships that passed in the fog. Brenda humbly agreed and swore to make amends.

"I don't want to be fifty years old with a house full of children who all have different daddies. I know that it's done, but I don't have to be the one doing it."

WISDOM FROM BRENDA!

"Besides your mother would kill me," she laughed.

"She's your mother now," Sarah informed her.

"You know, sometimes bad things do turn out to be good things in disguise."

MORE WISDOM FROM BRENDA!

"What about you, Sarah?" Brenda asked, "You do want to get married and have kids, don't you?"

"Don't you start now. We're talking about *you*. Let's just stick to the subject at hand, shall we," said Sarah coyly yet emphatically.

"I'm just saying...What about you? Maybe even you and the English man will make it after all," Brenda asked demonstratively.

"Yeah, yeah, yeah. We're just friends," Sarah shooed her question, yet it still lingered in the air.

It was precisely the type of thing Millie would ask her. Coming from a friend, though, it had an altogether different feel. She knew that Brenda didn't want her in actuality to run out and get herself pregnant. Sarah knew that Brenda wished her friend could experience the feeling of having so much love welling up inside. It dawned on Sarah that in essence that's what Millie was trying to say all these many years. The fact that it sounded more like a demand instead of a request may have everything to do with how Sarah perceived the entire issue of marriage, motherhood and men. It had just occurred to her that maybe it wasn't so much a matter of her supplying the family tree with fruit. Truly, Millie's delicate but pushy persistence would have led anyone to that conclusion. Millie's wishes would have been better sold had her appeal been more appealing. It never crossed Sarah's mind that it might be of some benefit to her to do what Millie vehemently suggested. That she would largely find something irresistible in the process even with the demands that it would impose on her life. This whole business with her mother had more to do with submitting to one of life's greatest mysteries. It was as simple as saying, *"Try this ride, you might like it."* Yet all this time Sarah swore that the fates had conspired to conform her into some ideal homemaker, mother and wife.

It suddenly occurred to her that this was not the type of subject she usually found herself having with Brenda. Such insight was flowing out of her that it made Sarah a little uneasy. Would she have to apologize to her mother for always trying fix her up on *some* date with *some* guy and that she had some nerve to complain? Was she doing it for her own good? She wanted her to be happy? Sarah had often heard Millie say that children bring meaning to a life.

"Are you going to Karen's today?" Sarah asked, still deep in thought.

"Yeah, she's gonna' give me some of her baby stuff, books mostly. I'm serious about being completely ready. For real. Will I see your face there?"

"Sure, sure, I'll be there. Remember, I'm your ride. Give me an hour before I can admire the new you in the flesh, okay," Sarah joked.

"It's a date."

After she hung up the phone Sarah got to thinking about the changes they had experienced in their long friendship; to think that they didn't even like each other when they first met. Now, Brenda was practically family. This latest incarnation was by far the best, Sarah thought.

It was weird. They were all going over to Karen's for a garage sale she was hosting. It would be the first time they would all be together since that night at the hospital. Karen warned them to bring lots of money because everything she owned was up for grabs. She invited everyone in her neighborhood and promised it would be an event to remember. Catered refreshments would be served and live music would be played. It sounded more like a block party to Sarah or maybe more precisely a coming out party. Karen was positively transformed too. She went from being evasive, withdrawn and sullen as she was when she arrived back into New York, to being open, friendly and extremely optimistic. She was once again the Karen they all remembered from high school. She was the strong one. She didn't take any guff from anyone then and that attitude was back and in full effect. She made it quite clear to anyone who challenged her that she was once again not afraid of anything. Each day of Norman's absence gave her a little more courage than the day before. Lately, she'd tell anyone who asked about Norman's whereabouts that she hadn't heard from him since she nearly blew his head off. She said the same thing to the cops when they knocked on her door looking for him. Norman's boss was concerned, not so much with Norman's absence from work, but more so with Karen's nonchalant attitude about his whereabouts. His office had called several times and Karen just kept telling them that she hadn't seen him since the almost fatal shooting. Crystal advised Karen to at least act like she was worried for the sake of appearances. The police made her produce witnesses of her whereabouts at the time Norman was last seen and at one point Karen swore someone was following her. They all knew that someone was definitely going around town asking questions about her. A man approached Crystal at her church. He hadn't properly identified himself and before Crystal realized that she was actually being interrogated, she had divulged to this complete stranger that Karen was angry enough to kill her husband. When

Karen heard this from Crystal's own quivering lips under a mountain of apologies, she figured it was Norman's boss who had hired a private investigator. Karen called him cheap because after three days the following suddenly ceased. No one could understand why Norman's boss would look for a worker who hardly ever showed up for work and when he did come in, he was too drunk to be effective. Karen found out later after receiving Norman's paycheck in the mail, that Norman's boss was not a man, but in fact, a woman.

This new information led Karen to paint a whole other kind of scenario in her mind too. She came to the conclusion that Norman was having an affair with his attractive but obviously deem-witted boss. He bullied her and tried to control her like he did with Karen, and she inevitably grew tired of his crazy ass and searched for ways of getting rid of him. Karen came to these conclusions by reading a Post It note attached to the check that simply said, *"Thanks, Karen. I owe you one!"* She felt a tinge of pain at the thought of Norman having sex with another woman until her bank told her that she could cash the check without his signature. She called Crystal immediately upon leaving the bank to tell her that money *can* make you happy.

"It's da' 'word' that makes you happy, not da' cash," Crystal corrected.

"It's the gottdamn cash - *trust me!*" Karen said, laughing.

Then she asked Crystal to sincerely forgive her poor choice of words and promised to clean up everything in the future including her language. She made Crystal swear to convince Rob to come and, of course, bring with him a wad of bills to her garage sale. Karen hadn't realized that Crystal and Rob had been inseparable ever since they met and that Rob would do anything for her including buying everything on sale at Karen's house just to impress his new love. Crystal managed to dodge around the topic of Rob for a whole two seconds before blurting out the fact that she and he were practically engaged. She didn't want to hold anything from Karen necessarily but understandably felt uncomfortable discussing her wedding plans in light of everything that had happened. To her surprise, Karen insisted that she tell her every detail.

Little did Karen know but now that Crystal had permission to talk about Rob, there was no getting her off the phone. She told the same story every time too. Rob was not her type, she'd say. She was the spiritual one, right? She was the church girl who knew better than to fall for some guy that she met at some club. She told everyone that she felt more than a little guilty at even going to the club in the first place. She made sure that Karen was aware of the fact that if it weren't for Brenda's pregnancy, she would have been home rolling her hair and eating Ho Ho's that night. She also told Karen repeatedly that the fact that there was no way she was supposed to be considering marrying him was understood. Any man who questioned his faith in God was immediately crossed off her imaginary list. Fortunately, for Rob, Crystal was not the same person that she used to be when she met him. After her "date" with Terry, and she used the term loosely, she made an important discovery about how erroneous her belief system was pertaining to men of God. She never considered the gray areas that lay between conviction and preference. Up until Terry, she honestly thought that she'd have no problem finding herself a husband-to-be at church, not that she was looking. She just naturally assumed she'd settle down to a normal respectable life with a couple of adorable, well behaved kids and live in a grand old house that had plenty of room for entertaining their ever increasing list of sanctified friends. She envisioned them traveling every year to the same hotel in Jamaica, the Holiday Inn Beach and Resort, entrance onto the beach of course. They'd be known as Mr. and Mrs. so and so and all the local merchants would welcome them just like old friends each time they'd visit.

When Crystal first started going to her church she felt as if she'd landed smack dab in heaven because the preaching made her weep and there were so many eligible single men in the congregation. They were all so well dressed; all had decent jobs and careers, and all drove around in nice cars. All that and they were saved too. Crystal thought her only decision would be which one to say yes to. She didn't even realize it at the time but she had elevated them to a status that rivaled deity. One by one though, they began to show her that she was wrong and that they were indeed only human. That was a cruel reality that she didn't want to face up to. To make matters worse, everyone knew of Crystal's little delusion to self except Crystal. Karen just figured that in time, like children who discover that Santa Claus doesn't exist, that Crystal too would come to a similar conclusion about "perfect" men in church. Crystal referred to that sad agonizing period in her life as a rude awakening. Rob came along and lifted Crystal's depressed spirits showing her something that had never occurred to her — that church is found in the heart. Simple. No matter where Rob went, he took the gospel with him. When they danced together that night at the club, he represented the character she had longed for but somehow missed in the men she dealt with. Rob explained to Crystal later that until he met her he doubted there were any righteous women in the church and that's why his faith was wavering.

"'Ah' guess wee' h'lped each 'awther," Crystal sang into the phone.

She paused and marveled at how God had brought them

together, she and he both needing to see someone Godly because their dreams were in despair.

"Now we have two things to celebrate," Karen suggested brightly.

Sarah was obediently stuffing her wallet with singles when the doorbell rang. She shuffled over to it in her house slippers thinking that it could only be one person, her mother. However, whoever it was had their back to her.

"Who is it?" she finally asked when she was certain that she couldn't make out a face.

"It's me," Matthew replied with such familiarity it moved Sarah to notice.

She opened the door and tried not to give the impression that she was in any way delighted to see him. Earlier in the month, she had hoped he'd call so they could once and for all go out on a proper date. She wouldn't have guessed in a million years that he'd just show up at her front door one morning out of the blue. He looked gorgeous. He smelled good too. She noticed that right away as he stepped in and pecked her on her cheek. She told herself not to let him see her blush and coo like a teenybopper but her feet weren't steady in his presence. All he did was enter her house and she had to use both of her sweaty hands to close and re-latch the lock. She wanted to ask him right away why the visit but hesitated as not to appear overly anxious. Something told her to pace herself. It pleased her that he didn't just boldly come in, plop down and make himself at home on her couch. They had some talking to do. Instead, he paced about the floor and tried to pick up on her mood and countenance. It became relatively obvious that he preferred to approach her cautiously. That was okay by her although it made her uneasy at the same time. She wasn't used to being studied. He paused and waited until she spoke first.

"Tea?" she managed.

"Yes, thanks," he replied.

As she walked into the kitchen, he eased out of his jacket and hat and draped them across the sofa arm. He paced some more but this time wandered over to her stereo and books, shaking his head admiring her collection of compact disks. It pleasantly reminded him of her, colorful and anything but boring, mostly jazz. When Sarah walked back into the living room he took his time joining her at the coffee table. He lingered taking in his surroundings. Finally she walked over and handed him a cup of Darjeeling. Their hands lightly brushed allowing them a moment to drink each other in. Sarah urgently wanted to kiss him right then but wasn't quite sure how he'd take it. It was evident to her that he liked her. He had said as much to her at least once before. He had kissed her very passionately on the dance floor and held her tightly and lovingly in his arms. At least to her it felt as if he was holding her in a loving way.

On the other hand, he equally gave her plenty of reasons to doubt his feelings toward her too. For one, he always traveled with some sort of female companionship. Plus, he thwarted her romantic advances and practically ran out of her house. Yet, she was certain that he at least found her attractive. There was nothing other than that though. And that wasn't enough to cause her to fall in love with him. She disappointedly broke their stare and retreated back into the kitchen. She didn't feel much like fooling herself. Matthew was beautiful to look at, sure she thought and she did feel all a flutter when he was around but other than that, she couldn't see them having any kind of future. She was the smart one, right? There was no way she was going to fall for a full-fledged playboy. The more she thought about it the more resolute she became in not allowing her emotions to get the better of her. She kept telling herself that lots of men are capable of sweeping a girl off her feet but how many of them stay around to pick her up. 'No, no, no,' she thought. She was not going to be his next conquest. At that moment of resolve, Matthew came up behind her. He placed his empty cup on the counter and indicated that he was ready to talk.

"You know, I came here…" he began.

"Yes," Sarah replied.

She didn't even want him to finish his sentence. She didn't want to have to stoop so low as to tell him that she wouldn't be his latest love interest but if he pushed her, she was ready to do just that. It was too ironic especially with her standing there practically barefoot in her own kitchen. All she kept thinking about was how it was going to look with her pining away over a man who everyone knew was an obvious player. She couldn't bear to think of how she would then be the single girl who wasted two or three years with some guy who never could make a commitment to her. Not only would she be the lonely one but she would also be the poor dumb one who took a chance on someone like Matthew.

"No, no, no, no, no," she couldn't believe she said it out loud.

He simply looked at her and smiled. She was being dramatic. He adored that side of her. The lady who was normally so pulled together was being frazzled and losing her cool. It made him molten to think that he could get to her that way, penetrate her thick wall of defenses that she tried so hard to maintain. Her showing some weakness endeared him to her even more.

"Look Matthew, I…" she started, "I know we have something between us…and…" she tried.

She stopped mid-sentence. Suddenly she found it hard to continue. The words 'something between us' left her lips and went unswervingly to his. They both felt bonded somehow as by an invisible force. She shrugged in an apparent weariness of defeat and leaned back against the granite counter top. She needed something sturdy to brace her trembling body. He watched her, gently his eyes roamed around her face, her form. It frustrated her that she couldn't even remember what she was about to say. It was so important two seconds ago and now all she wanted was to be held. He placed his hand on her hips, leaned in and pressed his lips to hers. Sarah didn't know how long they stayed in that position. All she knew was that her tights felt as if they were on fire. She came to a quick conclusion that she was in trouble as his right hand slid down her side and his left hand scooped behind and braced her head.

Karen wheeled Yolanda out of the house. Yolanda would have loved nothing more than to glide down the driveway to see what the metal chair could really do. She knew better than to ask Karen if she could steer it herself, who hovered over her like a hawk. Sarah, Matthew, Crystal, Rob, Brenda, Millie and Jacob greeted them warmly as they approached the front gate. Yolanda hadn't regained her strength yet but she was in good spirits. Miss Oliver, now their official family friend, was off by the freshly trimmed grass smiling in their direction. It took some doing, but Karen was facing up to things in their sessions. Once again Miss Oliver renewed her vows as a therapist on the alter of her graduate school degree. Karen motioned for her to come over and join them. Miss Oliver did so by meeting them halfway as they made it to the chain-link fence. Karen was having *the one and only* yard and open house sale. Everything inside and out could be bought, bartered for, or even given away. Matthew, Rob and some of Karen's male neighbors lingered by one table in particular. On it was a set of bowling balls and other sports enthusiast items. At the end of a clothes rack was the Hawaiian shirt that Norman wore to Millie's party. It still smelled of bourbon and stale cigarettes. In fact, everything on that table was Norman's personal belongings.

"Whatever happened to your husband?" Miss Oliver asked as she perused Norman's things with the guys.

"He run off," Karen said with an expression that could only be read as indifference.

Sarah, Brenda and Crystal believed that sooner or later she'd weep for him but not today. Today she was the perfect hostess, welcoming old friends and some new ones to her open doors. They all enjoyed themselves that day. Everyone dug their hands in and rummaged through the sale items, playfully haggling with Karen for the best deals. That day she practically gave everything away for free. **THE END**

FINALE

*F*ar off in the distance on a one lane road is a sign that reads "Welcome to Utah." A truck slowly passes the sign and as it does, a figure appears as if out of nowhere that was previously blocked from view. The figure approaches the sign. Although it is getting closer and closer, it's still difficult to make out what or who it is. As the sun begins to set, finally it's clear enough to see that it's a man. He is jogging along the graveled edge of the road. Another truck passes and the man dodges off into a field, shielding his eyes all the while from flying dust and debris. The man does not stop but continues to run right pass the state sign, down the road until all that is seen of him is a small, tiny speck.

About the Author

Beverly A. Burchett placed second in the Billie Holiday Theatre Poetry Contest and thusly her love of writing was spurred. She's a graduate of the famed High School of Performing Arts, and has acted in a number of national commercials as well as a few popular films, including "Fame", and "Joey Breaker." Her latest works <u>Queen Kinni</u>, <u>Open Doors</u> and <u>Random Arts of Kindness, a journey</u>, are available in stores and on-line at www.blackcurrantpress.com. Beverly's also a published lyrist, who resides in New York.